Sins of Our Father

The St. Claire Series

Jessica Wright
Lara Wright
Jaclyn Parks

J.L. Wright

Copyright © 2023 By Jessica Wright (Author) Lara Wright (Co-Author) & Jaclyn Parks (Co-Author)

All Rights reserved. No part of this publication may be reproduced or transmitted in any form without the written permission of the author, except the use of quotations in a book review.

This is a work of fiction. Names, characters, places, and incidents either are the product of the author's imagination or are used fictitiously. Any resemblance to actual persons, living or dead, events, or locales is entirely coincidental.

Editor: Jaclyn Parks & Jessica Wright
Cover Designer: Lara Wright

ISBN: 979-8-9896-1140-9

ACKNOWLEDGMENT

To my loving husband, Richard, and children Nathan, Lucas, and Brayden; the four of you are my steadfast. Thank you for supporting me while I experience my dream. I love you all endlessly. You're my every reason for my existence.

To my sisters and co-authors, Lara Wright and Jaclyn Parks, whom without them this book would not be possible; although we haven't known each other from birth, the connection we have is otherworldly. You both have become the part of my family that I never knew I needed, and I will love and protect you until my last breath... and then some. To me, you are both just as much a part of this as I am. Thank you for the endless laughs and tears, as WE created something beautiful.

And last, but certainly not least, to my readers. Thank you for opening my book and taking a chance on me. I am forever grateful.

WARNING

Sins of Our Father is a fictional dark romance meets fantasy where the two worlds collide. If you are looking for a safe read, this book is not it. Reader discretion is advised. The contents of this book are not suitable for all audiences, but for dark ones like me, please come, let me feed your soul.

Some content of this publication is dark with triggering situations including, but not limited to, graphic violence, torture, death, extreme sexual exploitation, mental illness, self-harm, suicide, nonconsensual consent, witchcraft, vulgarity, narcissistic behavior, fire, blood play, and more.

Contents

Title Page	
Part One: Elizabeth James	1
1	3
2	10
3	22
4	31
5	44
6	59
Part Two: Olivia Rose	69
7	78
8	87
9	95
10	109
11	118
12	125
13	139
Part Three: Nyx Harper	145
14	146
15	155
16	167

17	177
18	187
19	198
20	205
21	211
Part Four: New Orleans	220
22	221
23	229
24	236
25	247
A Few Weeks Later	254
26	255
27	264
Sneak peek into The St. Claire Series: Sinful Scars …	272

Part One: Elizabeth James

My Dearest Elizabeth,

If you're reading this, then I am gone. Please know that I love you with everything that I am. I wish I had more time with you to help you discover yourself, but that's not the case, so I will start with what is most important. You are half witch. I know it may seem impossible, I thought so too when Augustus told me, but I have witnessed it first-hand. Even as I write this, I feel your power growing in my womb. He thinks you're evil, but I know different.

Your father wasn't always a bad man. The man I fell in love with would have never left us behind; yet here we are. He's a powerful man Libby, unlike anything I've ever seen before. I don't know what his intentions for you are, but I know it cannot be good. My only regret is leaving you with no one. I have taken as many precautions as I can think of to give you your best shot at life. I visited an elder today, Agatha Hawthorne, at her coven in the city and had her cast a protection spell over you. When you're ready, she is located off the trail in Hitt Hills Park in Seattle. There you will find what you are looking for. She will have more answers than I can give you right now.

I can't imagine your life has been ideal in state custody, but it was the only option I had given the circumstances. Cancer is a thief, I hate that I have been robbed of the opportunity to watch you grow up. I'll be loving you until my last breath ... and then some.

Love, Mom

Daya James
1/4/1993

1

I turn the page over and over in my hand like I have a million times before. It has haunted me every day from the moment my eyes met her words. I was sixteen and very unsure of who I really was. I was different. Everyone could see it. I could feel it, but I didn't know why.

I think back on how India would constantly bully me. You would think being in foster care together we would have shared kinship, but no. She was my biggest critic and lived to torture me. She enjoyed feeling superior. She was tall, lean, and blonde and I was... well, the shy, weird kid.

One particular day, she was making fun of a stuffed bear on my cot that I had had for as long as I could remember. She grabs it up, stands on my bed, and begins dangling it above my head. I told her to give it back, but she wouldn't. It's the first time I experienced rage pulsating through my veins. It felt like an out of body experience; the lights began to flash and the air around me thickened, gripping my throat like a vice.

I jumped up in an attempt to yank the stuffed bear from her hands, but it became more of a tug of war; It finally gives. Cotton falls like snow everywhere and it was demolished. The little bitch laughed as I scurried on the floor gathering remnants of what was left.

As I gathered the cotton and pieces of tan fur, I saw it. A small, yellow folded up sheet of paper; it had been hidden inside my bear.

Could this be a joke?

But it was simply a fleeting thought. I knew it was real the moment my fingers grazed the note. It's in a lot worse shape now. Almost falling to pieces, as many times as I have unfolded and then folded it back up. I shake my head, willing myself out of my daydream. Enough of the trip down memory lane. It's been fourteen years now.

Get ahold of yourself Lib. You're going to be late.

I silently make a promise to myself, as I have multiple times before, that I will go into the city, confront Agatha, and get the answers I have been longing for.

I've got to stop reading this so much, the words aren't going to change.

I place my letter back on my nightstand and head to the bathroom to get ready. I'm sure Tink will already be downstairs waiting for me.

That's the best attribute of living in the loft above my bookstore. The commute is nonexistent, and I own it. It's my greatest accomplishment. After I aged out of the foster care system, I spent my nights in the bed of any guy I wanted to siren. The couple of hundreds of dollars the system gives you doesn't go very far. I'm not proud of it, but it gave me a relatively safe place to lay my head, food to eat, and a quiet place to study. The only good thing to ever come from being a ward to the state is having free access to education. By the time I was twenty-five, I found myself publishing my first fantasy novel, moving to Bainbridge Island, Washington and even opening my antique bookstore. At the time I was unsure of my decisions thus far, but five years in and business is thriving. It is a sight to see and still takes my breath away.

Hidden in plain sight, right on the corner of the town square, the architecture looks like it was molded from a Thomas Kincaid painting. Small and quaint but packed with so much history and culture. Windows lined the entirety of the front surrounded by red brick with a cream-colored sign above *"Grimoire"*. Inside we have two breakfast tables on either side of the door, placed there purposely to capture the natural lighting for those who like to read a small piece before buying. I wanted to keep the charm, so the walls are lined with wooden shelves. We have sconces dimly lighting the entirety of the store, a couple of dark cherry wood tables are placed throughout with our bestseller novels displayed atop, with our checkout counter almost in the center. This month my newest novel, *'The Onyx'*, happens to be one of our bestsellers. It's the first time I have had a table dedicated to myself.

In the front Tink runs the desk. I couldn't ask for better help. She's one of the few who know my secret. Rather she figured it out. Very observant, that one. I met her in college, and we hit it off. After graduation I hired her. She jokes now that she was meant to find me, and that this bookstore is her passion. She is the only person I consider calling a true friend. Her birth name is Tina Macabi but due to her petite 4'11 stature and pixie cut; I nicknamed her Tink. I thought it was witty. She liked it, so it stuck. She bounces around like a fairy, so I find that ironic.

We are a sight to see; I'm a full-figured plus size and just shy of 5'5. I'm highly self-conscious, but I'm not naive enough to think that I lack beauty. I was granted curves exactly where they are meant to be, a warm olive skin tone with blue-green eyes, rosy, red cheeks, and warm brown hair that falls just below my shoulders. Tink is your more traditional beauty; she's tiny, with blonde hair, big green doe eyes and porcelain skin. Traditional stops there though; her face has more holes in it than in my entire body, but she rocks it. I have a nose piercing and a couple holes in my ears but that's the extent. We share similarities though, in the way we dress, our love for ink therapy, and our need for good, no strings attached, dick.

After washing my face, I throw on a bit of mascara and some gloss, I prefer low maintenance and a fresh face; I'm not a girly-girl. Opting for my favorite pair of distressed jeans, that have worn rips in the knees, a black lace bra, and a vintage Metallica tank, I take a look in the mirror, and adjust my nose ring.

That'll have to do.

I open the blinds to let the light filter in my apartment in a last-ditch effort to keep my plants alive and then head out the back door and down the stairs that lead into my office in the bookstore. My office is my favorite place to work. I have a small desk in the center, but the walls are lined with cherry wood shelves as well. This is where I hold all the older, more ancient archives. These are not for sale. If there is anything you need to know on Witchcraft or Wicca, you find it here. Not many know I have access to such powerful knowledge; I like having that secret to myself. Although, I have searched high and low, in every book here, I always come up empty. There are no answers to who I am.

I will figure it out one day.

I quickly walk through my office, push open the door and then use the code to lock it and head to the front.

"Good morning your majesty. I was beginning to think you were never getting up". Tink bellows as she leans lazily against the counter.

"Why do you insist on calling me that? You know I'm not a fucking princess, right?" I say smiling.

"Oh no ma'am, you are the Queen Witch".

She laughs as she bounces off to the back to receive our new shipment.

I swear if I didn't know any better, I would think that girl has an unhealthy obsession with witches. I take my place behind the counter and open my latest book, just as the bell above the door chimes.

I feel his energy before I even lift my head. The contrast between the darkness of the store and the morning sun shining through the storefront windows requires me to give my eyes a moment to adjust.

Sweet baby Jesus.

He's got to be at least six-foot-tall, in his early to mid-thirties and just my cup of poison. A sleeve of intricate tattoos run the full length of his right arm, traveling up until they disappear beneath his black t-shirt. I want to trace each one with my tongue.

Jesus Lib, get ahold of yourself.

I dare to take a deeper look. His fitted jeans strained across his quads. Converse shoes have never looked so fucking appealing.
Dear lord, I may combust right here.
I readjust my stance and my center warms.
Fuck, why am I wet?

I have seen a lot of men, but this one is literally etched out of my dreams. He has shoulder length dirty blonde hair and blue eyes so light that they are almost gray; he has scruff but not unkept. His body is everything from what I can see. What I would do to see the rest of it! The energy radiating off of him I can't place, but at this point I'm not thinking straight. I think I've finally had enough of being the girl that always second guesses herself... and HIM... He is a delicious vision of danger and sin that I'd love to take a bite out of.

He walks towards me, and our eyes meet, every ounce of confidence that I had moments ago dissipates. My pulse is ringing so loud in my ears that I don't even notice Tink has made her way back up to the front.

"Hey Boss, are you going to offer him some assistance or continue to eye fuck him?" she leans in and whispers.

I feel the heat rise to my cheeks as I swat her away. I round the counter and close our distance.

"Hi, welcome to *Grimoire*. Can I help you find anything?"

Why did that come out so high pitched and more importantly why do I care?

"Well, Love, originally I came in for a book to bide my time, but I think I might have found something way more intriguing". He says with a lifted brow.

He has an Irish accent that has me hypnotized. I look over my shoulder as if he was referring to something other than me, but I come up short.

Isn't he bold?
I have always been shy and unsure, but he has me speechless.
"Did you just roll your eyes at me?" He looks at me smirking.
"Maybe, does your cheesy attempt at flirting always work?" I counter.

"I saved that line for you Love, but I'm starting to see that I'm going to have to work harder. How's this? You want me; It was radiating off you the moment I stepped in the door. I felt your energy. Maybe, try not to be so obvious little lady." He says with a wink and smirk.

Ass.

Who in the hell does he think he is? Wait, did he say he felt my energy? Great. Another fucking witch. Of course, he's a pompous ass.

"I'm not your 'little lady'. Do I look *little* to you? Let me guess, just a terrible attempt at a fat joke? So, are you buying anything or are you here to be a comedian?"

His smile fades and is replaced with seriousness.

"Love, those were never my intentions. You cannot be thinking clearly. You're anything but fat. Now don't you get me wrong; you look like you're a hand full, but I'm up for the challenge. What's your name?" He leans in as if a magnet is pulling him toward me.

"Lib... Libby James and you are?"

"Finn O'Brien, maybe you've heard of me. I'm the guitarist in Misfits." he says, as he puffs out his chest.

I'm sure I look at him dumbfounded, because he's quick to add.

"It's an alternative rock band out of Galway, Ireland. I was assuming because you're wearing that Metallica tank, very well I might add, that you know good music. My mistake". He smiles.

How do you compliment and insult someone in the same sentence?

"Let me know if you need help finding anything Finn O'Brien." Exasperated, I turn and head back to the counter, making sure to put a little sway in my hips. Fuck if I'm going to be the only one hot and bothered by this encounter. If I'm sure about anything it's that tonight me and my trusty dildo have a date with an image of a certain tattooed, Irishman attached.

"Shut the fuck up, do not say a word Tink."

She skips over with a shit eating grin plastered across her face. I know I'm failing miserably at not smiling.

What the hell was that about?

"Oh, come on boss lady, siren him. You know you want to! He would be a perfect addition to your 'quick fixes!'"

She knows I'm shy and self-conscious until I want something. Then it's a one and done; no time for anything more. One thing my mother's letter taught me was to never trust a man. So, a hot weekend affair is always my safest bet.

Too bad today is Monday.

"I'm not interested." I say a little snippier than I intended.

Tink raises her hands in surrender with a playful smile, so I know this is all but over. Finn looks to be perplexed as he scans different titles in our 'fantasy' section gliding his fingers across my latest edition *'The Onyx'*. I blush and look down, picking up a book and trying to focus on anything but him.

The door chimes again as he exits, no words and he didn't even buy anything.

What a dick.

I catch a glimpse of the sweet ass I could have had. I'm starting to think Tink was right; probably not though, because he looks like a drug I could easily become addicted too. Sin drips off him and I just want a taste.

No Lib, you under no circumstances are to partake in that catastrophe.

2

It's damn near five p.m., and I'm still feigning for the Irishman. I can't get his face out of my mind. I've never been this pulled to someone's features ever.
Fuck it.
"Tink, I'm taking an early day. I have to get out of here."
A couple hours early shouldn't hurt.
She knows I pay her substantially more than any place around, so she doesn't complain. I'm about to burst, and wringing wet, when I finally make it up the stairs and into my apartment. I don't make it far past the door before I'm stripping off every layer of clothing. They're like lava against my skin. Walking over to my sliding glass door that overlooks the town square below, I pull the blinds. I hardly ever use the front door to the apartment because of the easy access to the bookstore through the back stairwell, so I almost forget that it's even there. I'm sure no one can see me, but I still feel the need.

It's an open floor plan studio. My bed and dresser are on the far side of the room beckoning me.
God, almost there.
I turn off the lamp, the only light in the apartment aside from the natural light feeding in, and lay on the bed positioning myself on my pillow. I reach into my top drawer, frantically moving my hand around until I grip it. My pulse quickens and the energy in the room changes.
I just turned that lamp off. Why is it flickering?
I feel like I'm losing control, but it feels so good it hurts.

Looking at the toy in my hand, I press the button to turn it on. My dildo buzzes to life and it speaks to my soul. I take it in my mouth first to get it wet; Although at this point, I shouldn't need it.

Yep, don't need it at all.

I position the thick head at my slit, teasing myself, and slowly plunge the length into my center. Every muscle gripping down on the toy, slowing my pace and then speeding it up again; my body telling me to savior the sensation, but fuck it, my mind is ready to release. I pick up the pace and I can see my climax as my vision darkens. With my other hand I pinch one of my nipples; I'm moving like a mad woman about to come undone. Right when I'm about to cum, I scream his name.

"Fuck me Finn".

From the shadows he steps out.

I'm mid orgasm, acting oblivious, I pretend not to see him. Quickening my hand, I grip the dildo harder, feeling the vibrations pulsating into my core. My blood is running hot and I bare my hips into the bed, crying out as the orgasm overtakes me. The lamp now flickering, casts an eerie glow across Finn's face. Chewing on his bottom lip; he lets out a deep growl. My body is rocked with the aftermath and I'm breathless.

"Don't Stop." he urges.

Reality finally hits me. Panic sets in and I begin clawing at my down comforter, willing it to cover my exposed body. I sit up and envelop myself in the down. I don't scream though, secretly knowing the whole time he was watching. I could feel it, his gaze on my skin like the hot sun.

What the fuck Lib, this turns you on? You're about to be murdered and you're turned on!! If you get out of this alive, you're getting a fucking psychiatrist.

"What the fuck are you doing in my apartment?"

I stammer, my breathing goes rigid, still feeling the aftershock of that earth shattering climax. I was fine with being seen, hell I wanted it to be him touching my body, thrusting his cock deep inside me, but why did I have to say his name?

I did say it out loud, didn't I?
I was so caught up in the moment.
Now, there is no hiding my attraction.
As if it ever was.

He walks around the bed, turns my side lamp on, and sits down slowly. Turning his body toward me, he reaches out and touches my cheek and I swear the heat from his touch goes straight to my pussy. I shift and the comforter falls to my waist.
Fuck it, let him look.
I arch my back just the slightest to accentuate my double D's. I may be self-conscious, but I have beautiful tits.
"I asked you a question." I stutter.
"With all due respect Love, I will give you your answer, but I'm going to need you to put a shirt on, because right now all I want is to devour every inch of you. I want to throw away that fucking dildo that I'm now envious of, and really make you scream."

My body is humming with energy. It's like a nervousness I've never felt before. My skin is crawling, in the most delicious way.
What is this man doing to me?
"I can't imagine you have a good explanation, so you can get out!" I bite.
"Please give me two minutes."
I wait in silence.

"When I walked out of *Grimoire* this morning and rounded the corner, it was like a magnetic pull. The staircase leading to your side balcony was glowing. Love, I'm no stranger to another witch's energy but yours summoned me. It was like a drunken elixir. Before I knew it, I was taking the fire escape two steps at a time, landing outside your door. Lighting my cigarette to ease my mind and collect my thoughts; I fought the urge for what seemed hours. Standing on your balcony, I peered out over Bainbridge. It is a lovely place, Bainbridge, but not quite as lovely as your hypnotic eyes."
"Stop trying to flirt with me." I spat.
He clears his throat. "I turned away from the rails, prepared to

leave and noticed the handle glowing. I pushed on it, and it was like fate. It was unlocked."

Lib, what the fuck? When did you unlock that door?

"Walking in, your delicious smells of chamomile, peonies, and books filled my senses. I wanted, no, I needed to find out why I am so drawn to you. Tell me Love, Is this a cheeky attempt to siren me?"

Dear Lord, I could listen to him talk all day. Snap out of it!

"With all due respect, if I wanted to siren you, I wouldn't be the only one naked in this bed right now." He smirks.

Where did that come from? I'm not courageous. There is something about this man that speaks to my confidence.

"That can be arranged."

He sneers. He looks in my eyes and leans in toward me, so close that our noses are damn near touching. I feel his breath warm against my lips. My nipples respond, hardening, aching for his attention.

He slowly speaks again.

"Tell me what you want! "He whispers in a deep rasp.

"I want you to leave."

I lie. I fucking lie.

"You're lying."

He brings the pad of his thumb to meet my bottom lip as his eyes drink me in. My body is literally shaking. No man has ever made me feel this way. It's like my body is betraying me.

"You, I want you," I whisper, attempting to look anywhere but in his eyes.

"Well now, was that so hard?" He hums as he leans in, and our lips meet.

Explosive energy pulses through my body. I can't think straight. This is the first man to ever seek me out. The combination of the softness of his lips and the hardness of his urgency has my powers threatening release. I'm usually repulsed by smokers, but his taste has me weak; the perfect mixture of tobacco and mint.

I'm an illusionist. In the bedroom, I can make a man see

what he desires, masking all of my flaw and distorting their vision. They don't recognize the extra weight I carry in my thighs, the stretch marks that run along the inner sides, or the 6-inch scar in between my tits that runs vertically, perfectly centered. I received that gem from one of my many foster moms. She was nice enough at first, but when she would drink, she would convince herself that I was fucking her boyfriend.

Yeah, just what every twelve-year-old does.

It was a broken beer bottle and a very scared little girl.

If only I had noticed my powers, then....

My mind trails off. But I'm brought back to reality as our kiss deepens, losing my whole thought process.

As we release each other, breathing altered, my brain begins to regain traction.

This isn't good Lib. Think. You didn't put up an image for him. He sees you, flaws and all. Why isn't he running? Don't I disgust him? Fuck it.

This feels too dangerous. Maybe letting him see me will have him running for the hills after he gets his release, and I'll get to fuck the *famous* Finn O'Brien, I laugh in my head. Win, win for the both of us.

"Turn off the lamp!" I demand.

"No, we aren't doing that. You're taking control here, but I'm damn well going to watch you take it." He responds.

I usually let others take control once I siren them. What am I supposed to do here?

He reaches and finds both of my hands, stands, and then pulls me to my feet. My comforter drops and I'm completely naked as the blood rushes to my cheeks. Stepping back facing me, he drinks my body in. My eyes fall to the ground. He brings his hand to my face and lifts my chin until our eyes meet.

"You are the most beautiful creature I've ever seen love." He growls.

"No, stop. You don't have to say that." I say shyly.

"Do you know what I see? Physically I see luscious brown hair that I cannot wait to get my fingers wrapped around, eyes that hypnotize me, lips that are so soft I never want to come up for air. I see the most gorgeous set of tits that have my mouth watering, thighs that I cannot wait to have wrapped around my head, and the most beautiful bare pussy I've ever laid eyes on. I can promise to take you to heights you've never been, if only you will allow it Love." He slowly licks his lips, as if imagining my taste on them. He continues.

"Emotionally, I see insecurity, years of damage, and brokenness. All I want to do is fix it if you will let me."

He reaches down and takes off his shirt, never leaving my eyes. The tattoo that was teasing now on full display. It reaches the full length of his arm and down one side. That along with his chiseled abs and "v" pointing to my destination has my mouth watering.

He comes closer and grips my left hand and pulls it toward him, resting it on the large bulge in his jeans.

"This Love, is what you do to me."

I all but come apart. Before I know it, I am pushing my hand down the front of his jeans, encasing the girth of his dick. I'm surprised to find a bead of cum *and something hard* already waiting on the tip.

Maybe he is really turned on by me.

With my other hand, I quickly go to work unbuckling his jeans and pushing them to the floor. His cock bobs free and I go stoic for a moment.

Is this for real?

He has the most perfect cock I've ever seen and that hard *something* is his prince albert piercing.

Thank the Gods. This is going to be fun if he knows how to use it.

I grip his length and take him into my mouth. His head falls back as his cock stiffens. Running my tongue down the under length, I feel a groan escape him. I release his cock and just to tease, take one of his balls and give it a quick suck, before taking his length into my mouth again.

"Fuck Love. Hungry, are we?"

I begin to hum and quicken my pace, feeling the cold metal of the ring glide across my tongue. He begins fucking my mouth. My eyes go teary as remnants of my mascara fall.

Gods he's huge.

I feel his hand in my hair, beckoning me to slow down.

"Calm now Love, before I spill down your throat."

I pull myself away.

Damn he tastes good.

His eyes now dancing with amusement.

"What?" I ask unsure.

"I'm not normally like this, why do I feel like I can do anything with you?" I whisper.

"Because you can. I am yours to command, take your power back Lib." He says as he finishes undressing.

Mine to command.

Is this some sick joke?

He will be long gone tomorrow, I'm sure of it. I remain between his legs, looking up as if I'm waiting for his permission to continue.

"Stand up, I'm the one who should be kneeling before you. A body like yours deserves to be worshiped, I will bow at your altar. I am nothing, if not yours."

I rise.

Then he whispers. "You're in control."

I take in every inch of him my body humming with need. Fuck it. I can no longer hold back. I close the distance and our lips meet hungrily. Trailing his fingertips lightly down my sides, he wraps me in his arms and in one swift movement lifts me up, his hands gripping my ass and I wrap my legs around his waist.

"Where to Love?"

"I don't know." I respond shyly.

"You're in control Love! Fucking where?"

Breathy I respond. "Balcony!"

Simultaneously the door slides open with force followed by a gust of wind.

I don't even register the energy pulsing through me until he laughs and says, "Calm down, save your magic for later, we're about to create our own."

He kisses me and carries me out of the apartment. The air is crisp and a bit chilly for late August. I take a deep breath trying to find my nerve. The sun is just starting to set, and the street below seems quiet.

So far, so good.

The balcony consists of the wrought iron railing in the front that adjoins the fire escape leading below. I have a lounge chair and a small table against the wall at the far end that butts up to the sliding glass doors.

He sets me to my feet and kisses me urgently. Stepping back, my bare ass hits the cool glass behind me. He pulls away from my lips and lowers himself, first stopping at my breasts as he painfully and greedily sucks my nipples, taking one in his mouth at a time.

"OH MY GODS!!"

He begins trailing kisses down my body as my clit throbs in response. Soon settling eye level with my pussy, he grips my hip with his right hand, and runs his free hand behind my left thigh, lifting my leg and resting it over his shoulder. Turning his head, he begins trailing kisses along the stretch marks that I am painfully aware that he sees now.

"So fucking perfect." He licks across one and begins to nibble as I let out a gasp.

"Harder."

He bites and I grab his hair willing more.

"Harder I said."

I feel my flesh break and he pulls his face away. Small trails of blood appear where his mouth was just seconds ago. He stills for a moment.

Maybe I pushed too far.

"Again!" I scream urgently.

He doesn't procrastinate, biting just underneath the first mark; this time not holding back and drawing more blood. I am shaking with a mixture of pain and pleasure. He comes up for a reprieve and as I see my blood on his bottom lip, I reach down, running my finger across it and then take it into my mouth. The taste is intoxicating. He drops his right hand from my hip and runs the pad of his middle finger through the trails of blood now dripping down my thigh and then puts it to his own lips.

OH MY GODS! There is no way he is about to do what I think he's going to do. My inner monologue screams.

He does. He places his finger with my blood on his tongue and begins sucking it off.

Don't you dare fucking cum Lib.

He slowly withdraws his finger letting it pause on his bottom lip. My mouth waters. He lifts his hand beckoning me to taste.

"Such a sweet girl."

I bow down dipping my head and lock my eyes on his as I take his finger into my mouth. On release, he adds another finger and dips them back in. He pulls his fingers from my mouth, and they are dripping with a mixture of his and my saliva. He finds my pussy wet and waiting and inserts those two fingers.

"Fuck, Love you're so tight."

Starting off slowly, he begins to fuck me with his fingers until pleasure is moving through me like a cyclone.

I'm so close. Not yet.

Streetlights flicker below. He frees my needy pussy of his fingers to give me time to take control of my magic. I have a moment's notice before his mouth is devouring me again, lapping up my juices. I feel a moan escape his mouth.

"How do I taste?" I ask.

He pulls away long enough to answer. "Like my own personal hell, Little Devil."

Then he dives back in.

"Take me to bed," I say demandingly.

"You don't have to tell me twice."

He pulls away from my dripping center and stands.

I miss his mouth already.

Lifting me up, he throws me over his shoulder, as if I'm as light as a feather. Smacking my ass, we enter the apartment, heading straight to my bed.

Laughing. I'm laughing. What the actual fuck?

He tosses me on the bed shaking his head in amusement. A smile playing on his lips.

"What now Love? Take control. What do you want?"

I look up at him unsure.

What is he trying to prove?

I'm the submissive one. I guess I'm not right now.

Standing still as a statue, we're in a standoff, but I finally give in.

"I want you to fuck me Finn. NOW!!"

He smiles, giving a silent approval, moving between my legs. Lining himself up at my slit, I feel the cool ring and let out a small whimper. I'm sure he notices my arousal, because he grips his cock and moves it the length of my cunt, pressing into my clit, knowingly driving my need for him. A smile plays on his lips as he quickly moves to my opening and slowly begins to push inside of me. The head is barely in when I'm writhing beneath him.

"You're so big." I stammer.

He pulls the head out and I instantly feel empty. I watch his spit drip down right above my clit. He fists his cock as he rubs it through the saliva and repositions himself.

Well, that's fucking hot!

"Tell me when Love. Be ready because I won't hold back."

I'm squirming now with anticipation.

"Please Finn."

That's all I had to say. He slams into me, thrusting with so much force my vision darkens, and I lose myself. The lamp flickers casting shadows across Finn's face, mixed with his glistening sweat, he looks like a god, and I'm in his heaven. Pausing he reaches for my left arm and rests my hand on my pussy. My clit pulses.

"Touch that pretty little cunt for me Love."

I comply.

Stretched and filled, trembling beneath him, I arch my back

beckoning him to take me into his waiting mouth, as I work my clit. Hot breath and then his teeth lightly graze my nipple, I'm in ecstasy and threatening my release.

"Fucking bite me Finn."

What has gotten into me, I'm a fucking animal. I'll probably never see him again after this. What the hell? Might as well make it worth my while.

He doesn't hold back as I feel my flesh break and he begins to suck. He continues to slide in and out with shear force urging me to release but I'm still not ready. Running my left hand down the length of his back, I dig my nails in feeling every muscle working and my pussy tightens in response. With my right hand, I grip his hair and pull. He growls.

"Get off!" I shout.

He pulls out of me and raises to his knees looking at me with bewildered amusement. Smiling up innocently, I look at the dildo that I just recognized was still on the bed from my earlier rendezvous. His eyes follow mine as they land on my toy.

"Didn't I say I wanted to toss that thing?" He cocks his brow.

"Well, maybe just this once, you could tag team." I play, batting my lashes.

"You're killing me woman."

I smile, seeing I got my way. I roll over and pull myself up onto my hands and knees, poking my ass out to give him a good view. Crawling up the bed, I reach up and grip my headboard with one hand, holding myself up and with the other I reach for the dildo. Turning it on, I slip it into my wet pussy and begin rolling my hips.

Finn clears his throat. "It's a damn beautiful sight, but what about me?"

Is that a streak of jealousy I hear? Don't lose your nerve now Lib. You're in control.

I look over my shoulder.

"Now Love, I have more than one hole, don't stop now."

I smile, mockingly using his own words against him. Throwing my head back, I moan just to show him how much I'm enjoying this.

He wastes no time as he positions himself at my ass. First, I feel his tongue at my slit, working it slowly back to my opening. I feel his tongue flicker across my hole and shiver at the sensation. He pulls away and spits, his saliva runs down as he spreads me. Then, one finger slowly inches his way inside until it accepts him, then he adds another, stretching me. Once I relax and fall into him, he lifts up and positions himself. Feeling the piercing first, then the fullness pressing into me, I still, allowing my body to take him. Tears threatening my lids, I begin to use my, almost forgotten, dildo again to help dull the pressure. We shift and get more comfortable.

He's so large.

My vision blurs as he slowly inches further in and we find our rhythm. First pain and then sheer pleasure wrecks my body taking me to heights I've never been.

I guess he made good on his promise.

Each thrust has him dancing on my G spot. Between his cock and this dildo, I'm losing control. The bedside lamp begins to flicker as we pick up the pace, closing my eyes, too lost in my climax. He lets out a growl and I scream as my body jerks uncontrollably. I feel his hot load release deep inside me and I lose my vision and all control, as I hear the bulb shatter.

3

I collapse breathless, collecting myself and recovering from that marathon I was just a part of. "Shit, that was fun! I hope I have some more lightbulbs." I laugh, moving to the side of the bed.

I sit up and will my legs to work, shakily standing and make my way into the bathroom. Closing the door, I take a deep breath, turn on the water and glance in the mirror.

"What just happened?" I ask myself.

He will probably be gone before I even go back out there.

I clean myself quickly and begin rummaging under the cabinets until my hand lands on the box of lightbulbs. Before walking out, I slip on my silk robe, leaving it open. I'm surprised to find him lying on the bed when I walk back out into the room. Partially covered, the down landing just below the start of his "v" with both hands resting behind his head.

I would never get tired of this sight. On second thought, no robe.

I think to myself as I let it fall to the floor.

He's a one and done.... But why does he feel different?

His eyes are closed and his breathing back to normal. I look at my cellphone; It reads 9:16 p.m.

Fine. I'll let him nap. But as soon as he wakes up, he's gone Lib. Yeah, yeah, I hear you.

I walk around the bed to the dresser, screw in the lightbulb and my eye catches my mother's letter. I exhale, releasing the breath that I didn't notice I was holding, and pick it up. I'm careful not to wake my visitor as I sit down beside him. Opening the letter, I begin to read... I'm halfway through the note when I feel Finn scoot in behind me and put his hand on my lower back. Then he sits up and looks over my shoulder.

"What are you reading there Love?"

I have a battle within my head whether to share or not. I don't know him after all. Either I feel safe in this moment, or I'm still sex drunk, but I answer.

"It's a letter from my mother."

He goes quiet, waiting for me to offer more.

When I don't, he says.

"I won't push, and I know you don't know me. But I sense you carry a lot and never get the chance to share. I'm safe Love. You can trust me."

That safety net just broke.

Trust. My ass.

I lose my shit. At this point, I am seething.

"Trust you? I don't even fucking know you! My mother trusted my father and he left her to battle cancer alone, make hard decisions about my life, all because he was too much of a pussy to stick around. Look where trust got her. Now look at me, laying in a bed naked with a man I don't even fucking know. Not to fucking mention one who snuck into my house and was snooping around like some creep. Yet, you want me to trust you?"

Why did I just unload all my trauma on a man I barely know?

No one knows my history and I am usually good at keeping it to myself. Why is he different? I keep rambling, angrily. It comes out like word vomit.

"You think you can waltz in here with your Irish accent without being invited, fuck me, and demand I trust you. Fuck you!"

I do not do trust and I do not do sharing. It shows, because here I am throwing the fit of the century, after an epic orgasm. Tears are streaming down my face as Finn wraps his arms around me trying to sooth me. I fight against his grasp.

"GET THE FUCK OUT!" I yell.

I'm at the point of hysteria. The newly replaced bulb shatters again as my chaos pulses through the air.

Finn stops fighting, releasing his hold on me, and stands up to get dressed.

"You won't get rid of me that easy. Make no mistake, I *let* you be in control this time. It won't be like that next time." He clenches his jaw.

"There won't be a next time!" I scream at him, chunking my dildo at his head.

He easily dodges my pathetic throw and walks to the door. I hear it open as I fall back into the bed covering my head with my comforter. The door slams. I lay there sobbing, feeling like the biggest fucking idiot, until I feel my eyes go heavy.

I cannot believe I just fucked a man that broke into my apartment, you need help Lib.

My last thoughts are of Finn O'Brien, and I drift off to a restless night of sleep.

I wake, reaching out before opening my eyes, but find my bed is empty.

Of course it is, you kicked him out.

I roll my eyes. Since when do I care?

I reach for my cellphone on my nightstand, letting my eyes adjust and I read the time. 7:43a.m. The feeling of emptiness surprises me. I'm used to being alone, but this feels different. My mind trails off.

Shit, Tink is going to ride my ass. Late, two days in a row.

I rush to get ready and head down to the bookstore. Tink is smiling.

"I see someone needed their beauty sleep." She winks.

'Spill it Tink." I roll my eyes, knowing she is up to something. She rolls her eyes.

"Okay. Fine. So, your Irishman came in this morning and left you this." She says, and hands me a folded-up piece of paper.

"I may have read it already, I'm sorry, but you should go. I got the bookstore." I roll my eyes and huff dramatically.

With that, she turns away and scurries off to the back of the store. I take a deep breath.

What the hell?

I open the note.

> Love,
>
> Ok, so I get it, you got a mean streak, but see here, I have never felt the magnetic pull that I feel when I'm around you. Fight it if you must, but you're my own personal drug that I cannot get enough of. Last night I seen pain in your eyes when you read the letter from your mother, and apparently, I fueled that fire. I get we don't know each other, and I know I am asking a lot of someone who I can tell is used to being alone, but would you give me a chance? I'm away now and hate that I left on such odd terms. I had to catch my flight. The life of a musician unfortunately. I am away a lot, but I could see sticking around a place if I found something worth sticking around for. I think that 'something' is you. I'm going to be playing a gig in two weeks time in Sequim. It's a local bar there called "Pour". I know the owner and he pays well. He wants to give the locals a good show. And I want to show you a piece of me. I'll pick you up at 6pm. I know where you stay. If you should need me before then, I took the liberty to add my number into your contacts when you went to the bathroom last night. Maybe set a lock on your phone, Love.
>
>   Finn O' Brien
>
> Mo shiorghra

I pull my cellphone from my back pocket almost in disbelief

and go to my contacts. Sure enough there it is. Not only that, but my messages were open and any guy I have sirened in the past, if I had his contact or message him, they were deleted.

Red Fucking Flag. What the actual fuck?

I quickly go to google translate and type in the odd word written at the bottom of the letter.

MY ETERNAL LOVE.

What the fuck have I gotten into, and why do I kind of like it?

"No!" I raise my voice as Tink heads towards me. "You know my rule. I siren. Then we're done. End of story."

"You didn't siren him though. He told me himself."

What an asshole!!

Tink keeps on and on and by ten o'clock I've finally agreed to accompany him. Just to shut her up. That's the only reason.

Yeah right!

Me
Fine if you really want to take me, let's play 20 questions. Might as well get to know each other.

Finn
Sounds like fun! What do you want to know love?

Me
Why me? Why not Tink?

Finn
Because it was YOUR soul crying out to me.

Smooth talker.

Finn
My turn. What are you most scared of?

That's mighty personal but I guess we are jumping right in.
I make him wait awhile just for theatrics.

Me
I'm scared of acceptance. Equally just as scared of not being

accepted.
What was it like growing up with your parents?

Finn
Oh, you know the regular. I had a pretty standard upbringing until my family exiled me for choosing my music. I haven't spoken to them since I was 18. What about your childhood?

Me
Loaded question. Are you sure you want to know?

Finn
I want to know everything about you Love.

Alright buddy. You asked for it.

Me
Well, I told you some when I went off about trust. (sorry about that lol) My mother died of cancer soon after I was born. My father went MIA. I'm guessing having a kid wasn't in the cards for him. I was placed in four different foster homes, each one worse than the one before, until I ended up with Sandy. She is the one who left the scar on my chest. She would drink and convince herself that I was sleeping with her boyfriend. After I went back to the group home, I aged out. Not a lot to tell really. Your turn?

Finn
Damn that's tough. You sure did good for yourself Love. I'm about to go help get our set ready. I'll give you one last Question. Make it Count.

Don't think too deep, something simple. Safe.

Me
Why do you want me to be in control so much?

Finn
Because I want to see the potential you're afraid to let show. Bye now Love. See you in two weeks.

Two weeks later

"You know you like him. Hell, he texts you multiple times a day. He knows more about you now than me at this point. When's the wedding?"

I'm so not up for her shenanigans.

"Are you nervous for tonight?" Tink asks.

"Can we just focus on the store?" I respond smiling.

As our day takes off, Tink and I get busy catching up with the bookstore. Sales are great but could be better.

"Hey Tink, want to shut the place down for lunch? I could use some sushi."

"Hell Yeah, you know I can eat my weight in that shit."

She's practically bouncing up and down. I smile as we head to the door, lock up and start down the sidewalk. We decide on one of our favorite sushi bars and spent thirty glorious minutes, just talking as friends do.

"So, catch me up! Back to Finn's note; I've been dying to ask. He said, "last night" in it. Did you fuck him? You've been so close lipped about your 'encounter'," Tink smiles.

"Jumping right in huh?"

"Well, it sounds like you did."

"Yes girl! Okay. We fucked. Is that what you wanted to hear? It was wild, in fact, he was in my apartment when I got there, but then he pissed me off and I kicked him out." I admitted exasperated.

The bite of sushi falls from Tink's lips. That shut her up for a moment. She recovers though.

"Stalker much?"

"I don't know it was kind of hot. Spontaneous even. Nothing I have ever done before. I didn't even distort his vision."

"Girl, I have told you all along that you never needed to, but you don't listen to me." She rolls her eyes. Changing the subject I say, "I love the bookstore but sometimes it is really nice just to get away." She nods in agreement.

"I'm considering branching out and bringing in some novelty items to see if they sell. What do you think?"

"I think that's a great idea." She says, bouncing in her seat.

"While I'm in Sequim I will check out an apothecary there to see if they have anything that our customers may be interested in."

If I have to go, I might as well make good use of my time.
Fucking him. No Lib. That was a onetime thing. I sigh.
For fucks sake. I'm Fucked.

We finish our lunch and as we are walking back, something catches my eye. We get closer to the front door of "Grimoire", and I notice a single black stem rose placed in the handle. Plucking it out, I see it has a burgundy ribbon wrapped around the upper stem with a small, plain cream-colored card attached. Inside on one side it says *fragile and delicate, easily broken!* the other has the letters *"ASC"* and nothing else.

What the fuck is that supposed to mean?

There is an energy radiating off of the flower and it is not a good one.

"Is it from lover boy?" Tink asks mockingly.

"Um, I don't know. I don't think so. All it says is **ASC** and **fragile and delicate, easily broken.** Could it be for you Tink?" I say laughing nervously.

Something about this rose is familiar and the moment I saw it, I knew it was for me.

"Tink I'm going to make a phone call really quick. I'll be in, in just a minute." Tink cocks her brow and enter the bookstore, clearly shaken.

Real smooth, Lib. She knows who you're calling.

I pull my cellphone from my back pocket and hit the call button before I can come to my senses.

"Well, Hello."

He picks up on the first ring. Surprise etched on his voice.

"Did you put a rose in the handle of my door at *Grimoire*, it drips with bad energy. And what does ASC even mean? Is it some Irish acronym I'm not aware of?" I ramble, exasperated, and filled with an uneasy energy.

I explain to him that me and Tink stepped out for lunch, that we almost never do, and what we found when we returned.

"Someone knew we would be gone; I just know it. Was it you? I feel like someone is watching me, but nothing seems out of the ordinary." I say frantically looking around.

Your panicking Lib. Get ahold of yourself.

"Wait, calm down Love. What are you talking about? I'm still a few hours away. Maybe it was left for Tink." He says.

"No, I felt the energy. It drips of dark magic." I say defeated.

"I cannot come right now but put up some protection and I will be there around four. Lock up the store and you and Tink let no one in until I get there. That's an order."

I thought I was the one in control.

"I'll figure it out. Nothing will harm you. Your Mine Love."

He says jealousy dripping off his tongue.

I don't even correct him because I'm so caught up in everything going on around me.

I belong to no one buddy.

I begin chanting my incantations and soon have a protection barrier cloaking *Grimoire*. Walking in, I lock the door and move my attention to Tink. She looks at me puzzled and I explain to her that something doesn't feel right. She doesn't fight me on it. We decide to use the time to restock, to busy ourselves.

4

It's almost two p.m. and as I'm busily stocking a shelf, Tink calls over to me.

"Lib." She clears her throat as she taps her wrist.

"What?" Playing like I don't know what she's insinuating.

She rolls her eyes.

"Get your witch ass upstairs and start getting ready, before I carry you myself."

I laugh at the image in my mind of Tink attempting to carry me.

"Fine." I smile surrendering.

"Oh, wear that black mini skirt with the slit. He will die!"

Shaking my head, I run up the stairs laughing.

My hands are visibly shaking with excitement as I step into the shower. I've almost forgotten the threat that seems to be looming over me. Beginning to let the hot water fall down my skin, I think of Finn and feel the heat travel through my body pooling at my center. Before I know it, I'm grabbing the chorded shower head, lifting and propping my right foot on the edge of the tub. I begin letting the water run on my clit as I spread my lips.

Oh Gods it feels marvelous!

Changing the setting to pulse, images of our first night dance through my mind. I let the warm water bear down on my now throbbing clit, grabbing my breast into my hand, pinching my nipple. I shift the water, giving me a short reprieve to let my orgasm build. The image of Finn biting down on my inner thigh flashes through my mind as I return the water to my center.

I run my hand down my wet body and slide a finger, then two, into my hungry pussy. Greedily pumping, meeting the pace of the pulsing water, I'm taken over by sheer climax; writhing under the water as my body convulses. Coming undone, pleasure takes root in every inch of my body.

Ok I'll give you a beat but pull yourself together Lib. You're running behind with your senseless need to orgasm every time you think about him.

My thoughts interrupt my bliss.

I roll my eyes, wash off quickly, and step out of the tub.

I spend way more time than I've ever allowed myself; styling my hair, making sure that every curl is in place. I actually take the time to do a full face of makeup.

Who am I?

A girl that wants another mind-blowing climax. That's who!

I opt for that mini skirt Tink raves about, my deep sage green cami, no bra, *because who needs one with these tits,* and a light suede jacket. I dress it up with my gold crescent moon necklace, Hamsa bracelet, and my nose ring. I walk over to my dresser, but I decide differently.

No panties either.

I smirk at myself. I don my favorite pair of black thigh high boots and I take a look in the mirror.

That'll do.

Just as I grab my purse, I hear my cellphone ring.

Damn, where is it? Oh yeah, bathroom counter.

I run toward the sound and pick it up. "Hello". I whisper.

"Well Love, you sound breathless. How about breaking down that barrier so I can be the reason for that?"

Little do you know; you already are Finn O'Brien.

"Absolutely! I'm on my way down now."

I say way more enthusiastic than I would have liked to. Locking my office, I head to the front of the store.

Gods he's delicious.

He's leaning lazily against the counter talking to Tink. He

doesn't notice me yet, so it gives me a moment to drink him in. My mouth waters. He's wearing a dark gray beanie, a button-down black shirt that's open at the chest, some faded blue jeans and boots. He looks every bit of the starving artist that he is. I notice that in the last two weeks his facial hair has grown into a perfectly manicured beard. I can't wait to run my fingers through it. I lick my lips and I step out of the shadows.

He looks up and stops talking mid-sentence and I smile innocently. Tink turns her attention to me, and I swear her jaw drops to the floor. Finn is the first one to speak.

He clears his throat, and then lets out a rather raspy "Wow!"

I cast a glance at the floor. I don't know how to take a compliment, so I recover with, "Wow, yourself."

We both close in the distance and then I'm in his arms. We kiss each other with such urgency that we forget Tink is there for a moment. I bring myself back down into reality.

"Sorry Tink."

She just claps her hands and bounces up and down like a child.

"So, I was telling Tink that I felt the same energy off the rose. I don't know what it is Love, but you've got to be careful. In fact, while I'm in town, outside of the gigs I'm obligated to, I will be staying with you. Hope you don't mind."

More of telling me than asking.

I know I look at him like I'm deranged.

"Excuse me? Last I checked I am a witch that has been capable of staying alive for thirty years, so that won't be necessary." I bite out.

"I wasn't asking." He states matter of fact.

And then crushes my lips with a needy kiss before I can further protest. I come up for air.

"We barely just met."

Tink butts in with, "Maybe it's a good idea."

I look at her with a 'shut the fuck up' glare. I can't rightfully stay mad at her though because I know she's more freaked out about the mystery flower than I am.

"Fine." I manage, defeated. "But let's get out of here. I got a stop I want to make in Sequim."

"Yes Ma'am. After you."

Sequim is beautiful. Just as I remembered. I don't come here often at all, even if it is only a little over an hour away from Bainbridge. I make a mental note to make more travels.

We begin down the sidewalk of Main Street and I feel a strong buzz of energy pulling me. It seems familiar and safe, but I cannot place it. Coming to the entrance of Salt and Sage Apothecary, we stop at the door. The reviews do not do it justice. It's captivating, a place that calls to my very soul.

"Do you feel that?" I ask Finn.

"Feel what?"

Oh well, he doesn't press, and I don't say. We enter the shop and I feel like I need to look at everything. "Welcome to Salt and Sage. My name is Jinny. Can I help you find anything?"

This little petite human buzzes. She's dressed like your average gothic, but she reminds me a lot of Tink.

"I'll just take a look around." I say with a smile.

There is everything from oils and crystals to candles and figurines. My eyes land on a basket filled with Onyx crystal and I think to myself that these would be a great novelty item to promote my latest edition. Readers will eat this up. I give myself a mental pat on the back. I knew this place wouldn't disappoint. Making my way to a display table that has the most captivating figurines atop, my breath catches on their beauty; I feel drawn to these items. I catch their Onyx eyes looking straight into my soul, as if they are trying to communicate something with me. Blown glass dragons; they're magnificent, the detail unlike anything I have ever seen, etched with vibrant colors of reds, oranges, and yellows. I'm eye level with these creatures.

"Jinny, are these products of Salt and Sage?"

"Oh no ma'am we special order out of La Connor for

those. There is a place called Rose and Ember. Their work is unmatched. If you're ever out that way, they have a very unique store. You have to make an appointment to visit unless it's the weekend, or you can order direct. I can give you the contact information if you would like."

She grabs a pen and post it and begins writing the information. I stash the post it in my bag for safe keeping until tomorrow, I plan to call first thing.

"The Onyx crystals?"

"Yes, now those are ours. They are wonderful at absorbing negative energy. Nyx is the very best at what she does."

Well, I guess that works out double for me, for my readers and my looming threat.

"Can I place an order, please, to have them shipped to Bainbridge Island?" I smile.

"Oh, yes ma'am. Just fill out this form and we will get to work on that order for you."

As I'm filling out the form, Jinny begins bouncing up and down covering her mouth. I look up at her with a questioning gaze. She points at my name on the form.

"Your Elizabeth James' like the author of *'The Onyx'* Elizabeth James? I thought that was you, but I wasn't sure. Just wait until I tell Nyx. She owns the place. She will be so jealous that she wasn't here."

"That's me." I say shyly.

I don't do well with fans. If it wasn't for that one press release, no one would know what I look like. Finn is now standing beside me and lets out a laugh.

"Imagine how I feel. To know I get to sleep with this beauty and she's my *all-time* favorite author."

Oh my Gods, I want to just die. He such a pompous ass.

He puts his arms around my shoulder and leans in and kisses me on the cheek. Jinny swoons and I'm left in the wake of it, tongue tied. She's about to lose it. Reaching under the counter, she pulls her copy of *'The Onyx'* out and asked me to sign it. I quickly scrawl my name inside the book jacket, pay for my order, and rush for the door.

As we walk out of the Apothecary, Finn leans in and whispers.

"Are we here for work or play?" He questions.

"Are you Jealous?" I ask him slyly.

"She asked for your autograph, not the famous musicians," he said with a grin.

"This was for work, now we can play!" I smirk.

He smacks my ass and then grabs my hand as we go around the corner and start down a rather dark alley lined with brick buildings on either side.

We step into 'Pour' and I automatically love the atmosphere. It is so full of everything, with decor and pictures from all over.

"Hey Finn, the boys are building up the stage and getting set up. You probably want to give them a hand."

I hear a middle-aged man say. I look in his direction and he's quite delicious himself for an older gent. I smile.

"Hey ya Morgan, do me a solid and see that my lady gets a good drink and an even better seat."

"What can I get for you, pretty lady?"

He's a charming guy.

"I would die for a Margarita, Hun." I say as I follow him over to the bar.

He hands me the most delicious margarita I have ever put to my lips, downing it, and asking for another.

"Wow, I hope you can hold your liquor ma'am. I make `em strong. What's your name?" he inquires.

"Libby James, but everyone calls me Lib."

"Nice to meet you Lib. I'm Morgan. Welcome to 'Pour'."

He takes my arm and leads me to a booth left of the stage, I have a seat and then look at my cellphone and the time reads 7:28 p.m. as Morgan makes his way to the stage. It's not overcrowded but every seat seems to be filled.

Please be good.

I become nervous for them.

"Welcome to 'Pour'. We have a special treat for you tonight.

Please join me in welcoming 'The Misfits'."

The band walks out on stage; breath taking, all of them. My eyes, though, lock on my Irishman. The first set of songs are originals. Finn is in his element. I notice each muscle tense in his forearm as he strums his guitar, heat pooling at my center. I'm so caught up and hollering with the crowd that I don't notice Finn moving and taking place in front of the center microphone.

"I brought a special guest tonight. Normally I leave the singing to my lad, Jon, but tonight I got to make a good impression."

Then he winks at me. I'm regretting not wearing those panties now, because I am about to flood this booth.

He begins singing a cover of Death Cab for Cutie's, *I Will Possess your Heart*. I lose all control. Our eyes lock and it feels like it's just the two of us. I feel the lyrics as he sings.

The crowd erupts with cheer as the band makes their exit. I don't know if it is the liquor or Finn's voice, but I'm about to combust when he finally makes his way to me.

"Wanna get out of here?' He whispers, his voice dripping with sin.

I shake my head yes and he grabs my hand. Their lead singer Jon yells after us. Turning around and making eye contact, I can see this encounter will not end well.

"Aren't ye going to share ye little pet with us, Finn? You never bring us playthings anymore."

Finn gives a glare that stops Jon in his tracks.

"Don't you speak of her like that again Jon, I will break your fucking face. She is mine and I do not share."

Jon turns as white as a ghost and holds his hand up in surrender.

"I was jest playin' there Lad."

He stutters in his thick accent; his blazing eyes saying

otherwise. Ignoring Jon, Finn turns his attention to me.

"Are you ready to go?"

"Absolutely."

When we walk out of 'Pour', the nights' chill hits us and my nipples harden in response. Catching Finn look down and take notice; a smirk begins to play on his lips.

"What do you want to do Love?" I go quiet because he knows.

"What do you want to do Love?" He asks again more urgently.

"You!" I smile.

"Then what are we waiting for?"

I look at him in surprise.

"What do you mean? We at least need to get back to Bainbridge." I say.

"No! Now!"

There is no sound of sarcasm in his voice as he slowly backs me into the brick building.

He looks around as if to gesture.

"We're in a dark alley Love. You can distort images. Distort us while I take you right here, right now."

He whispers into my neck, his lips grazing my skin. I can feel my pulse beating in my center, my wetness damp against my thigh.

I feel him smirk into my skin when he sees that I'm not putting up a fight. Chanting an incantation as his lips caress my neck, the energy lifts across us. I gently push against him and remove my jacket. A shocked expression comes across his face as I take off my cami and I stand there topless.

Good he wasn't expecting me to play his game. Check.

He kisses me deeply diving his hands into my hair, the brick biting into my naked skin, and the erotic sensation making my knees weak. Inhaling, I take in his scent of tobacco and sage and my senses ignite. Power pulses out of me, the illusion holding steady. His hands move from my face as they trail softly down my sides. Getting to the hem of my mini skirt, he lifts with both hands until it is bunching at my waist.

"No panties."

He growls, slowly skimming my wet pussy with the pads of his fingers.

"That's my naughty girl."

Losing no time, I grab his belt and take it from his waist and toss it aside. Unzipping his pants. I let his cock bob free.

Gods I've missed this.

Squatting I begin sucking his cock like a mad woman. I pick up rhythm; his hand gripping my hair beckoning me until I reach his shaft, as he pumps deeper and harder into my mouth. The tears threatening my lids make their release and run down my face. His piercing touches the back of my throat, and my clit throbs at the thought of what else it could touch. I hum softly to keep myself from gagging. Finn pulls my head back away from his cock, letting me know that he is ready.

Thank the Gods I wore these heels tonight.

Kissing and reaching down aimlessly, as my back is plastered to the brick, he touches my wet pussy.

"Oh, fuck Finn". I gasp.

"Just the way I like you Love. Wet and waiting. What do you want?"

I know I'm in control, so I don't waste time fighting it.

"Fuck my pussy Finn."

He doesn't hesitate. Widening his stance, he lines his cock up to my slit. I use the wall behind me as traction as he slams his dick into me, sinking deeper and deeper. He uses both hands to brace himself on the wall until I grab one arm guiding that hand to my throat.

"Choke Me."

I lift one leg and wrap it around him as he grips my neck. He's holding just enough pressure to darken my vision. I hear faint talking in the distance, but I am too distracted. Each stroke is causing a fire to build inside me. I'm about to lose control. I start shaking as the orgasm takes me; Finn releases my neck just as my climax peaks. My pussy muscles tighten around him. Simultaneously, thunder rolls in the night sky and I let out a cry.

"Yes Finn."

He continues to thrust as my body convulses. I feel the illusion starting to fade. Slowly I collect myself and whisper.

"I want to finish what I started and suck you dry but I feel my power weakening, so the image won't stay much longer, and your band... is literally twenty feet away. This may have to wait."

Finn looks me in the eye and says.

"Fuck it. Let em watch. Especially that dick, Jon. He needs to know your mine."

A smile plays on his lips.

Is he for real right now?

Every fiber in my body is on fire for this man. No way would this be something I would even dream of doing but this is different. I am stronger with him.

With that, I released the image, lowering myself to my knees, and begin sucking Finn's dick. The band has now stopped talking and just stares with a mix of confusion and intrigue upon their faces. Except for the lead singer who looks to be seething. I meet Jons eyes and will myself not to blink as Finns cum spills down my throat, lifting my middle finger in the air.

Fuck you!
Checkmate.

"Tonight was epic."

I say as I lay on his chest reminiscing about the activities from this evening. I run my fingers, mindlessly through his chest hair, pausing to look up.

"Thank you Finn."

"Whatever for Love?"

He looks at me puzzled as he strokes my back softly.

"You took me at my most vulnerable and gave me confidence. I can't explain it, but you push me to push myself."

He smiles a lazy smile and then kisses my forehead.

We lay in silence for a while, and I catch a glimpse of my

mother's note on my dresser. I fight the urge to reach out and grab it. Instead, I look at Finn.

"I think I'm ready to go."

"Go where Love?"

"To visit Agatha. Would you go with me? I can talk to Tink tomorrow and have her watch the store."

My heart is pounding in my ears.

"Of course, I'll go with you Love. The sooner the better. We will get the answers you need, and you can finally put that burden to rest."

My eyes are weak and for the first time in forever, it feels like I have a peaceful night of sleep.

"Morning, Tink."

I gear up for the question that she will inevitably be asking. She props her elbows on the counter and rests her head in her hands.

"Tell me everything."

"Whatever do you mean?" I bat my lashes playfully.

"You know exactly what I mean. How did last night go?"

"Well, we fucked in the alley after he sang to me, so there's that."

She has to pick her jaw up from the floor.

"You slut."

She says as she grabs me and starts jumping up and down hugging me. I'm laughing when the phone rings and I break our embrace.

"Grimoire, how can I help you?"

Silence, heavy breathing, there is a low growl, and an almost inaudible.

"Your next."

"Who is this?"

I say as I look over at Tink who now has a concerned look on her face. The phone disconnects and I'm now just listening to a dial tone trying to collect my nerves.

"Must have been some kids trying to prank call."

I say, trying to cut the tension. I decided not to tell Tink what was said, knowing the threat was intended for me. I feel anything but calm. Looking at Tink I notice she shares the same sentiment. I decide since I have the phone in my grasp, to go ahead and give Rose and Ember's a call. I cannot wait to see what they can come up with for what I have envisioned.

"Can you hand me my purse Tink?"

I rustle through my bag and finally find the post it, grab the phone and dial the number.

"Good day from Rose and Ember, my name is Alex, and who do I have the pleasure of speaking with?"

Well, this guy is the bubbliest person I've ever spoken to.

Instantly, I am calmer.

"My name is Elizabeth James. I got…."

"SHUT UP, SHUT UP.OH. MY. GOD. The Elizabeth James?"

"Yes, I…" He cuts me off again.

"You are fabulous. I own everything you have written. Do you remember that time…."

He's rambling but his voice alone makes me happy. I giggle and clear my throat.

"Oh yes, darling, I'm sorry. Sometimes I just get carried away. How can I be of your assistance?" He recovers.

"I was in Sequim last night and went into Salt & Sage. I inquired on a set of figurines and was given this contact information. I own a bookstore here in Bainbridge and was wondering how much trouble it would be to place an order. I envisioned maybe some small fairies and wolves, keeping up with the themes for my fantasy readers. I'd be willing to pay generously."

"Girl, O will be thrilled to do some work for you. Something to tie into your new book? She has a series of wolves already made, but I'm sure she will want to do something custom for you. Pricing won't be an issue. Honestly, she undercharges, but she makes up for it with a special request with every order. She requests a picture of the product display as part of her payment."

Oddly I'm intrigued.

"Also, she works quickly, but she's working on multiple pieces so it could take a bit, but for you I'll see if I can sweet talk her into squeezing you in." He says flirtatiously.

Charm will get you everywhere Alex.

I chuckle, "No need to rush Hun."

We talk numbers and details a bit longer before I hang up the phone.

Cheaper than I expected for the level of detail that dragon had.

"We will have two orders coming in Tink, one from Salt & Sage and one from Rose & Ember."

I attempt to change the subject because Tink still looks pretty shaken up.

"Did we get anything good in the mail while I was gone?"

"Not really, same stuff. Another convention invite."

I just shake my head. It's not that I purposely ignore them, it's just that I'm not a people person so I would rather not.

"So did anything else happen last night?" Tink asked.

"Not really. Oh yeah, I meant to ask. I was thinking I would take a day off Friday if you could take care of the bookstore?" She smiles.

"Sure thing boss. You got a hot date?"

"Not exactly. I'm finally going to go visit Agatha."

Her smile fades and her facial expression grows serious. I've shared my letter with her, and she knows that I have been struggling mentally with it.

"Are you sure you're ready?" she asks, concern filling her eyes.

"Well not really, but with all these weird incidences happening around me, I need answers and I have a feeling she will know exactly what is going on."

I blow out a breath of exasperation. We work the rest of the day in awkward silence. I think Tink knows I just need time to think.

5

Friday

The misfits played a gig in Seattle last night, so Finn agreed to meet me here this morning. I step off the ferry and my nerves are buzzing. It's rather chilly for September in Seattle but I have a feeling that I'm shivering for a different reason. Finn is there waiting, as promised, looking ravishing as always. My mouth waters.

"Well, hello Love."

He says as he takes his jacket off and places it on my shoulders, over my own. Sensing my anxiousness he says.

"C'mon Love, you've got this. You're in control."

He drapes his arm lazily around me. With that we turn and head in the direction of Hitt Hills.

"Hurry. Please hurry!"

I hear a panicked voice in my head.

What the hell was that?

"Hurry!" She is screaming.

I fall to my knees with my hands covering my ears as a piercing sound takes over my senses. I cannot hear anything going on around me. People stop and stare, but I don't care. Finn is squatted down in front of me grabbing my arms. The shrill sound subsides, and I lower my hands.

"What's wrong Love? Come back to me. What's going on. Damn it, speak to me!"

Concern etched on his face. I don't know why but I am sobbing. He lifts me to my feet, still searching my face for answers.

"You didn't hear that? She's screaming. I have to get to her."

I don't know how I know but I know it's Agatha summoning me. I take off running. Finn wastes no time as he follows me. I feel the magnetic pull beckoning me as we start into the entrance of Hitt Hills Park. We are running for what seems like miles. We get right to the outskirts, and I feel it. There is a cloaking spell. I know what it's like to distort images, so I know this is the work of another illusionist.

"There's a barrier up", I say as I catch my breath.

"Yes, I feel it too. It's rather weak. Do you think you can break it?" Finn asked.

"I can try."

Holding out my hand, I feel my powers pooling, ready to release. I begin to chant, focusing on bringing down the barrier. He's right. It is weak, but I'm still not strong enough.

"I can't." Tears sting my eyes, "But I have to get to her."

"Yes, you can."

Finn steps beside me grabbing my hand and reaches forward. He starts chanting and I join in.

"In the realm of shadows, I stand tall,
Summoning the power to make this shield fall.
Barrier of obstruction, I command thee,
Dissolve into nothing, set the path free."

Within seconds we feel the release of the barrier and what looks like an old, abandoned house comes into view. I look at Finn and we share a moment of skepticism but then I'm off, taking the steps that lead to the front door two at a time. The house is a dull gray wood exterior, boards are nailed covering the windows. This was possibly a beautiful Victorian house at one point. Now it seems to be a sad shell of what it once was.

I grab the door handle, twist and push with all my might,

expecting some type of resistance. Instead, I nearly fall into the front door.

Unlocked. Weird.

There are cobwebs everywhere. The smell of dust and iron fills my nostrils. I take my cellphone from my back pocket to use for light and notice Finn do the same.

I come to a complete halt once the door closes behind us. I feel something I can only describe as thick and sticky underneath my feet, knowing before I even look. Tilting my phone toward the floor, I see dark crimson congealed blood pooling at my feet, a body, neck gaping open, lay maybe 10 feet away from me. My head goes dizzy, and knees start to buckle. Finn catches the sight I'm sure because he grabs me before I make it to the ground.

I'm going to be sick. Hold it together Lib. She needs you.

Finn bends next to, what looks to be a middled age man, to assess the situation. Clearly the man's throat has been slit. Dark blood crusts on the edges of the gaping hole. It's oddly shaped, *like a crescent moon,* I think to myself. He checks for a pulse and says what I already knew to be true.

"He's Dead."

I stare into his vacant eyes unable to look away.

"Maybe we should get out of here." Finn says, startling me from my trance.

"No. I feel her. She's here."

"Okay Love. Let's find her then."

We step over the body as we both start searching rooms for any evidence of Agatha. I come to a halt when I get to a door right off of the kitchen. She's there, I just know it. I open the door to a set of stairs leading to what I assume is a basement. Swallowing hard as I walk through the doorway, I begin down the steps.

Lib, what the fuck are you doing? Are you trying to be the next murder victim?

I ignore myself and finish descending the stairs.

I see light but I can't tell just yet where it is coming from. A complete contrast to the rest of the darkened house. There are no cobwebs to be seen, but the smell of copper and iron is strong.

The wall is cold and damp to the touch, and I use it to center myself before I go any further.

Be strong Lib, Agatha needs you.

I look around the corner and at first, I see nothing, a bright light so bright it is threatening to shatter. There is a single bulb swinging from a chain descended from the ceiling. My vision registers and I can't breathe.

Bodies. They're everywhere. There has to be at least twenty of them, their bodies twisted and mangled, like an animal ravaged them before discarding them and moving on to the next. They form a circle, their blood trailing towards the center of the room where an older lifeless woman is bound to a chair. She looks like she's been tortured for information, her body covered in what looks like a thousand tiny crescent shaped cuts, each placed specifically for pain and not death. Chains are cutting into her flesh around her wrists and ankles. Her fingers and toes are purple where her blood has pooled to her extremities.

On the wall in front of her, written in blood "ASC".

Suddenly her head lulls back, exposing the large crescent shaped cut on her throat, blood dripping from her cracked lips.

She's still alive. Oh my Gods.

"FINN!" I scream. "Down here in the basement."

With a quick flip of my wrist, the chains release and I catch her as her body falls limply from the chair. Moving her to the floor, I hold pressure on her neck. I hear heavy steps racing down the stairs. Finn looks at me with a shocked expression.

"What the fuck happened here?"

He asks more to the universe than to me as he looks around in bewilderment. He makes it to my side and takes over holding pressure. I will every ounce of power I have, but I don't know what I can do. I can't heal. Agatha grabs my arm and stares into my eyes.

Beware, He's coming for you. Nothing will stop him!"

I hear in my mind.

She turns her head toward Finn, her eyes growing wide. She looks like she's trying to speak, but her last breath is taken from her, the light in her eyes vanishing into the darkness that now consumes them.

"I'm sorry! I'm so sorry." I cry. "I should have gotten here sooner."

Why Lib, why did you wait so long? You're always so scared to do what needs to be done and look what happens!

I sob as I cradle her lifeless body. Finn releases the pressure from her neck and gives me a few moments to grieve her loss before he grabs me and pulls me into his safe embrace. I let him hold me as I stare at the sticky blood on my hands. We sit there for minutes, maybe hours. I can't be sure.

"What do I do now Finn? The bodies of her and her coven. They will have a field day covering this story. I have to do something. I have to cover this up. I can't let them be found like this."

I don't know why I feel such protection over Agatha, but I especially can't let her be found like this. Not after everything she did for my Mom.

He understands exactly what I am implying.

"We have to destroy the house. Will you help me?"

"Always. For you, I'd burn this world down." Finn says.

I don't know if it's just the moment, or the situation we're in, but I am thankful for his words. I take one last look at Agatha, her tortured face now etched in my mind, as Finn helps me to my feet. We ascend from the basement and exit the house. The moment we are out of the house, the vice grip that I didn't realize was threatening my air supply is released. I can breathe.

"Are you ready love?"

"As ready as I will ever be." I answer nervously. *Damn it Lib, stop being afraid.*

I quickly cast a circle, centering myself and Finn inside. I lift my hands, feeling the power like I never have before. I'm furious, I'm sad, and I feel like I just lost the last connection to my mother. The wind starts howling in the distance. I close my eyes and all I see are their decimated bodies, and the letters scrolled across the wall in their blood. Fury flows through my veins as energy pulsates through me.

I call to the Gods.

"In this circle of power, we summon your aid.
Invoke the elements, let justice be paid.
For the innocent souls, their blood has been spilled.
With your purifying flame, let their fear be stilled. "

Lightning strikes the house, a spark flashes and fire spreads across the roof. I feel its warmth in my hands, shooting from my core to feed the flames. I turn to find Finn staring at me in shock, he's struggling to hold his footing. The wind is whirling around me and the house. It's then that I realize he is not doing any of this. This is my chaos.

Yes Lib, let your chaos burn.

I turn back to the house, my hands still outstretched, radiating energy, glowing like I've never seen them before. The house is engulfed, the flames reaching higher, licking at the sky, casting an eerie glow that can probably be seen for miles. The intense heat radiates outward, scorching the earth. I continue my plea to the Gods.

"Strengthen our will, in your powerful name.
Let the earth be cleansed, in your cleansing flame.
Turn this tragedy into a purifying pyre.
Burn away these sins, bring forth my desire."

I drop my hands as tears roll down my cheeks. I fall to my knees as most of the surging energy in my body dissipates. The wind goes still. Finn reaches my side and holds me as we watch the house burn. A loud crash sounds as the house collapses sending embers into the air.

"That's enough love." Finn whispers.

I call to the Gods one more time.

"Spirits of the West, I summon thee,
Bring forth the rain, from the deep blue sea.
Let clouds gather across the sky,

Bring forth the rain, let the fire die."

The sky opens and rain falls from the heavens, washing away every fiber of evidence that took place. I kneel there and stare at my hands. They still have energy pulsating through, but every drop of blood is gone. I look to the clearing sky, now noticing the energy still surging through my body. I need to release it. I look to Finn, his face etched into an indiscernible expression.

What just happened?

The ferry ride back to Bainbridge is quiet. Once we are back on common ground, Finn breaks the silence.

"What happened when you got off the ferry this morning?" He asks delicately.

He's going to think your bat shit Lib.

"I heard her. Agatha. In my mind. I can't explain it."

He just nods, a perplexed expression on his face.

"You must think I am crazy." I throw up my hands in defeat.

He grabs my arms to slow me and pulls me into him.

"No, I just think we need answers now more than ever. You're receiving black roses with the letters "ASC" and now I just saw those same letters spelled out in a witch's blood. An elder, no less, who you were summoned by. Also, you've been receiving phone calls. Yeah, Tink told me."

I'm going to kick her ass.

Might as well get it all out there.

"Agatha said one other thing as she was dying." I whisper, not quiet meeting his eyes.

"What did she say?"

His facial expression is hard as stone. I feel his body tense against mine.

"She said, "Beware, he's coming for you. Nothing will stop him.""

I see anger in his eyes.

"I don't fucking know who "he" is, but I will fucking rip out his heart."

We walk into the bookstore and Tink is bouncing up and down, per usual. The feeling of normalcy washes over me, and I bask in it.

"I wanted to call you last night, boss lady, but it was late. So... When I left work yesterday, I didn't really want to go home. I went down to the bar to unwind. I just wanted a drink and to just relax."

She is rambling and I'm here for it after the shitshow that just happen.

"When in walks the most beautiful person I have ever laid my eyes on. I mean your beautiful too Lib, but not in the 'I want to sleep with you' kind of way." I giggle.

"I disagree." Finn interjects and I playfully elbow him in the side.

"Any who, blonde hair, blue eyed bombshell. She just got out of a bad 'situation-ship' and needed a drink herself. We talked for hours. I almost pulled a 'you' this morning and was late."

Tink is smiling ear to ear now. She never talks of people like this. Usually, it's just no strings attached, and we compare dick sizes.

What is happening to us?

"Wait a minute. You said 'she'. I thought you were 'strictly dickly'," I say playfully.

Finn raises his hands in surrender. He begins to laugh as he turns away. Looking over his shoulder he says.

"I'll be over there being anywhere but, in this conversation," as he points to the other side of the bookstore.

"I don't know, she's different. She sees me Lib." Tink says with a sigh.

"Well, when is the wedding?" I use her own words against her.

"Shut up!" she says laughing.

"So, what's her name and when do I get to meet her?" I say with my brow cocked.

"Her name is MK, and you can meet her ...oh... in twenty-three minutes when she comes by to walk me home." She grins.

"Oh, I almost forgot. How did it go with Agatha? And why are you two wet?"

I feel my smile fade and tears spring to my eyes.

"Oh god, I'm sorry. What did I say?"

She looks over my shoulder to where Finn is now taking his place at my side. He rests his hand on my lower back waiting for me to respond.

"No answer, she wasn't there and it rained on us." I whisper in a small voice.

What's wrong with you Lib? You don't keep things from Tink.

I justify it with the fact that I do not want to worry Tink any more than she already is. Also, the threat isn't aimed at her. We know that for a fact now.

"Hey Tink, how about you take a long weekend? Come back Tuesday. Take these next few days to get to know MK. You've been working really hard lately, and you deserve it. All expenses paid."

"Do you mean it Lib?" the sheer excitement dancing across her face.

"I do. I can handle things here."

Almost, as if perfect timing, the bell above the door chimes. I see Tink's face, and I know right away that this is indeed "MK". Tink walks around the counter and closes the distance between her and MK. She leans in and kisses her cheek.

"You're early. Come meet my friends. MK this is Lib. She's my boss and my bestie." She gestures to me. "And that," She points at Finn, "That is Finn, the dick that tricked her." We all laugh.

"Keep talking and I'll trick Love here, into taking it back on your long weekend." Finn says with a grin.

"Fine." Tink holds her hands up in surrender, playfully.

"Go ahead and get out of here, I'll close up."

Tink smiles. We bid our goodbyes as Tink and MK leave.

"They're cute. I hope Tink's able to settle. She needs that." I say out loud more to myself than to Finn.

"Well, what about you? How do you feel about settling?" Finn says as he walks over to the windows and begins lowering the blinds.

My mouth goes dry. I search for words, but they don't come. He walks to the door and turns the lock.

Catching his eyes I whisper.

"There's still three minutes left until close."

"Not tonight! I know the owner. I'll take it up with her." He smiles, joking.

He walks over to me and lifts me up and sits me on the counter. Taking my head in his hands, he kisses me more urgently than ever before. I feel the energy radiating off of him and through me. Our touches are electric. Finn begins trailing kisses down my neck. He pulls away long enough to find the hem of my, still damp, shirt and lifts it over my head. Once it's off he dives back into my neck. He comes up for air.

"We were so powerful out there today."

We? Who is this we? That was all me.

My thought subsides as he begins kissing right at my collarbone and he bites down with force. I feel my flesh break and I let out a small whimper.

"Yes Finn. Don't stop."

But he does. He pulls back and licks his lips. Searching my eyes he says.

"What do you need?"

"What do I need? I ... um... I need you to be in control tonight."

I expect to get an argument. Instead, he surprises me.

"Go get a chair." He points towards the breakfast tables.

"O... kay."

I hop down off the counter looking at him puzzled. My nerves are literally vibrating.

"That's Yes Sir or Yes Daddy, to you."

Sin dripping off his voice.

Daddy kink. Ok Finn. I like it.

"Yes Daddy." I say playfully.

"That's my naughty girl. That should be all I hear from you tonight other than the sound of you choking on my cock." He growls.

I gulp. I've never seen this side of Finn. He's obviously been holding back. I love that he pushes me to be in control, but this, I could get used to.

Awkwardly, I carry the chair back over to where he is standing. Looking at me with lustful eyes, he begins to undress me. I reach for his shirt, and he grabs my wrist.

"No not yet."

"Yes." I say still playing.

He reaches behind me and smacks my ass.

"Yes, what?" he demands.

"Yes Daddy!" I squeal, heat building in my center.

I'm now standing completely naked in front of him. "Sit! Where are the keys to your apartment? Speak."

"Why?" I wonder aloud.

"You have one more time of disobeying me, naughty girl, before I lay you across my knee and spank your ass. Don't question me, just answer."

Well Gods damned if that doesn't sound hot!

I don't ask further because my body is buzzing with anticipation; every nerve ending on fire. I need to know what comes next.

"You can go through my office. The code is 431#."

Why did I just give him that? Tink doesn't even have it.

It seems like it is taking him forever. I sit, with my ass on this cold wooden chair, and smile at how ridiculous this must look. He enters with a handful in tow.

What the fuck is he doing?

He literally brought down a basket in one arm and a cup in his opposite hand. I suppose he got thirsty as he was packing my house up. I laugh to myself.

"You ready to have some fun?" He smirks.

"Yes."

He clears his throat.

"I mean, yes daddy." I say, licking my lips.

"Good Girl."

He reaches into the basket and pulls out my scarf. Walking around me, he places the scarf around my eyes. He stands me up and pulls me across his lap, face down.

"Did you think you can disobey me without consequences?" My nipples bead to the point of pain. A small giggle escapes me and then I hear the loud smack, followed by pain. My center warms as my pussy muscles tighten. I feel his cock pulse beneath me.

"No Daddy."

He pushes me to my feet. Grabbing my arms he shifts me.

"Sit."

I obey; my ass and back finding the cold wood again. I hear him undo his belt as my senses heighten. He grabs my arms and pulls them behind me and begins tightening the belt, binding my wrist taunt.

"Are you okay with this Love?"

"Oh my Gods yes … Yes Sir."

"Good girl."

I am so wet. I have no idea what's coming, and the anticipation has me more turned on than ever. He runs a brush through my hair.

What the fuck?

I think to myself as he parts my hair into two sections and begins braiding it. As if he knew I was about to question what we are doing he says.

"I need to get your hair out of the way for what's to come."

"What's to come?"

"Shhh Love. Let me ask you. Do you think I would hurt you? Speak."

"No." I whisper.

"No what?" he says with a tug of my hair.

"No sir." I say with a quick shake of my head.

"Good." He says offering nothing more. I hear footsteps as he begins to move but I don't know what he is doing. I smell a match and hear him blow it out. Then I feel his presence close by again. I hear a lot of things being moved around, getting no warning before I feel it. It burns painfully at first, but then igniting everything within me. The wax drips down my collar bone and begins to cool.

"Ohhh Fuck, Yes Daddy. That feels so good."

"Oh, you like that?"

But he doesn't wait for an answer or for me to recover. He pours the hot wax, this time right above my nipples. it drips and cools. A new sensation as it hardens against my areolas. He must be on his knees because he grips my ankles and spreads my legs. With no warning I feel at least two fingers inside me.

"Love, you're soaked. Tell me this is what I do to you? Speak."

"Yes, I am so fucking wet for you daddy."

He finds his rhythm and I'm writhing in the chair. He pulls his fingers out.

"Taste how sweet you are Love."

He says as I feel his fingers at my mouth. The taste is tangy and sweet as I suck my wetness off him. He pulls away for a second and then I feel the warmth of the wax again. This time running down my left thigh.

Oh God it feels so good.

Wasting no time, he dives into my pussy, and I lose it. Now I know what the cup was for. Between the hot wax and the ice that he is currently swirling around my clit, I am losing all control. I cannot hold back any longer. I scream, wiggling my hips and moving into his tongue. My muscles tighten as I come undone. I will the belt to drop to the floor. At the same time the scarf falls from my eyes.

That'll do, I needed to see him.

"You just couldn't stay put, could you Love? Tsk Tsk" he asks with a devilish smile on his face.

"My turn."

I say as I stand. Finn gets to his feet, then grabbing his shirt, he pulls it over his head never taking his eyes off mine.

He takes off his boots and finishes undressing as I drink him in. He is a god, I swear it.

"Sit."

I say using his words against him.

He does but adds.

"I'm still in control. Do you understand?"

"Yes, sir."

"I guess it's time for me to choke on that cock, Daddy."

I grab the cup of ice and put a piece into my mouth. I get to my knees, grabbing his dick, I waste no time. I feel it pulse beneath my hands and warmth pools at my pussy. Using my tongue to guide the ice, I run it over the tip and the ring before sinking down over his length. Soon the ice is melted, and I begin taking more and more of his cock until tears threaten my lids and I'm gagging. He forces my head down as he thrusts upward.

"Yes, you suck that cock, baby. You're my whore only. Do you understand?"

I hum my answer against his dick.

His words have me weak, and I am dying for him to be inside me. I pull my head back and I get off of my knees.

"I have control over things that are mine. My life. My choices. They are mine." I bend and reach forward gripping his dick and I say, "And this. This cock is mine."

I turn around allowing him to help me get lined up and I sit down on his length. It takes me a moment but soon I'm bouncing and moving my hips as I ride him. He grabs the braids on either side and pulls until my face is looking at the ceiling.

"Yes Daddy."

He meets each one of my movements with a thrust. "Ride that cock Love."

"Whose cock does this belong to?" He rasps.

"Me." I say breathlessly.

He moves one hand from my braids and reaches around and grips my pussy as he slides in and out of me.

"And who's sweet pussy is this?"

"Yours."

"That's a good fucking girl."

He pulls his hand away until it comes back down with a slap against my needy cunt.

My vision darkens and I swear I see stars. We both moan and fall apart as I feel his warm cum spill out into my pussy.

Yep, definitely yours Finn O'Brien.

6

Scared. Eyes full of warning. She's scared. Dying. "Run!"

I sit up startled out of my restless sleep, tears streaming down my face.

Inhale, exhale, come on Lib.

I reach for my phone, the face reading 3:33 a.m. Great, the Devil's hour, that doesn't freak me out at all. Well one thing is for sure. I can't go back to sleep right now, so I try to be quiet while I sneak out of bed. I find myself standing at the sink in the bathroom, dousing my face with cold water. I look up into the mirror.

"What were you trying to tell me Agatha?"

I say out loud to my reflection.

"Focus on Me. You need to know the danger that is coming for you sweet girl."

Her voice rings in my head; laced with warning.

Placing my hands onto the counter to brace myself.

Why do I have this connection with her? No one has ever communicated with me like this.

I think to myself. I stare into the mirror, my hands growing warm, glowing as my power pools. I am pulled away and a vision appears; a small woman kneeling on a dirt floor. It isn't me but we look a lot alike; she's thinner, more fragile, and bald. Her face is mine though. Even with the pale skin and dark circles around her eyes you can tell she is beautiful. She looks sick, very sick, and really weak. Crying, looking down into a blanket in her arms, between sobs she speaks. Her voice, even in this moment comforts me.

"My God, do I love you little one. You are perfect. Your Aunt will take good care of you and place a protection over you. It is a danger for you to stay within the coven, but one day you'll make your way back and she will be here to pick up the pieces. I love you, Elizabeth."

Shifting, she lays down onto her side, pulling her knees to her chest while still cradling the infant.

Me and that's my mom.

She lies sobbing and then her body goes limp as she releases her last agonal breath, the sound horrifying. The only sound now is a blood curdling wail released from the blanket. A silhouette forms walking up to the scene I am now entranced in. I recognize her. She is younger but that is her.

Agatha. She's my aunt?

Reaching down she lifts the blanket and kisses the baby, *me*, on the forehead.

"Shh, now! I've got you, sweet girl. I vow to you that as long as I live my big brother will not harm a hair on your head. Forgive him, for he knows not what he's done."

She begins to chant an incantation and the connection breaks. I glance into the mirrors, tears streaming freely down my face. I don't fight them, welcoming the pain to leave my body in any form that it can. Agatha is speaking to me, even now from beyond the grave.

She wanted me to see the last encounter with my mother, but why?

Finally collecting my nerves, I head back to bed determined to get some sleep before work. Something feels off. My sliding glass door slams open with a gust of wind that follows. I rush toward the balcony, and I spot it as lightning flashes in the sky. A single black rose dripping with crimson. A small card attached with one word.

"RUN!"

"Love, are you okay? What the fuck just happened?" Finn sits up startled.

I don't say anything. I am paralyzed in place. The tears come again, and the sobs escape me. Finn rushes to my side, now seeing what has me held in place.

Finn runs to the balcony, grabs the rose, makes his way to the trashcan, and tosses it in. Walking away to the sink and washes his hands, he directs his attention back to me.

"Someone is trying to mess with you." He says, anger filling his voice.

I'm still standing like a statue, unmoved. He comes back over, closes and locks the door. Lifting me up, he carries me back to bed. I curl up next to him, my head on his chest. I don't say anything right away.

"Do you want to talk about it?"

"I don't know…" I deeply exhale. "I haven't been able to get Agatha out of my mind. I close my eyes and I can see her face. I know she was trying to warn me about something, but now I will never know. And now, this. What did I do so wrong?" A tear falls from my lid to Finn's chest.

"I'm sorry Love, maybe you'll get answers soon enough."

He grabs my chin and lifts it to meet his eyes, pausing.

"Lib, I Love you. Your mine."

My mind goes dizzy.

Did he say what I think he just said? Do I even know what love is?

He tightens his grip around me. I know I have a strong pull to this man. Stronger than anything I have ever experienced. Maybe that's what this feeling is. I let go.

"I think I love you too Finn."

And that thought scares me more than my looming threat.

I lift myself up and straddle him. He meets my lips and electricity pulses through us both. Both of us hungry for this, needing it. My hair wraps around his fingers as he pulls me deeper into the kiss. Releasing me, he stares into my eyes.

I miss his mouth already.

He's not telling me something.

"What is it?" I ask.

"Love, I have to leave. I know it's bad timing, especially now that this shit keeps happening. I leave Monday for Canada. I'll be gone for a month. We have a tour that I'm obligated to."

I just shake my head in agreement. Life of a musician. I've been independent all my life so why does this come as a blow to the gut? He searches my eyes looking for a response. I don't quite meet his eyes because I know if I do he will see that I want him to stay.

No, you don't, you're a fucking badass and you're in control. Lib needs no one.

I truly am at war with myself. I decide not to tell Finn about the vision I just had in the bathroom. No need in making things worse now.

He moves me from on top of him, gets out of bed and starts rummaging through his duffle bag, pulling out a long black rectangle box.

"I have you something. I have spelled it with protection, for while I am gone. I know you are perfectly capable of taking care of yourself, but it would make me feel better, now more than ever, if you would do me the honors of wearing this." He says as he circles the bed.

I sit up on the side as he opens the box and my breath catches. "It's beautiful."

It's a black chained necklace with an emerald pendant. The emerald green has a hypnotic swirl to it and it is breathtaking. I stand and turn around and lift my hair. As soon as the necklace grazes my skin, I feel its warmth and familiarity. I let it envelop me. It falls just to the top of my scar. I twirl around and give him a little show.

"Well, how does it look?"

"Like it was meant for you. Gods your beautiful." He says as he lifts me and throws me on the bed.

"We aren't getting any sleep tonight."

I wake startled. I must have fallen asleep on the couch

sometime late this morning. I reach for my phone; it reads 5:23pm.

Wow my whole day is about gone.

I feel his energy before I even see him, as the apartment door slides open; him carrying a brown paper bag in tow.

"Oh, good Love, you're awake. Go take a shower. I'm making you dinner tonight." He says smiling.

"I'm sorry I must have fallen asleep on you." I apologize.

"Don't worry about it Love, now run along, while I get things started."

I hop up and head to the bathroom. Feeling my stomach rumble, I notice I am rather famished. I stand under the hot water as the steam rises around me. I feel my muscles loosen; I'm pulled into my own head for a moment until the aromas from the kitchen invade my senses. I am brought back to reality. It smells delicious.

I rush out of the shower in a haste only half drying myself off before pulling on Finn's black t-shirt and my black panties, making my way out of the bathroom still drying my hair with my towel. Finn is facing the stove and chopping up produce and begins tossing it into the salad bowl. At some point while I was showering, he took off his shirt and is now standing barefoot in my kitchen cooking. My center warms at the sight of his faded blue jeans resting just shy of his hip bones. I lick my lips.

Damn Lib, why must you be such a slut?

"What have you got there? It smells amazing."

"Well Love, the pasta is almost finished and I'm currently working on the salad."

He says walking toward the sink to wash more produce. I hop up on the counter of the bar so I can watch him work. He looks like a natural in the kitchen.

As he begins washing the produce, I about lose it. The grip he has, as he strokes the length of the cucumber in his hand has me in a choke hold. As if he feels my eyes on him, he cuts off the water and turns to look at me with a devilish grin.

"Have you not had enough of me Love?"

He places the cucumber next to me on the counter and rest his hands on my thighs. I bite my lip at the contact of our skin.

"I will never get enough of you." I reach for him, but he retreats.

"I have a better idea."

He lowers himself between my thighs. I drop my head back and reach for the back edge of the counter anticipating his next move. He slides my panties to the side as I place my feet on his shoulders, opening myself to him. He runs his fingers between my slit. A moan escapes. Slowly pushing two fingers into me, he leans in to circle my clit with his tongue. The pleasure tightens my core. I rock my hips into him, moving my ass off the edge of the counter, allowing him further access to my pussy. I moan deeper at his touch. I feel him smile into my cunt as my center pools.

I am lost in the ecstasy of his movements. My head snaps forward as I feel a cool sensation push into my center. My eyes widen as I see him looking up at me while thrusting the cucumber that had just been on the counter into my wet pussy. I am in shock, but the sensation of the slickness causes me to tighten around it.

He's fucking me with a cucumber! Why am I into it? Fuck it!

I drop my head back and let the euphoria take me.

"Good girl, you take it so well."

He growls from below me. I climax at his praise. He pulls the cucumber from me and licks my pussy deeper. My thighs shake and the orgasm rattles my soul. I sit up looking down at the man that just destroyed me with fucking produce.

He wipes his lips and walks back to the cutting board with a sinful smirk.

No fucking way.

He chops the cucumber into pieces and tosses it into the salad.

Oh, my fucking Gods.

We sit at the table in a playful conversation about the produce encounter that just unfolded. I look at my salad, smile up at Finn wickedly, grab a piece of cucumber and toss it into my mouth.

"Fuck this!"

He growls standing from the table as his chair falls to the ground. He strides towards me; grabbing me up, he lifts me over his shoulder and tosses me on the couch.

Looming over me, he rips my panties off and throws them on the floor.

"You're mine!"

He grits threw his teeth, unzipping his pants, and then thrusts his cock deep inside me.

Monday

We've stayed in the apartment all weekend. We've fucked more this weekend than I have in my entire adulthood, and that's a lot. I didn't even open the bookstore Saturday. It isn't like me at all.

What is this man doing to me?

I don't know if it is because I wanted the last two days uninterrupted with him or all of the threats. Either way, it's been a good respite when my mind doesn't trail back to Agatha and her haunting death.

"Take a shower with me Love."

"Absolutely, just let me finish my coffee."

Sleep hasn't been good to me, so I live on caffeine and sex these days.

"I'll go get it started."

He winks at me and my pussy warms.

Calm down bitch, your going to end up with the grand canyon for a vagina at this rate. Shit Lib.

I walk into the bathroom. Steam in the air, I pull the curtain back and to my surprise, Finn is fisting his cock. I smile.

"Don't get me wrong, I could get off to this sight but what are you doing that for?"

"Just trying to get use to my new normal for the next month while I think of you my love." He smirks as he slows his pace.

"On second thought this just will not do."

He grabs me, still in my sleep shorts and sports bra and pulls me into the tub. I yelp and I'm doubling over in laughter as he rips my wet clothes off of me and tosses them out. Facing him I look up. He moves my, now wet hair from my face.

"I'm going to miss you, Pretty Girl."

"I'm gon...."

But before I can get my thought out, he turns me around and pushes the center of my back until I have my hands plastered to the wall. Roughly, he grips my hair and pushes his cock with force into my pussy, from the back. Pain pulses through me, as tears threaten to fall. The pain feels so good as he thrusts deeply until I'm screaming his name. He reaches around gripping my breast as he keeps up at a punishing rate.

"Oh God, I'm cumming."

"Yes, fucking cum on my cock. Tell me this is the only cock that will ever be buried inside of you like this again."

My pussy muscles tighten around him, but he's still moving like a mad man.

"Tell me!" He growls.

"Yours, only yours." I choke out breathlessly.

I feel the heat of his cum fill me.

"I'm gonna miss you too."

I've only made it to noon, and I'm bored out of my mind. Finn left after our shower this morning and I opened the bookstore, but business is slow today. Tink is still on her extended weekend with MK, so I'm left alone to my thoughts. I've already restocked.

What else is there to keep me busy?

I grab all of the mail out from beneath the counter and a black envelope falls to the floor. It has prestigious white calligraphy written across.

Elizabeth St. Claire

That's not my fucking last name. And no one calls me by Elizabeth anymore. Oh well. Maybe they know something I don't. Very intriguing.

I.S.A.O

INTERNATIONAL SOCIETY OF ALCHEMY & OCCULT

Location: **82305 Tulane Avenue, New Orleans, LA 70112**

Date: **October 28, 2023 – October 30, 2023**

On Behalf of The International Society of Alchemy & Occult, we would officially like to invite you to attend and participate in our convention. The conference will be held In New Orleans at Humanity Hospital. Although vacant since Hurricane Katrina, the realtor has agreed to open the doors to allow our conference. The setting is perfect for all factions.

The purpose of the 3-day conference is to bring together researchers from around the world who are interested in exploring the links between the supernatural, phenomena, wicca, and many more factions. We plan to touch on all magical practices.

Should you require more information on our convention, please visit our conference website at www.secretsocietyDDCL.com. Thank you. We look forward to seeing you at the conference.

Sincerely,

THE INTERNATIONAL SOCIETY of ALCHEMY & OCCULT

Thomas Woodwind
(Conference Coordinator)

I pick it up and read over the invite. It's a convention for all occupations dealing with the occult. Something was pulling me to this letter. I can feel the energy radiating off of it at my fingertips. I shoot a message to Tink first.

Me
I think I'm going to go to this convention in New Orleans. There is something special about this one. And honestly, I could use the time away from here.

Tink
I think it's a great idea. When is it?

Me
It's on October 28th.

Tink
Well, I'll give you an extended weekend lol

Me
Thanks. You're the best!!!!!

Now to Finn.

Me
Hey, I'm actually going to go out of town. There is a convention in New Orleans, and I think it will be a good way to clear my head.

Finn
See the amulet is already working to protect you. Have a great time.

Finn
I miss you already and I cannot wait until our eyes meet again. It will be magical. That I have no doubt!!

Well, I guess we're going to New Orleans……..

Part Two: Olivia Rose

"Oh my goodness!!!" I squeal. "Eliza he's absolutely perfect! Mom is going to fall in love with him." I say as I scratch underneath the puppy's chin. He's a beautiful 12-week-old Cavapoo. His cute little brown curls and tiny ears remind me of a teddy bear. Eliza clears her throat and says, "Are you sure getting her a puppy is the best idea? He can be a handful. He's already been returned once, and I'd hate to see it happen again."

The puppy in question is currently chewing on my fingers. He has sharp little teeth, but I know he can be trained on what not to chew on.

"I'm sure. She needs something special to bond with, and unfortunately, I am just not that something," *or someone,* I think to myself.

"Well alright then. Since he's already been bought and returned, there isn't much paperwork, but he is already named and registered, so if you want to change it, you'll have to go through the AKC."

Eliza hands me the folder with all the puppy's documents inside. I open it and look at the certificate, *August Theodore.*

"Well, that's an interesting name you have there, August". The dog looks up at me and barks. "At least you know your name," I tell him as I scoop him up in my arms. "Thanks a lot Eliza. You don't know what this means to me."

She smiles and waves as August and I leave for the bus stop. It's almost 7pm. I told mom I'd be home by 7:30. I can't wait to surprise her. She is never going to expect it.

As we wait for the bus, I shift August to my left arm and dig in my bag.

Where is the damn ribbon? I know I put it in here. Ahhh there it is.

I pull the ribbon out as the bus pulls up. The door opens and I'm hit with a blast of warm air. I didn't even notice it was cold outside until now. I climb the stairs and swipe my transit card. The driver grunts his acknowledgment at me as I move to the middle of the bus and sit down, placing August on my lap. I slowly work the ribbon around his neck and tie a frivolous bow.

He's not the dog I would've picked for me, too small, but he's perfect for my mom. The perfect little lap dog. Something to give her purpose. For the first 18 years of my life, I gave her purpose, but when the clock struck on my 18th birthday, it's like the lights went out in her eyes. Her purpose was over. I've tried everything these last 3 years to bring that light back. I really hope this works.

We pull up and August and I exit the bus. He begins squirming in my arms, so I set him down to play in the yard for a moment as I just stand there. My feet feel glued to this spot. I was just so excited on the bus, but as I stand here looking at our house, a feeling of dread washes over me. Just once, I need Mom to be happy with me.

I look at our house. It's nothing special. It's a two-bedroom southern style bungalow. Mom complains about it all the time. I turn my face up to the night sky. The waxing crescent moon just barely visible.

I just really need this to work. I need Mom to be happy before I go.

I bend over and scoop August up in my arms, plaster on a smile, and head for the front door.

As I open the door, I am immediately hit by the smell of apples and cinnamon. I smile to myself.

Mom must've made me an apple cinnamon cheesecake for my birthday.

"Mom, I'm home." The lights in the living room instantly turn on.

"Olivia, your early. Give me just a few more minutes, okay?" my mom yells from the kitchen.

"Sure Mom. I'm just going to go wash up, but then I have a surprise for you."

I turn the lights in the living room back off with a flick of the wrist and head for the hall bathroom and close the door behind me. Setting August down on the floor, I wash my face and freshen up.

"Ok, ready when you are," Mom calls to me.

I scoop up August and head toward the kitchen. I can hear mom singing. She rarely does that anymore, but I love to hear her voice. I stop for a moment in the hall to listen, but she stops singing as she hears me. I walk into the kitchen, and she turns around with the apple cinnamon cheesecake in her hands with one candle burning in the center.

"Happy Birthday Olivia Ro... what on earth do you have there?' she yelps out.

"Surprise Mom!"

I blurt out as quickly as possible. I give her a big smile, but she just stares at me and the dog in my hands. My smile slowly fades away. August whimpers and licks my chin.

"Mom. Are you going to say anything?" She lets out a loud huff.

"Olivia, I don't know why you didn't consult with me first. What do I need a dog for? Just something else to clean up after and trip over in this tiny fucking house."

I stand there speechless for a moment, regretting my decision to bring the dog here.

"I'm sorry mom." I say quietly. "I thought it would be nice to have someone to come home to, especially when I move out."

My mom gives me an exasperated look.

"Olivia Rose you are not moving out of this house. You are finally done with college and working a decent job, you are going to stay here and repay me for all the years I spent raising you. You already know this. We've discussed it multiple times. I'm done working for that sexist pig. You are going to take over the bills and let me enjoy life like you did for the last 21 years."

I just stare at her. It doesn't do any good to point out I was a child for much of that time, or that I was in college getting my bachelor's in business the last 4 years and working a full-time job to pay half the bills. Or that we never discussed it, she just demands it and expects me to obey.

"I'm sorry mom." I say again, dropping my gaze to the floor. There is nothing else to say. Mom always gets her way.

"It's fine. We will figure out what to do with it. You'll just have to take care of, what is it, a boy, or a girl?" She asks.

"A boy." I told her. "His name is August."

In what felt like a slow-motion moment of life, mom drops the cheesecake, or should I say, slam-dunks it to the floor. Glass shatters, cheesecake splatters against the cabinets, the stove, the fridge, and our legs. My mother takes a step toward me, lifts her hand, and strikes me against my cheek. Blood rushes to my face and my cheek swells with heat, and just like that, time returns to normal, and mom starts screaming.

"How fucking dare, you bring that bastard into my home. What the fuck were you thinking?! I thought college was supposed to make you smart, not stupid. I should've known better though, with all your stupid talk of making figurines and moving away to abandon me again. I raised you better than that. You bring that abomination here! And on today of all days. You stupid little ungrateful piece of shit. I should've known you'd turn on me. You think you're better than me because you're a witch like him. Because you don't have to work for anything, you can just snap your fingers and make it happen. You disgust me, Olivia."

She turns, grabbing a glass that was on the counter and throws it at my head. I duck just in time for it to miss my face, grazing my head instead. I drop August. I hear him yelp and scamper away, but I don't know which direction he goes. All I can see is red.

"I could've been famous you know. People came from all over the world to hear me sing. But that bastard ruined me, and then you, you..."

Blood is dripping down my face from where the glass split my head. My head is spinning. My mother's words start fading and I feel like I am in a tunnel. My blood is pumping so fast I can feel the heat from it. I feel dizzy, like I am going to vomit, and then the room goes dark.

I think I blacked out. My mother is no longer screaming. I don't hear her in the house anymore. Honestly, I don't hear anything except for the roaring sound in my ears. My body feels like it is no longer my own. I don't really know what's happening. Somehow, I am no longer in the kitchen. I look around and realize I'm in my bedroom.

How did I get here?

I turn to my bedside table and see the clock. 9:38. Two hours have passed since I got home with August, and other than the first 15 minutes, I remember nothing. I close my eyes for a second and take a shaky breath.

When I open them, I notice a cream-colored card with deep burgundy peonies on its surface and the words "Happy Birthday" written underneath it in fancy calligraphy, sitting next to the clock. I grab it and flip over the card and see -*ASC* on the backside.

Odd. Who is ASC?

Mom must've set it in here, but my head hurts too much to think who it could be from. I set the card back down and turn to the mirror. Other than a small cut on my forehead, I see no evidence of our fight from earlier.

What happened? How did I lose two hours?

I sit down on the edge of my bed, feeling my phone in my back pocket, and think about the words mom screamed at me.

A Witch like him. You bring that Bastard in my home. You disgust me.

She must've been talking about my father. I know very little about him other than he is a witch like me. My mother has always refused to speak about him other than to say he's the bastard that stole her stardom away and saddled her with me.

Sorry I'm such a burden Mom.

Any time I try to discuss my dreams of owning my own business, she reminds me what she gave up having me. That I owe her.

I sure wouldn't exist without her.

I guess I've at least learned his name. August.

Well Fuck.

I jump. I feel like something just snapped inside me, like a wave of power I've never felt before. I turn toward the door, I need to go check on mom, but my feet won't move. I stare at my bedroom door. Smoke is billowing from under it and filling the room. I start coughing, choking on the smoke-filled air.

"MOM!" I scream.

My skin breaks out in a cold sweat, the slow realization that the roaring sound was the fire ravaging the house behind my closed door, not in my head. I look around the room and start to panic. I have to get my mom out of the house!

"Mom I'm coming!!"

I grab for the doorknob and quickly pull back. I didn't even get my hand on the knob before I could feel the heat radiating off of it. Flames start licking up the door like they are tasting the wood before devouring it. The sight is mesmerizing, and I feel drawn to it.

The fire cracks, and I jump, the sound pulling me out of the trance the fire was holding me in. I turn and move toward the window and open it. The fresh oxygen in the room feeds the fire, the flames now dancing across the floor toward me. I press the screen out and start to climb out feeling the heat on my back. The fire keeps ravaging on.

Suddenly arms wrap around me and drag me out of the window.

"New Orleans Fire Department, I've got you Firefly."

I push against him and start yelling.

"Mom, I've got to get my mom."

The firefighter continues to hold me and drags me into the front yard away from the house.

"Miss, I need you to calm down. How many people are in the house, do you know where they are?"

The house is completely engulfed in flames now. I see firefighters rushing out of the house. Water is spraying on each side, the red lights from the trucks dancing against the flames. The fire screams, fighting to break free from the home and engulf everything in its path.

"Mom." I say in a broken voice and collapse on the lawn.

Something in me feels like it breaks, as the sky opens up and rain starts pouring down.

Soaked to the bone, I stand and stare at the remnants of my home.

"It looks like candles were left burning in the back bedroom and caught the curtains on fire."

I hear the firefighter that has identified himself as Captain to me say.

I just nod at him.

Mom never burns candles. She hates them.

"I'm deeply sorry for your loss miss. Is there anyone that we can call for you?" I shake my head no.

I continue to stare at the house.

I killed my mother. I killed an innocent dog. Why aren't they arresting me? How can they not see that I'm a danger to society. I can't control my powers. I can't be a Witch.

"Firefly, I think you're in shock." I hear him say.

I turn and look at him.

Firefly? I must be hearing things.

He has the kindest sea green eyes I've ever seen. I don't deserve kindness right now.

"I'm fine." I mumble. "It's just a lot to take in. My home is gone, my mom, the dog." My voice cracks. "It's all my fault."

He looks at me with sad understanding eyes.

"It was an accident. You are strong. You'll get through this. Please let me know if we can call someone for you."

He reaches for my hand and squeezes.

"Everything is going to be okay."

I pull my hands from his and turn away without a word, walking toward the sidewalk, sitting down on the wet concrete. I can't listen to him anymore. He doesn't know anything, if he did, I'd be in the back of a squad car or be hanged from the gallows.

The fire is almost out, but the smell still permeates the air. I don't think I'll ever be able to forget the smell. I look down at my hands and clench my fist.

What am I going to do now?

As if the Gods hear me, I notice a half-burnt page from a magazine next to me on the sidewalk. Surprisingly after the downpour, it's dry. I turn it in my hand. It's a beautiful picture of a field filled with bright pink tulips. "La Conner, Washington, Tulip Festival" the headline says.

I pulled my phone out of my back pocket. Miraculously it's still there after all the commotion. I turn and look at my childhood home. Every terrible thing my mother ever said to me comes flooding to the surface. Swiping a tear from my eye, I try to think of the good memories too but come up empty handed. I turn back to my phone and before I could change my mind, I type in La Conner, Washington bus fare into the search engine.

I think it's time for a change.

7

Power flows through my hands. The glass dragon's wings slowly come to life.
A little more heat, a little more sand and ash. Just a touch more color.

Alex sits in the hammock swing in my studio watching me work. He acts as though he is mesmerized by my magic, like it's the first time he is witnessing it, every time. I smile. I remember his first time. His reaction was a bit more excited than he is right now, but the stare is the same. I don't use magic, except in my work, and Alex loves to watch. I don't get it.

I suppose I am a sight to see. Flaming hair, almost nuclear in color, it sits high on my head, curls spilling out of the messy bun. Sweat beading my brow, my sky-blue eyes radiating with power as I generate heat into my hands. Energy pulsating the air as I work. I spin the glass over and over, slowly working the wings into shape. The muscles in my arms are straining against my skin. Looking up I see Alex with an expression of envy in his eyes as he looks down at his biceps and flexes. I almost let a small laugh escape me. He's in the gym five days a week to keep his chiseled physique.

"Are you admiring yourself over there?"

I smile mockingly, and flex back at him as I set the dragon down on my worktable.

Alex laughs at me and locks his eyes on my newest creation. The onyx-eyed dragon is a magnificent creature, exuding an aura of power and grace.

"Wow, O you never cease to amaze me. It's like you took a dragon and merged it with a phoenix. This is definitely the coolest dragon you've done yet."

"I sure hope so. It's the last one of the dragon series the shop in Sequim ordered. I need to finish getting it cooled and boxed up with the rest of them before Marco gets here for the shipment." I say with a wink.

Marco has been our delivery guy for the last three years. Alex has been yearning for the man to ask him out already. So far, no such luck, but unless I'm dead wrong, Marco wants Alex as much as Alex wants him.

"You know, you could just ask him out yourself," I say smiling.

"I'll make a deal. "I'll ask him out as soon as you get yourself a date". He retorts.

Checkmate.

I feel my eyes darken and my smile vanishes. The lights above our heads begin to flicker.

"I don't need a man to make me happy," I spit out like venom.

"Open Mouth, insert foot. O, you know I didn't mean it like that. It's just... a date isn't going to kill you. Live a little. Find a hot guy and take the plunge. I'm not telling you to fall in love or get married, but bitch you need some dick. If that's not appealing, I'll take you to the new sex shop downtown, at least have an orgasm."

I feel heat rise to my cheeks and burst out laughing.

"Alex, what am I going to do with you?"

He walks toward me and puts his hands on my shoulders.

"You'll either love me forever or turn me into one of your figurines."

"Ha, now there's an idea!" I smirk.

"I was joking!" Alex jerks his hands back and asks, "Can you actually do that?" his face a little panicked.

"Are you nervous?' I laugh, letting him stew a little. "Actually...I don't know. I've never tried anything like that before on a living thing. There is only one way to find out." I say jokingly.

The storefront doorbell signals. "Saved by the bell." I smile at Alex. "Why don't I wrap this up and you go tell Marco I'll be just a minute?"

Alex looks a little nervous, but he starts walking toward the door.

"You were joking, right?"

He calls out over his shoulder. I just smile and turn away to start cooling the dragon.

Man, I love fucking with him.

I close the box with the last dragon secured safely inside. I tape the lid and put the shipping label on top.

"There, that's the final piece."

I say to myself. I can't wait to see the picture of Salt and Sage's display that they will send me. I look over at my cork board. Hundreds of pictures from different stores pinned in a gigantic collage. In the center is a single black and white newspaper clipping of my mom, Delilah Rose, standing behind a mic on the stage of a jazz bar in New Orleans. It's the only picture I have of her.

I'm sorry mom.

Bile rises in the back of my throat. I hate that I'm always drawn to look at her picture when I finish a project. I wish she could see me now.

In the almost 6 years since she's been gone, I moved to La Conner, Washington, and used the insurance money from the house and her death to buy this building. It took some time, but I eventually started my business, Rose and Ember, and made a life for myself here. The first two years I did everything by hand, without magic. I think I needed time to heal, knowing that I unintentionally killed my mother and August the last time I unknowingly used it.

That's how I met Alex. Trying to heal myself, I took a local yoga and meditation class. Alex was the instructor. We clicked instantly. We hung out every day for six weeks. We had one drunk night where we made out for a while before we both busted out laughing.

I remember him looking at me and going,

"You know I'm gay, right?" to which I replied, "You know I only date straight men, right?"

We died laughing, and then I told him I was a witch and he never questioned it. We've been living together ever since.

    I pick up the box and start heading toward the arches when Alex walks through.

"Come back to test the waters?" I say to him teasingly.

He ignores my question.

"Hey O, there's someone in the office wanting to see you." He says with a grin.

"Oh, not Marco?"

I question, knowing there is no way it is Marco. Alex would still be up front flirting with him.

"Who is it?"

"You'll see."

He says as he starts jogging up our apartment step. I watch him until he's out of sight. My stomach suddenly clenches.

    I push through the doors and walk to my desk, setting the box down on the counter as I look around the storefront. Dozens of four-foot shelves line the floor filled with pieces that haven't been sold, picked up or put on consignment yet. I make everything from porch swings to bed swings and frames to dining room tables and television stands. I can design pretty much anything that uses metal, glass or wood. I haven't hit a roadblock yet in my artistic abilities, though I'm always looking for new ways to push my limits. I smile and look around the building, but I don't see anyone.

Hmmm, I guess they are looking around.

I walk around the counter to go look by the furniture when I see him.

    "Fuck me!" I yelp out.

I can't stop staring into the biggest brownest, most soulful eyes I've ever seen. He stares back at me. His face is chiseled like a statue that demands attention. His broad chest and powerful limbs accentuate his tan muscular body, looking hard as stone, but agile like he's ready to pounce at a moment's notice. Despite his imposing size, he has a kind demeanor thanks to those soulful eyes. I yearn to touch him.

"You startled me."

I say to him, but he just continues to stare at me with those watchful eyes. My body is aching to move, wanting to stroke his exquisite chest. I don't know what's come over me. We continue to stare in silence. I slowly start stepping closer.

What on earth are you doing Olivia. Are you fucking crazy?

It's like there's an energy pulling me closer until I'm standing right in front of him.

"Hi."

Hi, really Olivia? That's your opening line.

I roll my eyes. He cocks his head to one side and looks at me, his face relaxing into an open-mouthed smile. I take that as a good sign. I reach out nervously, holding my hand beside his face for a moment, when he leans in and starts rubbing his face against my hand.

"Well, hello there handsome boy, who might you be?"

I squat down so I can look at the tag on the collar, but he proceeds to slather my face with his gigantic tongue. Laughing, I fall over as the dog excitedly gives me kisses like he's known me all his life. This mastiff is massive!

"Well, my Gods, do you let everyone kiss you like that when they meet you for the first time, or is he just really lucky?"

I gasp at the sound of the voice behind me. I try to scramble to my feet, but the dog is towering over me and isn't letting me off the floor.

"Who the fuck are you?" I yell snidely.

I can feel my face turning as red as my hair.

"I'm Marcel. I see you and Odin are already closely acquainted."

He answers as he steps out from the fantasy collection aisle. My mouth goes dry.

How fitting. My Gods, who is this man?

From my position on the floor, I can see he's every bit of six foot tall and then some. I can feel my stomach clench again.

For fucks sake he's exquisite.

His jet-black hair is a little long on top, a piece falling down his forehead stopping short of those beautiful large almond shaped ocean blue eyes. He has a beautiful olive complexion with skin as smooth as marble. His lips.

Gods be damned those lips.

They look soft and full. I let my gaze travel down his body, resting on his torso. My word, his arms look bigger than Alex's and that's saying something. His chest is as broad as Odin's and looks to be just as muscular, if not more.

I continue my once over and notice his long thick fingers before moving down his narrow waist and thick thighs. I can see a very prominent bulge in his black jeans, my mouth waters and my center warms.

Jesus Christ Olivia. What the fuck is wrong with you? Maybe a visit to the sex shop is in order.

I finally scramble out from under Odin and scoot back.

"Why are you here?"

He stops inches from me and rests his hand atop Odin's head. The dog is so massive his head comes right up to his waist. Perfectly inline for me to look at the dog, and the bulge in his pants.

Great.

He ignores my question.

"When I came to this town, I knew I was coming for work, but I didn't realize I was coming for pleasure too, Ma chère."

I pulled my gaze away from Odin, and a bulge I'll be dreaming about later, and looked up into his face. Something familiar itched at the back of my brain, but I don't know what it could be. I'd remember if I ever looked into eyes like his before.

"Listen here asshole, I'm not your chère, and I asked you a question. Two actually. Who are you and why are you in MY SHOP?" I'm almost yelling at the top of my lungs now.

I see Alex looking out the picture window in our apartment that overlooks the shop. He looks like he's smirking.

Alex what the fuck did you do?!

Odin moves away from the ridiculously gorgeous asshole and lumbers over to my side. I instinctively lay my hand on his head as Mr. Asshole takes another step towards us.

"Always lovely to meet a Witch, but one as stunning as you?" he says with a devilish smile, "Todays my lucky day."

Who the hell does this guy think he is?

"I'm Marcel La Croix," he said holding out his hand, interrupting my thoughts.

"My assistant called yesterday about us meeting to discuss the details of the St. Croix piece."

OH FUCK ME.

He represents a new client.

Oh Alex, you may find out if I can turn you into a fucking figurine after all. A damned donkey!

I quickly put a smile on my face.

"Ahh yes, I'm sorry, you, you just startled me," I stutter out. "Wait, did you just call me a witch?"

Did he just say what I think he said? "I'm sorry, what?" Marcel inches closer to me and smiles that devilish smile again.

Gods be damned, he has a killer smile.

"Listen belle, you don't have to pretend with me. I could feel your essence almost six blocks away. If you wanted to keep it a secret, you should've at least put up a ward or a sigil to let others know it's a secret."

I just stare at him and try to take a step backwards, but Odin's boulder size body is blocking my path.

"You do know what a protection ward is don't you?"

I shake my head, unable to find my voice, my breath coming out faster with every word he says. I've never met another Witch before, let alone been called out for being one.

Why does he keep coming closer, why is my body so warm?

Marcel continues stepping closer, his body mere inches from mine, "Ma chère, you have much to learn."

I would've sworn at that moment that he was going to try to kiss me, but I'll never know.

One minute I'm standing there staring at him, and the next moment Odin shoves into me so hard I go flying into Marcel. As soon as our bodies touch, electricity shoots out between us like lightning and strikes the lights overhead. Glass shards rain down, and Marcel throws his hands up causing me to fall to the ground. I look up and the glass is suspended in the air. Marcel whips his hand to the side, the glass following suit and slamming to the ground.

"What the fuck!" Marcel whips his head around to glare at me.

"I call you a witch, so you fucking attack me?"

Again, I am scrambling to my feet in his presence, "I didn't attack you! I was going to ask you what the fuck that was. I work with fire, not electricity, and I don't use my magic outside of work," I say with a huff.

"Clearly I can see why," he says implying he doesn't believe that I didn't do it.

He reaches into his pocket and takes out an envelope.

"Look, I was bringing by an invitation to the local art exhibit. They have some pieces my client wants you to see for inspiration. Maybe you'll have better luck keeping your powers under control in public. I'll meet you there at 8. Oh, and wear something nicer than that, okay? It's a black-tie event."

He throws the invitation on the counter, snaps his fingers at Odin, and they saunter out of the storefront.

"O, what the fuck just happened?"

I hear Alex calling out to me as he runs down the stairs.

"Are you okay? One-minute the two of you are standing there and the next there's lightning shooting across the room and glass raining down."

I stand there staring at the door that just closed.

"O!" Alex yells at me.

"I... I don't know. He thought it was me. I don't think it was me, but...what else could it be?"

I stare at my hands.

Am I losing control? Last time...Last time I killed someone.

I look up at Alex and tell him, "Maybe you shouldn't stay here."

Alex shakes his head.

"O, if you say it wasn't you, it wasn't you. You would know."

I feel my shoulders start to shake before the tears start running down my face.

"Mom."

It's all I can get out before I crumble to the floor against the counter. Alex sits down next to me and gathers me into his arms.

"It's all going to be okay honey. I've got you."

But is it?

8

"**B**itch, how is it that you can wield the perfect figurines with the flip of your wrist, but cannot eat Chinese food with chopsticks?"

Alex asked doubled over in laughter. He has spent the better portion of the day attempting to cheer me up. After the catastrophe this morning, he convinced me we needed a mental health day. So, for Alex that meant shopping until our arms could carry nothing more and ordering in for dinner.

"Not all of us are that *experienced* with *"sticks"*.

I say back playfully as I attempt to pick up my sweet and sour chicken. I fail as usual and look up just in time to dodge the pillow Alex flings at my head. Laughing, I start to tell Alex of my conversation with Marcel this morning.

"Does he really think he can insult me and then demand me go to some art gallery that he's hosting. That's ridiculous, right?"

Alex looks at me with an amused expression, so I know this is about to be bad.

"Well, bitch he did say it was for a client. What will it do to your reputation if you start flaking now? Plus, he's hot."

I give Alex a kill me now look.

"Girl, I'd suck the fart out of his asshole if he'd let me." Alex deadpans.

I literally choke on my soda.

"Jesus Alex! What am I going to do with you?"

"Love me forever? Use your magical powers to make me the richest man in the world? I'm already the most beautiful man ever so what else is there?"

I double over with laughter, rolling on the throw pillows.

Alex looks down at his watch, the diamonds on the Rolex dancing lights onto the ceiling.

"Bitch, you better hurry. He said 8pm and its 6:30 now."

He stands up and begins clearing the table.

"Plus, he did say that you basically look like a hag."

Unlike me, he couldn't dodge the pillow I threw at the back of his head.

"We, Bitch. We."

I say as I start to gather the rest of the food. "If I must go and endure his total ass-ery, so do you. It's a black-tie affair. Shall we go crash a party?"

We finish cleaning up the living room, all evidence of our dinner gone. I'm so glad Alex is as much of a neat freak as I am. I can't stand living in filth. We interlock our arms and begin down the hall.

We make it into my room, and it's a stark contrast from the rest of the apartment. I let Alex decorate the apartment due to his brilliant design skills and his passion for it. Most of the apartment is bright and bold, full of red, teal and dark wood accents. Many would think it's too much, but Alex makes it feel like home. It's cozy and warm with loads of pillows and fluffy rugs. I love how vibrant the apartment is, but my room is my quiet space and the one room I demanded I get to decorate.

I can instantly feel my mood start too somber. Black and gold are the focus. I love how at peace this room makes me feel. The large windows on each side of the bed covered with huge curtains help block out the light. I spare a glance to my bed, sunlight beaming down on the black and gold comforter from the skylight, while making our way to the closet. "Memento Vivere" is scrolled in iron and gold on my headboard. *Remember to live.* My daily reminder to choose life and not let my past define me.

We turn toward the floor to ceiling bookshelves and my ceiling hammock in front of the picture window, it slowly swaying back and forth from the fan above the bed. I long to climb in it with a good book, but I let Alex drag me into the closet instead.

We begin rummaging through, Alex on one side, me on the other. We share the walk-in closet that adjoins our bedrooms and the primary bathroom. The closet is as big as both of our bedrooms combined. I had it specially designed when we built our home above the store. There's just enough room in here for all our clothes, bags and shoes. Most of it I've never worn, but Alex loves his retail therapy and I always seem to add more to my wardrobe with every trip.

"Should I settle for the black dress?" I ask Alex.

"Abso-Fucking-Lutely not! You are bold, Olivia. What have I always told you? You weren't born to fit in, you were born to stand out!"

With that he pulls my navy-blue pantsuit out.

It screams sexy but reserved. I love it.

"You don't think it's too much?"

Alex turns and grabs a suit for himself. It begins as black and fades into a deep crimson red.

"Bitch, too much is our mantra!"

Alex smiles boldly and starts stripping in the closet.

"Marcel is going to shit a brick when we shine brighter than the art on display."

I smile, hardly able to contain my excitement. I join Alex and start changing into my pantsuit. We both decide on a light coat of foundation.

As if Alex even needs it with his beautiful chocolate complexion.

I attempted to put on some mascara and eyeliner, but Alex shoos me out of the bathroom. He's constantly telling me I don't need makeup, but I like to accentuate my eyes and hide my freckles in hopes to distract people from noticing my crooked lips.

If only I could have Alex's flawless face.

We look at each other with an approving nod.

Guess that will have to do.

We finish putting on our shoes and head for the door.
We look like trouble.

We pull up to a dainty strip right on time and I have to do a double take. I grab the invite out of my purse.
"Yep, this is the place."
I look over at Alex who shares the same inquisitive expression.
The sun has set but the street lighting allows me to see that it is an off-white building trimmed in dark sage. It sits between a museum and a wood merchant. Alex rounds the car and opens my door.
Over his shoulders I see Marcel standing at the front of the gallery, just outside the doorway with Odin. He is wearing a suit that looks like it was made only for him. My mouth waters. I'm so caught up I barely recognize Alex's outstretched hand. He clears his throat and laughs.
"See something you like already?" Alex asks with a lifted brow.
"Shut the hell up." I snip taking his hand.
Marcel is smiling and making small talk with a very attractive blonde. A twinge of jealousy catches me off guard.
What the hell Olivia?
Our eyes meet and I smile back. I watch as his smile slowly fades.
Dick.
He bids his goodbye to the blonde and makes his way over to me and Alex. I bend down to pet Odin.
At least one of them is bearable.
"Alex, and you must be Marcel. Our girl here has told me all about you." Alex says with a smirk as he extends his hand.
Marcel pauses but obliges.
"I'm Marcel, and what is it that you mean 'our girl'?"
"Oh No! Nothing like that babe. She's one appendage too short

for me," Alex says with a wink.

Dead, I'm dead. This is just going great. What was I thinking bringing Alex?

Marcel leans into my ear. "You don't fucking listen to directions, do you Ma chère?" He whispers.

"No, I do. But only when it matters." I say with more edge than I expect.

I grab Alex and pull him in the direction of the gallery. Once I step inside my social butterfly of a friend starts talking to everyone but me.

Thanks a lot Alex.

I wander off and find myself mesmerized by works of art from all over. The creativity level of some of these pieces are top notch. What I wasn't aware of was that the entire showcase tonight was blown glass. I'm in my own personal heaven as I walk along looking at each piece lining the walls.

I'm lost in thought looking at a chandelier when I hear an unfamiliar voice behind me.

"It's beautiful, isn't it? But it doesn't hold a candle to some of the pieces I have seen of yours."

"Thank you."

I turn and come eye to eye with the attractive blonde from earlier and attached to her arm is none other than Marcel.

Fuck my life.

He smiles a sarcastic smile and says, "This is my client of St. Croix Inc. Camille Mcintosh."

She is dripping with old money; you can tell right away. She wears a black strapless dress that reaches the floor, a split that rides to her upper thigh, and black gloves that go right past her elbows. She has a flashy diamond necklace and earrings. On closer observation I can tell she's a bit older than I am, maybe in her mid-forties, but attractive none the less.

I reach out my hand to introduce myself, and Marcel cuts in. "She knows who you are. She requested you after all."

I've had about enough of his condescending Gods complex.

"It's called courtesy, something you obviously lack." I retort as

Alex comes to a stop by my side.

I return my attention to Camille who is smiling from ear to ear.

"Oh, I like her Marcel. Finally, someone who won't take your shit." She laughs and takes my hand. "An absolute pleasure Miss Rose. I must say you are much more striking in person."

Marcel cocks his eyebrow at me with an expression lacking all amusement.

"Thank you, Mrs. Mcintosh," I say noticing her decorated finger.

"Please, call me Camille." She states as she takes my arm. "Come let's talk numbers. I am wanting chandeliers made like this one here, but much more extravagant."

She points to the one that I had my eyes on moments before.

"I want one for each room, but themed differently. I will pay above top dollar."

She goes on rambling, and I can't get a word in edgewise as she steers me through the guests.

"You must come to my party. My husband is the fire chief, and we are doing a charity banquet for the fire victims from the Kincaid fire last month." she boasts.

"Of course, that would be incredible." I spit out before she is even finished inviting me.

Any chance I can help burn victims I am there.

"Wonderful." She claps her hand. "It's a masquerade ball this Friday. It begins at 7pm but you can arrive at any time. Here, let me see your phone and I'll add my contact and the address. Please, bring a plus one."

"I'll accompany her." Marcel's thick French accent breaks in.

"Oh, that's just swell. I'll see you then."

She hands my phone back along with our official invites and turns away before I can further protest.

"Absolutely not." I glare at him and his audacity.

He grabs ahold of one of the invites and jerks it out of my hand.

"I'll take that. Look, I would rather bite my arm off than go with you, but I have been looking for a way to get my foot into that ball. There will be some very important people there and you Miss, are my ticket, so deal with it."

He is damn near touching my nose with his.

Who does he think he is?

"So shall I pick you up around 6:30 Ma chère?"

"No, you may not. Just because you weaseled an invite does not mean I would be caught dead accompanying you, you fucking dick."

"Oh, come now Ma chère, who doesn't want a date with a dick?"

I hear Alex snicker behind me.

Traitor.

"Oh please, we both know I'm not your type, and you most definitely are not mine!"

"Oh, quite the contrary Ma chère. You are quite delectable until you open that mouth of yours. I would say I could fix that problem, but I'm not even sure a good fucking would help you."

I hear Alex laugh and then recover with a cough. I turn and give him a 'go to hell' glare. When I turn back around, I see Marcel has lost interest and has turned to walk away, Odin matching his steps.

"Who the fuck does he think he is?"

I seethe at Alex.

"Bitch, if you don't fuck him, I will! You could cut that sexual tension with a knife."

"He's a complete ass with a Gods complex, I can't believe you think I would be interested in the likes of him. He fucking said I'm attractive until I open my mouth. What a fucking asshole! His precious ego just can't handle a woman with intelligence. He thinks a woman should only open her mouth to suck his cock." I rant.

My hands are trembling, and heat radiates from them. Alex looks at me like I'm trying to convince myself more than I am him. With a roll of his eyes, he holds his hands up in surrender.

"Sure, whatever you say O. I'd say cool your tits, but it looks

like you need to cool your hands." He says looking at my hands.
"Fuck off." I spat shoving my hands in my pockets.
Maybe I need to rethink turning Alex into a figurine.

9

Friday

"I see you have decided to go." Alex says with a smirk.

I am busy spinning the molten metal in my hands, focused on the mask. I've chosen gold, black and green to accent my emerald ballgown. Choosing it was a task in itself. It's a bit more risqué than I normally wear. It's strapless, a corset fit that hugs to my curves, two splits, one up each leg showing off, all the way to my upper thighs.

"Shut up. It's for a worthy cause. That's the only reason I'm going."

I give myself a mental pat on the back for how convincing I sound.

I get up from my desk, satisfied with how my mask has turned out. I place it down to cool and push pass Alex and out of my workshop. I need to get out of here before he sees right through me. All I have thought about for days is that perfect smile and his smooth voice. I lick my lips at the thought. When I am not thinking about him, I dream about him. I hate it because I hate him. He's everything that I despise.

So why is it that he can get my panties wet?

I make it up the stairs and to our closet and begin getting ready. I look at the gown hanging on the door frame and think to myself that it truly is the most exquisite dress I have ever seen.

I begin dressing and walk to my dresser.

No need in ruining that beauty with panties.

I decide to go without. I hear Alex in his room and beckon him over.

"Hey Alex, can I bother you to zip me up?"

He emerges in the doorway with a mixture of shock and amusement playing on his face.

"O, if only I were straight. You look fabulous."

I smile and thank him for his kind words as I grab the matching coat and slip it on. I rush down the stairs, pick up the mask, and head out the front door. There is a car waiting for me at the curb.

By the Gods, I will not be late.

"You really are drop-dead gorgeous Bitch!" I hear Alex yell from our kitchen window.

My energy level is high tonight.

I'm in control. I always keep it contained. The incident at the store was merely coincidental.

I take a deep breath and slip into the waiting car.

The car pulls up to two large ornate wrought iron gates. The driver reaches out and quickly puts in a code. As the gates open, he slowly drives into the circle drive. The house is breathtaking. A mansion, just like I would expect from a lady such as Camille Mcintosh.

The car rolls to a stop on the left side of the mansion. My door opens, and a gentleman waits, offering his arm. We walk into the house and directly in front of me is a set of descending stairs. A balcony overlooks the open ballroom below. It's just after 7, but the party is in full swing. A slower symphony of "Mr. Brightside" plays as I enter.

"Ma'am. Can I take your coat, and would you like me to escort you to your table?" The gentleman, who I see now on his nametag reads Ben, asks.

I hand him my coat and I watch as he hangs it in the coat closet to the left of the exit.

"No thank you. I have it from here."

He does a small bow and turns to walk away.

Fancy.

I descend the stairs and find an open area beside the dance floor to people watch. Camille spots me almost instantly and comes to my side.

"You look breath-taking. If I was fifteen years younger, I might be jealous." She says as she throws her hair over her shoulder and smiles back towards a striking man in firefighter red.

Must be the husband.

She turns back to me and squeezes my arm.

"Please do enjoy yourself."

She rushes off towards the next group of guests entering the ballroom. I imagine she must make an appearance for everyone, especially since it is a charity event.

I feel him before I see him. My pulse quickens and I hear his hum beckoning me to react. The heat on my neck makes me shiver as he closes in behind me and then I hear his whisper against my ear.

"You are ravishing tonight Ma chère. Now, can you keep that pretty mouth shut so I can enjoy it?"

I turn around, determined not to make a scene.

Damned if he doesn't look like he stepped out of the gates of hell to steal my soul.

The suit looks like it was meant to be worn by him and not the other way around. Black on black down to the breast handkerchief. His mask is also a simple matte black with no frills except for those blue eyes, I could drown in them. I think he catches me ogling him and smirks while I recover.

"You disgust me," I sneer, baring my teeth.

I slowly turn away. I need to find my seat and create some space between us.

Fuck why does he have to be so delicious, yet so fucking repulsive.

Every table looks to seat 6 guests. Most seats are already

occupied. I finally find my name in the crowd and exhale; or at least I do for a moment.

"Well, would you look at that? My name is right here next to yours Ma chère. Who would have guessed?"

I roll my eyes as he laughs and takes a seat. I look around to see if there are any vacant seats but come up short. Sitting down with a huff, I decide I am going to make the best of it.

"Good evening, Madam, my name is Victor, I'll be serving you tonight. Can I offer you a glass of wine?"

I oblige and take the glass, letting my hand skate across his.

"This is out of character for me, but I must say you are the most striking woman I have ever laid eyes on." I smile, blushing at the attention.

Fuck it. I want to have fun.

I bat my lashes playing into his flirtatious behavior. He smiles.

"Victor, you are too kind." Resting my hand on his arm.

"Madam, please call me Vic. I didn't catch your name."

He lifts my hand and kisses it gently with smoldering eye contact.

"Olivia." I hum out, lost in how smooth this man is.

Just then I feel it. Marcel's hand grips painfully hard into my thigh.

Bare skin, he must have gotten right past that split.

My pussy warms. My head snaps to him, I am glaring at him with a 'what the fuck do you think you're doing' look.

"She's with me!" Marcel says through gritted teeth, anger dripping off his words.

"No, I am not."

I try to wiggle away. He tightens his grip but then releases.

Victor puffs out his chest and says, "Is this guy bothering you?"

He directs his question toward Marcel. I begin to respond truthfully and then I feel Marcel push his hand between my thighs. He pushes until I feel his finger run the length of my slit and then he bends in toward my ear.

"Tell him no. Didn't I tell you that pretty mouth would get you in trouble?"

I pause and he pushes his finger into my pussy, and I writhe under his touch.

"No." I answer Victor as convincingly as I can.

He looks at me skeptically but turns away.

"You love the way this feels. Look how wet you are for me." Marcel whispers.

My body is failing me because I hate this man.

How can he do this to me?

With every restraint I can muster, I push back from the table leaving his hand idle. I stand, smooth out my dress, and glare in his direction.

"Don't you ever do that again!" I say seething.

He simply moves his finger to his mouth and licks it clean.

"It's sweeter than you are." His eyes darken.

My mouth falls open, speechless. I turn and begin aimlessly walking to clear my nerve.

"I see you're away from your little friend. It's break time for me. I would be honored if you would have this dance with me." Victor holds out his hand.

"I would love to."

I take it as we saunter out to the dance floor. I make sure to stay in Marcels vision just to fuck with him. I fall into step with Victor when I realize his hands have made their way dangerously close to my ass.

"Not so low on the hands." I say to Victor with a bat of my lashes.

"Oh, come on baby, you know you like it!" his tone clearly unaffected by the scene Marcel caused.

What is it with these guys not listening tonight?

The only problem though is that I don't like this attention from Victor. It feels cheap and sleazy. I am hit with a wave of intense energy.

When did Marcel make it onto the dance floor?

"No, she doesn't like it!" He growls.

"You again, look buddy, clearly she chose me." Victor retorts.

"Both of you outside NOW!" Marcels spits.

"Ok bud, we can go outside, but just know, only one of us will return."

Marcel doesn't say another word as he turns and heads for the exit. I don't know what makes me follow him, but I do. I have to almost jog to catch up. We make it to the gardens on the side of the house, a beautiful lit stone fountain in the center. This would be wonderful under other circumstances.

"Look Dude, these whores are a dime a dozen. Is she worth getting your ass kicked?" Victor says smug.

I don't know what comes over me, but I lay a punch across his face.

Fucker.

Marcel takes over and has him on his knees facing the fountains ledge before I know it.

"Tell me again, what did you just call her?"

"Nothing, man. I was just messing around." Victor sputters out, panic now consuming him.

"No Fucker, Say it! NOW!"

"Whore, I called her a whore!" He cries defeated.

"That's what I fucking thought you said! Olivia, come hold his head."

I don't know why, but I follow his direction.

"Stick out your tongue Vic. Let us see where your insults come from. Tsk look at it. I guarantee I can do a lot more useful things with mine."

Well, this is odd, but he is a little fucking twit, so I guess I'll play along.

His left cheek is pressed against the cold stone; I press hard and look to see what Marcel is doing. He pulls something from his pocket, but I can't tell what it is.

"See, Olivia here, is mine tonight, and no one disrespects what is mine. Those that try will have to pay the price."

Darkness edging into his voice. My pulse is racing, I'm scared, but my center is on fire. My brain finally catches up, and I see Marcel grab Victor's tongue as the blade comes crashing down.

I lift my hand from his head shocked at the scene unfolding. I'm glued to the spot I am standing in, unable to move. Paralyzed with fear, I watch Victor squirm and moan as Marcel cuts the tip of his tongue off. I will the vomit not to come. There is so much blood.

What the fuck. What the actual fuck just happened?

"You will never insult her again." Marcel says as he throws the severed tongue into the bushes. I hear him mumbling under his breath as he grabs my arm.

Was he just casting?

"What did you do?" I asked shakily.

"I made him forget. Now let's go!"

I dig my heals into the ground and try to free myself.

"No, what the fuck was that?" I demand.

"Me making sure he never fucking speaks again." He says like nothing just happened.

"You cut a man's tongue off for calling me a whore. Seems a little fucking extreme, don't you think?"

He releases my arm, stepping in close, he lowers his voice into a growl.

"He fucking touched you; he called you a whore, all while you thought it was some game. I don't fucking like that. I will not watch another man touch you."

I can't breathe. It is like he has taken the air from my lungs. This man who honestly, I can't stand, is telling me he doesn't want to see anyone else touch me.

Who the fuck does he think he is?

I can't just stand here and let him think I am his property.

"You are insane. I am not yours; I will never be yours. So, fuck off and find someone else to control."

I find the strength to move and storm off back into the party.

That man is a fucking psychopath.

Staring blankly into the bathroom mirror, I try to collect myself and rationalize the events I have just witnessed. That was the most ridiculous thing I have ever experienced. He cut that man's tongue off, and yet I am so fucking horny I can't control myself. My center burns with heat and the need for his fingers to play in it.

What is wrong with me?

I need to get back out there and mingle, but I am struggling with the need to rub one out first.

Get control of yourself Olivia.

Shaking my head I sigh, straightening my spine I turn and decide I will just take care of myself later.

The party is full of beautiful people, all dripping with old money. I may be self-made, but I do not fit in with this crowd.

Fake it till you make it.

I notice Camille talking with Marcel. She catches my gaze and waves me over. Sighing, I smile and make my way over to them, pretending like I didn't watch him go all knife happy with some man's tongue.

I focus on Camille as she banters about the benefit and how it really makes a difference in the lives of the victims. I try to ignore Marcel throughout the conversation, but the tension between us is thick, and the dark energy is radiating off of him.

"Olivia, I must admit when I hired Marcel to procure pieces for my chandeliers, I never expected him to find someone with your talent. Your work is like your soul formed each piece and that beauty is hard to find. Not to mention, you my dear, are radiant. Marcel, you need to keep this one close." She winks.

I blush offering her a grateful smile.

"Thank you, I love my craft and sharing it with those who can appreciate it."

I glance at Marcel, finally making eye contact. He is nearly vibrating with chaos. I raise my brow and smirk at him.

"Camille, if you would excuse us, I'd like to introduce Miss Rose to another interested investor."

"Of course! Enjoy the rest of the night." She smiles.

I look to Marcel and my blood is pumping so loud I can barely hear anything else. I feel my thighs slick with the intensity of his gaze growing closer.

I want him, now.

As if reading my thoughts, he laces our fingers and walks me back up the stairs. Not a word is uttered. He leads me through a door and the next thing I know he shoves me into the wall.

We are in a fucking coat closet.

My breath hitches and his mouth crashes into mine. I moan at the connection, my skin warms, and I feel as if I could burst into flames. I want him so bad; my body is threatening to burn us alive. I hear his zipper slide down; he hitches his left arm under one of my thighs, as he bunches my dress pushing it to the side; my pussy is dripping and needing to feel him. He positions his cock at my slit, and I damn near orgasm from the anticipation.

In the next moment he drives deep into me burying his face in my chest, letting out the darkest growl I have ever heard. Pleasure and pain rock through my center. I feel my pussy ripping at the intrusion of his thick cock.

Fuck! I might need stitches after this.

I grind into him; our movements are reckless and self-seeking; both chasing our own release. He reaches between us; using his thumb he circles my throbbing clit, the pressure is more than I ever use myself, but its intoxicating. The pressure inside me builds, yearning to explode.

I feel my center spasm and my orgasm is about to take me. My moan peaks as he drives harder and faster. I come undone. The ecstasy crashes around me and he roars with his own release; need still pushing him deeper into me. I nearly collapse from the sheer force of the orgasm.

We are still. The only sound is our heavy breathing. He releases my pinned leg and stares at me. I grab the handkerchief from his breast pocket. He watches me close as I wipe the mixture of cum running down my thigh off and then my still dripping pussy. Then with a smile I neatly fold it back up and place it into his pocket. His eyes blaze.

I smooth my dress and exit the closet without a word.
I fucking needed that.

"Miss Olivia, do you have a moment to come to the front? You have a delivery." Scarlett says through the line.

"Didn't I tell you not to call me Miss, I'm only 7 years older than you. I'll be out in just a moment."

I hang up and push away from my desk.

Scarlett Whitlock is a college student. She runs the storefront now due to the high demand. Alex and I cannot successfully run this place without the help. She has no idea I am a witch and I prefer it that way. While she works up front, I keep my skills hidden behind my office door. She just assumes I don't want to be bothered.

"What was that about?" Alex asks, rising from the hammock seat.

"Delivery." I tell him.

"That's odd. We aren't expecting anything today. Shall I go with you?" Alex is vibrating.

"Bitch, you know you're going out there to see if Marco is here." I say playfully. "Ask that man out already."

I don't wait for a response I open the door and head up front with Alex hot on my heels.

I see Marco making small talk with Scarlett and look over my shoulder with a smirk.

"I'm so getting you back for your shenanigans at the art gallery last week."

"Marco, dear. Me and Alex were just talking about you. What have you got there?" I am careful not to meet Alex's eyes.

Marco clears his throat. "Good things I hope." He says with a wink in Alex's direction, and I see him melt.

Well, this is new for Alex.

"Delivery." He says as he holds out a bouquet of peonies.

I take the arrangement and sit it on the counter. I feel an off energy as I begin searching for a card. I spot the card attached to the burgundy ribbon wrapped around the vase.

"BOLD & DARING – ASC"

What the actual fuck? I haven't seen those initials since the house fire. I can't breathe.

Time stops. I must get out of here. I slam the vase down and I feel my pain and anger build. My chaos threatening to release.

Contain it just a moment more.

I rush out the front door and start jogging. I assume Alex notices my state. I hear him faintly, screaming after me.

"O, Slow down. What the fuck?"

But I don't care. I do not slow my pace. I find myself a block over at the park. I make my way to the walking track. Running calms me. Looking at my hands, the heat starting to dissipate, I pick up the pace.

I finally feel like myself again when the wind is knocked out of me. Landing face first on the ground, I shift my weight and roll over to see what happened. I am attacked with wet slobbering kisses from Odin. Laughing, I reach up to give him a scratch behind the ears.

My bliss is broken with a clearing of his throat. I move my attention from Odin to Marcel who is straddling above my head. My eyes pause on the bulge in his pants. My mouth waters as I recall how good his cock felt inside me. He speaks and I am brought back to reality.

Well Fuck.

"Funny We keep meeting this way Ma chère." offering his hand. I allow him to pull me to my feet. "Unfortunate indeed." I say dusting my pants leg off and squatting back down to love on Odin.

"Not you Odin. Just your extra appendage." I snark glaring up at Marcel.

"What are you doing here?" I bite. "Are you following me?"

"Don't flatter yourself. Unfortunately, I have to leave for a week and Odin here, seems to hate the local kennel but I have no choice. I usually bring him here to the park to cheer him up before I leave."

Alex has finally caught up and pays the scene no mind.

"What the fuck O? I see that you're upset, but you got to give me something babe." He says exasperated.

"We can talk about it when we get home." I hope he can tell that I do not want to open up about everything here, especially in front of our new *friends*. He seems to catch on because he moves his attention to Marcel.

"O. I like that!" Marcel says.

"Um, no sir, you may be able to give her one, but I'm the only one who gets to call her that."

I let out an awkward laugh and just like that, I am calm again.

"Well, I'm just going to go back to the shop." Alex says, turning back and heading in the direction from which we came.

"So, you told Alex about our...coming together." Marcel says with a grin.

"Let me keep him." I blurt out, turning my attention back to Marcel, and quickly changing the subject. With everything going on, Odin would be a great distraction.

Marcel looks at me skeptically but says, "If you really don't mind, I think it's a great idea. I hate leaving him with people he doesn't know and for some odd reason he has taken a liking to you."

He genuinely sounds relieved.

"I can bring him by with his things around 8 if that's ok."

Well, his tone changed fast.

"Fine." Without another word, I turn and head back to the store.

I walk back in to find Alex and Marco, laughing in deep conversation and Scarlett doing her homework. I clear my throat, "Sorry for running out like that guys. It won't happen again." I wasn't about to try to explain any further. "I'll be upstairs if you need me."

I find Alex's eyes, beckoning him silently. With a small nod, I see that he has caught on as I turn to walk upstairs to the apartment.

Not even five minutes later, Alex walks through the door with a huge smile plastered across his face. He waves a small piece of paper in the air proudly.

"Guess who got a number and a date tonight?" he asks, hardly containing his excitement.

"Oh, my Gods. I am so happy for you."

I run over and hug him. He is all but bouncing with excitement. He pulls back still holding my arms and the atmosphere of the conversation changes.

"What happened out there O?"

I pause for a moment, trying to compartmentalize my thoughts and how I want to tell him.

"Do you remember how I told you that I received an anonymous birthday card right before the house fire?" He nods.

"Well, those same initials on the bouquet were on the card. Seeing that again brought up a lot of memories I would have liked to be kept buried."

Delicately he says, "Babe, at some point you're going to have to confront your past so that you can live in the present."

"I know. I need to go back home and force myself to get the closure I need."

He doesn't question what I am saying. We've had this conversation multiple times.

New Orleans will always be my home.

"You know, I received an invite, just the other day in the mail for a convention there. I almost wanted to take up the offer." I tell him.

"You should. Put it in the past for good. Maybe even do some digging to find out who ASC is O."

"Maybe. By the way, I offered to keep Odin while Marcel is away on business. Is that okay?" I ask.

Alex pauses but then rolls his eyes, smiling.

"Of course, anything for you my dear. So, when is that damn dog getting here? I swear O, if he shits in this apartment, I'm going to shit on your pillow." He plays.

I laugh. "He will be here around 8."

"Great, Marco is picking me up at 7. Are you sure you can handle being here alone with our friend Marcel. I mean you should be safe if you can keep him out of our closet." I swat at him playfully.

"Why must I tell you about everything, when you just hold it against me?"

Well not everything, the Victor situation is probably best left to yourself Olivia.

"Because you fucking love me Bitch."

10

It's right after 7 and Marco and Alex just left the apartment. I don't understand why I am so nervous. I continue to look at the clock.

This isn't like you Olivia. You don't get nervous. Pull it together.

I walk over to the bar and start looking through our pile of read mail to busy my time and I find the letter with my name on it from a New Orleans address. I pull the letter from its envelope and begin to read...

I didn't notice the first time I read this that the name on the front says:

Olivia St. Claire

Well that's odd...

> **I.S.A.O**
>
> **INTERNATIONAL SOCIETY OF ALCHEMY & OCCULT**
>
> Location: **82305 Tulane Avenue, New Orleans, LA 70112**
>
> Date: **October 28, 2023 – October 30, 2023**
>
> On Behalf of The International Society of Alchemy & Occult, we would officially like to invite you to attend and participate in our convention. The conference will be held In New Orleans at Humanity Hospital. Although vacant since Hurricane Katrina, the realtor has agreed to open the doors to allow our conference. The setting is perfect for all factions.
>
> The purpose of the 3-day conference is to bring together researchers from around the world who are interested in exploring the links between the supernatural, phenomena, wicca, and many more factions. We plan to touch on all magical practices.
>
> Should you require more information on our convention, please visit our conference website at www.secretsocietyDDCL.com. Thank you. We look forward to seeing you at the conference.
>
> Sincerely,
>
> **THE INTERNATIONAL SOCIETY of ALCHEMY & OCCULT**
>
> *Thomas Woodwind*
> (Conference Coordinator)

Surely this was meant for me. How many witches named Olivia can there be? Must be a clerical error. Maybe I could do this.

I stuff the letter into my purse for safe keeping just in case I grow the nerve. I head into the bedroom and grab 'The Onyx' off my nightstand and settle back on the couch and start reading, losing myself in my newest favorite fantasy.

My reading is interrupted by a knock at the door. I glance at the clock; 7:41p.m. Well, I guess they're early.

Showtime.
"Coming."
I open the door.
Gods be damned, it should be a sin to look that good.
Marcel has worn a suit at each encounter I have seen him, even in the park, so it shocks me to see him in casual wear. He's wearing light denim jeans that hang right at his hips, a tight-fitting black V-neck t-shirt with his chest hair peeking out, and a black backwards baseball cap to complete the look. My middle is on fire for this man.

"Well, are we just going to stand here, or are you going to invite us in?"

I now see the huge bag of dog food nestled on one shoulder and what looks like an overnight bag on the other.

"Right. Come on in." I stammer. Odin jumps up and begins licking my face, unable to contain his happiness.

"Odin, heel! I'm sorry, he rarely acts like this. You seem to be the exception." He says as he places the dog food bag next to the bar.

"Maybe he just knows a good thing, when he sees it, Sir."

"Maybe so."

Well did I just die and go to heaven or did Marcel just compliment me?

He walks over and squats making it eye level with Odin.

"You're going to be a good boy while I am gone. Olivia, here will take good care of you." He pets him on the head, and I melt.

"He's in good hands, I promise."

Marcel begins walking toward me and he doesn't stop. My back against the bar, his chest pressed against mine, my breath hitches.

"What are you doing?" I say in a rasp whisper.

He doesn't answer. He reaches around me and grabs my cellphone off the counter. Turning it toward my face to unlock my screen and backs away.

"I asked you, what are you doing?" I all but yell.

"I'm adding my contact. Should anything happen with Odin,

you call me, do you understand?"

"Do not chastise me! Of course, I would call you, but that won't be necessary."

"Oh, Ma chère. It is necessary. Do you have a restroom I can use? I do have a long flight."

Good, some distance.

"Down the hall, first door on the left. You can use my restroom. Its right through my room."

I feel my hands growing warm. It seems to be harder and harder to control myself around him. I look for anything to busy myself. Opening the bag on the counter, I begin rummaging.

"Let's see what all we have here." I say looking at Odin.

I take out a food and water bowl. As I look further, he has multiple dog toys, a leash, and a harness packed.

"Well, it looks like he at least likes you."

Taking out a large tennis ball, I toss it down the hall and Odin takes off. It bounces down the hall and into my room. He doesn't return right away so I go to investigate. I walk in and I am surprised to see Marcel lounging in my hammock swing facing the window.

"Well, this isn't the bathroom."

I walk over toward the swing and the window looking out. The moon is high and molded to the perfect crescent.

"Yes, the moon caught me off guard. It is rather beautiful; Wouldn't you agree?" He questions.

I step around him and peer out.

"It really is magnificent."

The beauty is interrupted as he pulls me back onto his lap. I let out a small yelp, completely caught off guard. I feel the heat from his breath reach my neck and my pussy warms.

"I haven't stopped thinking about you since the ball; how good it feels to be inside you. Then I think of Victor and how he called you a whore in such a distasteful fashion."

He reaches around my neck and applies the lightest pressure as I tilt my head back into him. He runs the length of his tongue along the side of my neck and to my ear.

"Ma chère, if you are to be anyone's whore, it is mine. Get up!"

I rise, turning to face him. I hope my shock doesn't show on my face.

He sure is bold tonight.

Marcel stands and begins unbuckling his belt.

"Take off your clothes."

"Who do you think you are demanding to..." But my voice is lost on his beckon.

The lights begin to flicker, and the room goes dark.

Great, the mighty and powerful witch has to boast. Two can play at that game.

I reach toward the direction of my dresser and with little effort I manifest a small flame. I release and all of my candles ignite to an alarming height before returning to normal, casting shadows across Marcels face.

"I fucking said, take off your clothes!"

I stand paused for a moment, a battle within my mind.

I do not submit.

Dear Gods, is he biting his bottom lip?

He obviously wants to play.

Game on.

I take off my shirt. Painfully slow, I unlatch my bra and watch it fall. Lifting my hand to my breast, I begin playfully rubbing my nipples. Marcel releases a deep growl.

Good it's working.

I look at him, never leaving his eyes, as I reach down and push my silk shorts to the floor. Marcel licks his lips.

"Bring that pretty little cunt over here." I walk up to him, never losing eye contact.

"Now what, Master?" I play.

"Master, Hmm I like that."

He lifts the belt and rests it around my neck.

"All you have to do is say stop and this ends." He warns.

My pussy is on fire.

No way am I calling it quits right now.

He secures the belt around my neck and steps back to drink

me in. I watch as he undresses. I can now see what I couldn't properly appreciate in the coat closet. Broad shoulders and a chest chiseled to perfection. He pushes his jeans down and his cock bobs free. My thoughts are taken back to the coat closet; the girth ripping me, the pain and then sheer pleasure.

"Now get on your knees and crawl to me, my beautiful whore."

I look at him with blazing eyes. I listen.

Why do I fucking listen?

He bends forward, grips the belt, and pulls it tight, beckoning me until I am I level with his bulging cock. I spit, watching my saliva drip from the head of his cock, I run my tongue underneath. He tightens the restraint and tries to pull back. Instead of heeding his warning to slow down, I grab his ass and I push forward until my mouth is full and he's hitting my throat. Tears springing to my eyes and the edges of my vision blurring, I move my hands, gripping both thighs and focus on my control.

My hands begin to glow, as I push a pulse of radiating heat out. It's met with his own magic pushing back. I feel electricity shoot through my palms and I begin to slow.

Shit that hurt but this is fun.

Marcel reaches down releasing my neck of the belt. I'm hit with relief as it loosens and gives reprieve. He snaps the belt across his hand. The crack of the leather further electrifying the atmosphere. Then he lifts me to my feet.

"Turn around, bend over, place your hands on the bed, and spread your legs. Do you understand?" I see flames in his gaze.

"Yes Master."

It comes out more of a whimper. I follow his instruction, leaning over and stretching myself across the bed. He glides his hands over my curves, I gasp as his hand slaps against my pussy. The sting is quickly replaced with his warm tongue.

Fuck that bitch is going to hate me, she just healed from our last encounter.

My thighs shake from the connection. Again, his tongue retreats, but this time his hand is replaced with the belt. Leather bites at my clit causing a feral moan to escape my lips. His tongue quickly returns, circling the stinging bud as I rock my hips into him, begging for more.

Yes, just like that.

Another lash cuts across my ass, and another, and another. The pain is almost unbearable. I have never been spanked during sex, much less whipped with a belt. My body is pulsating, I can feel my heart beating in my ears and my pussy.

"I tell you when you get more, do you understand me whore?" he commands.

I nod my head. A lash rips out across my back, biting into my skin.

"Answer me!" He grits through his teeth.

"Yes Master." I whimper, unable to say anything more.

His mouth returns to my swollen pussy, his movements are precise, a mixture of soft and firm strokes envelope my clit.

Oh, Gods I'm going to come undone.

I struggle not to rock back into him again but fuck this is intoxicating. I hear the belt buckle hit the ground. His pace slows ever so slightly. Then I feel the rough leather slide across my dripping pussy where his mouth had just been. I stretch further into the bed at the erotic feeling of the leather.

"What does my whore want?"

"Please!" I beg.

"Please what?"

"Please master, let me cum."

The need in my body overtaking my voice. I glance back to see him tightly wrapping the belt around two of his fingers.

Surely not.

His mouth returns to my cunt stroking faster than before and I am chasing my orgasm. I grind my hips into the bed as it builds higher and higher. He growls and then it happens. He shoves the two fingers he bound in leather into my pussy. I scream as pleasure rocks through me, and my orgasm overtakes me. He slams his fingers into me over and over again until I flood his hand and belt. My voice gives into a rasp as I come down from my high.

I just fucking squirted all over him. I have never done that!
I turn to find his eyes and he is dripping with desire and pride.
"Stay there." He orders as I hear him stand.
My legs are shaking, and I'm fighting the urge to roll over.
I want to watch him take me.

He rubs my ass, that I'm sure is cherry red from the belt. I feel the belt still wrapped around his fist now. I arch my back begging for more. A fist twist in my hair jerking my neck back. I gasp as he releases the belt from his hand; I feel the wet leather surround my neck again. Now it is a noose that he can tighten at will. Panic mixed with desire rushes through me. My pussy aches for his touch.

He lines up with my slit and, in one quick movement, buries his cock in my needy pussy. At the same time, he grips the belt and pulls back. My breath hitches as he pounds into me relentlessly, holding the belt taunt.

"Who's my good little whore?" He asks.

I don't validate him with an answer, enjoying this too much. He pulls the belt tighter; my vision going dark.

"Answer me." he demands.

I reach for the belt as my consciousness is nearly fading. Warmth springs from my hand, searing the belt in half. I turn my head and smirk at him letting him realize that I was in control this whole time.

"I am." I rasp, smiling.

I fell him come undone as he releases his load inside me. I find my own release, my body quaking with another orgasm.

Standing and regaining his composure, he grabs his clothes sitting on the edge of the bed. I roll to my side to watch this man go from sex fiend to businessman all in a matter of seconds.

"Sorry about your belt," I jab playfully.

"Sorry about your neck." He counters.

What's wrong with my neck?

I spring to my feet to look in the mirror.

Fuck.

Bruising just below the surface of my skin has begun to filter in.

Alex is going to shit.

"You did that on purpose, didn't you?"

"Every sub needs a collar from her master." He smirks. "When I get back, I plan on taking you out." he says smugly as he makes his way to the door.

I follow him out.

"Where?" I question.

"Don't worry about it and don't kill my dog while I'm gone."

He shuts the door behind him, and I see the deadbolt turn.

Asshole.

11

One week later

"I feel like I hardly ever see you anymore!" I pout to Alex. "You've been out every night this week with Marco." He puts his arm around me.

"And you have been in every night with this damn dog ma'am."

He smiles down at Odin as he scratches him behind the ears. I knew he would fall in love with him just like I did. Pulling me into a deeper embrace he says, "Also, you're really going to hate me, but Marco will be here in like 15 minutes to pick me up."

I stick out my bottom lip, but a smile breaks free. "You love him, don't you?" I ask.

"Bitch, I think I have from the moment I first saw that man."

I just smile. I wish I knew what that was like.

Alex, little do you know, you're the only person I've ever truly loved.

"I'm so happy for you Alex. I can't wait to help plan your wedding." I say with a laugh.

"Bitch I know you're joking, but it may be sooner than you think. You can bring your owner to the wedding." He says with a smirk.

"My owner?" I look at him flabbergasted.

"Hey, you're the Bitch with a collar, not me." He says as he finishes getting ready.

I reach for my neck. The bruising has faded, but it is still tender to the touch.

"Fuck you." I say with a laugh.

"That sex must be out of this world for you to be okay with that." he says, wiggling his brows at me.

"It's worth tolerating his arrogant ass at least." I say with a snicker.

There's a knock at the door and Alex greets Marco with a kiss.

"Hey Olivia. Sorry I'm stealing Alex again. We could always stay here." He says sheepishly.

"No Marco, you guys go have fun. I'm fine spending the evening with Odin."

Marco and Alex say their goodbyes and head out of the apartment.

Alex and Marco have been gone all of five minutes and I'm already bored. I look over at Odin.

"So, what do you want to do?"

He starts moving around the living room as if looking for something.

"Are you looking for your tennis ball, boy?"

I get up from my seat and begin searching the house. I make my way into my bedroom. Getting on my hands and knees, I look under the bed.

"Oh, come here, boy. It's in here."

I see him in the doorway and chunk the ball down the hall.

I start to get up and spot a red light shining out from under the ledge of my dresser.

What the fuck?

I walk toward it and on further observation, I realize it's a camera placed facing my bed. I get eye level with the camera, hoping he sees this. I smile my most devilish smile, back up and begin to undress. I reach into my dresser drawer to find my toy and, to my surprise, it's missing. As if on cue, my phone chimes. I know it's him before I even look.

Marcel
You really need to learn to pleasure yourself without the toys.

I don't respond, throwing the phone on the bed.
Fine, Fucker. You asked for it.
I position myself on the ledge of the bed and spread my legs, giving a perfect view to the camera.
How do you like that, you fucking psycho?
I begin circling my clit and the phone chimes again and then again. I look over my shoulder as it lights up.
Fuck it. You win!
Frustrated I get up, grab my panties and t-shirt, dress and reach for my phone.

Marcel
It's cute that you think you can play alone.

Marcel
You'll learn to draw out your pleasure one day Ma chère.

Me
You're a fucking psychopath.

Marcel
You have no idea.

Marcel
Oh, btw my flight lands late tonight. I don't want to keep you up so I can come by in the morning and pick up Odin. He is still alive, right?

Me
You should know since you're bugging my house!!!

Me
I think he's decided to stay with me. Rumor has it, his previous owner was a complete dick.

Marcel
See you in the morning Ma chère. And clear your calendar. After I drop Odin off at my apartment, I will be back to take you out.

I don't even bother with asking where because I know he won't tell me anyhow.

"Well, I suppose you'll be leaving soon Odin."
I hug the dog that has now curled up at my side and decide to text Alex.

Me
Hey not trying to interrupt but will you still be available to run the store tomorrow? Scarlett has her finals tomorrow afternoon.

Alex
Yes babe. I got the store. Where will you be?

Me
Marcel will be back. He is picking up Odin in the morning, but then he is coming back to pick me up and take me out.

Alex
And where is he taking you?

Me
Who knows.

Alex
Ooooh mysterious. I like it.

Me
Of course, you do.

The smell of coffee wakes me, I lay there trying to adjust my eyes. I hear Odin's nails tapping around in the living room.

Surely Alex isn't making coffee.

Grabbing the throw off the end of the bed, I wrap myself and follow the smell.

How the fuck did he get in?

He leans against the counter, coffee cup in one hand and his phone in the other. I glance at the time on the stove, 8am, why does he look like this at 8am? He's back to business in an all-black Armani suit, black button down, open at the collar and a blood red handkerchief in his breast pocket. My center tightens at the memory of what I did with the last one.

For fucks sake.

I shake my head at the intrusion. I clear my throat to snag his attention.

"Oh, you finally decided to grace me with your presence." he bows sarcastically.

"Oh, you must have decided you wanted to add a breaking and entering charge to your resume." I spit back. "How the hell did you get in here?"

"Well, you see I use this thing called 'Magic', you should try it sometime."

He waves his fingers as sparks dance across them.

I narrow my eyes at his coffee cup, willing my 'power' to do what I want for a change. His coffee boils over the mug scalding his hand causing him to release the mug; it crashes to the floor. I fight back the urge to jump up and down clapping with joy at my display, but I settle for a smirk.

I don't even care that I will be the one to clean that up.

"*Petite insolente!*" his eyes blaze.

Whatever does that mean?

"Eat some breakfast and get ready. I'll be back in a few hours to collect you. We will do a little shopping and grab a late lunch.

You will need your energy for tonight."

He turns grabbing the bag from the counter and Odin follows behind.

"You aren't going to clean this mess up?"

I gestured to the shattered mug and coffee splattered on the floor.

"Oh no, that was all you." He snarks closing the door behind him.

Asshole.

I find myself mindlessly going through the motions of getting ready for a day that I feel unprepared for.

Shopping?

What could he possibly have planned for the day, and the looming comment of 'you'll need your energy for tonight.', what am I agreeing to?

I sigh, flopping down on my bed, unable to decide what to wear. I grab my phone typing out a quick message to Alex, if anyone can help me figure out what to wear, it's him.

Me
SOS. Marcel is taking me out shopping and then a late lunch... what do I wear?

Alex
BITCH!!! SHOPPING?

I can hear his voice ringing in my ears as I read the text.

Alex
It's chilly today, grab that Champagne sweater with the camel-colored skirt, thigh high boots and my Chanel cross body bag!

Me
Champagne Sweater? Camel skirt? What?

Alex
BIIITCH... Cream sweater, brown skirt, tall black boots.

Better?

> **Me**
> **Got it.**

I pop up tossing my phone back on the bed. I rummage through the closet and grab the items Alex rattled off. I opt for my Kate Spade leather backpack instead of the crossbody. I hear my phone chime, I expect it's Alex asking for a picture of his ensemble, but it's not.

> **Marcel**
> **Be there in 5.**

12

Fuck.

I throw on the outfit and pin my curls into a messy bun. I'm still doing my make up when I feel him. In the mirror I see him standing in the doorway, an arm extended to the door frame just watching me. I apply a deep brown lipstick that gives the illusion that I have done more than I really have.

Why am I so nervous?

Turning, I lean against the counter and take in the sight of him commanding the space.

"I don't know if I'll make it all night."

He readjusts his pants against the thick bulge now very present. I arch my brow in curiosity.

"What is that supposed to mean?" I play coy.

"Oh, you will find out soon enough Ma chère. Now, let's go."

"Give me a minute more, geez."

I move towards him in the doorway, but he does not allow me to pass. My pulse quickens and I feel like I'm already panting.

"I said let's go." he grits through his teeth.

"Yes, I heard you. Now, if you would so kindly move your ass, I will grab my bag."

His hand that had held the door frame drops and grips my throat. I instinctively pull at his hand as he glares down at me.

"That fucking mouth of yours is a problem. When I tell you to do something you say 'Yes Master." Do you fucking understand me?"

My eyes are locked on his, and I'm not sure if I fear this man or if I'm turned on by him. The thought of not speaking crosses my mind, but his grip tightens, and his eyes tell me I should follow directions.

"Yes Master." I whisper, dropping my eyes.

"Good fucking girl."

My heart thrums in my ears and my pussy warms. He still holds my throat as his free hand now lifts the hem of my skirt. His fingers dance across the lace of my panties as he finds my center.

"Mmm," he growls finding my pussy is already wet and needy.

"This turns you on, doesn't it? My grip on your throat and the way I make you obey me. Your pussy loves this shit!"

All I can manage is a nod.

Why do I like this?

I am no virgin saint, but I am also not used to this caliber of play. This is intoxicating and I want more. His fingers slide my panties to the side and dive into my pussy; I let out a needy moan as he grips me, grinding his palm into my clit.

"Feel how your pussy weeps for my touch."

His eyes darken as my gaze finds his. I can't stand this man's ego, but fuck I want to cum. His pace quickens and I can feel my center grip tighter around him, ready to come undone, my head drops back and my lips part as a moan slips past them again. I am about to fall off the edge when his hand retracts. The sudden lack of sensation crushes me. My head snaps up to meet his eyes in shock.

"Oh, you thought I'd let you cum? No Ma chère, only once I am ready for you to cum will you get to enjoy yourself."

He straightens and looks like the ruler of hell. He releases my throat and moves to one side of the door, as if the toll has been paid and I can now pass.

Fucking Asshole.

My eyes blaze with frustration and fury, but I dare not let another word slip. I clench my jaw and move to step through the door as his arm slides out in front of me blocking the door once more.

"Remember this for the next time that you want to let your mouth run wild." He moves his arm away and I storm out to grab my bag.

I fucking hate him.

We spend the majority of the day browsing the shops around the town square. We talk about my life here in La Conner, I opt for the abridge version of my childhood, and how I know very little about my own magic. He tells me of his childhood in France and how he moved here after college to explore the art trade in the states. He also talks about how he comes from a long line of magic and that he was raised to master his practice.

I feel like a child, 'oh well I can burn shit'.

Though I honestly can't stand this man, he is supportive of me embracing my powers and also finding myself which makes me think he might have a soul after all. It's like I am getting a peak behind his heavy dark curtain he keeps closed, I like it.

Maybe he isn't always an ass.

"We should probably grab a bite, what do you say?"

He looks at me with a softened expression, this is not what I normally get from him.

"Yes, that sounds good."

"There is a bistro a few miles away, can I take you there?"

Is he asking my permission?

"Lead the way!" I insist.

It's a short drive, but I am grateful we drove. We park outside of a small bistro with tables on the sidewalk under a cute little awning. It is what I would expect to see in France. I can't believe I have never seen this place.

Who am I kidding, I never go anywhere.

The breeze is cooler than I had expected and a chill runs through me as I step out of the car, but then he's there beside me, wrapping his jacket around me; rubbing his hands against my arms. I look at him and smile; it is the first time I have seen this tender side to him.

I like this.

We are seated next to the windows in a cozy booth. The bistro is simple yet has a laid back atmosphere that is unmatched. My stomach rumbles, the aromas coming from the back are mouthwatering. I open the menu and its full of warm comfort food dishes with a French flare. There are so many options, and it all sounds amazing.

"Can I order for us?"

He peaks over my menu at me.

I blush at the connection.

"Sure, that would make this easier. Also, what is with you asking for my permission all of a sudden?" I push out of curiosity.

"Consent." he says casually waving over the server.

One word. He gave one word and its consent?

What is happening?

"I'm not always an asshole, as you like to think."

Shock strikes across my face as the server approaches. Marcel orders what sounds like enough to feed a small army. The server retreats and I am still left in shock about him knowing my thoughts.

"How do you know that? Can you read my mind?" I say in a whisper.

Laughter booms from his chest, echoing through the space. My face reddens, embarrassment floods my system, did I miss a joke? The embarrassment fades and is replaced with desire, his laughter brightens his features, and his relaxed posture is leaving me wanting.

"No Ma chère, I cannot read your mind, though that would be helpful," he winks, "but I can see it all over your face when I get under your skin." He laughs while leaning closer to me.

I mirror his position.

"So, what about this consent?"

"I want you to feel safe and understood during our play time."

"Okay, but I still don't know what you expect me to do."

I push, mainly because it's true. I feel out of my element.

"I want you to explore yourself, and it is obvious you have never been in a submissive sexual relationship before. So, I am trying to teach you, even if you do not follow directions well."

"Relationship?" My eyes widen.

"I'm not asking for your hand in marriage Olivia, I am asking to be your master. Let me show you what you are missing, what I can give you and how powerful you will feel after."

My body warms at his words, but I suddenly feel cheated by the use of my name. I have grown fond of my pet name. I want to explore myself, and the thought of doing it with him is thrilling.

"So how do I agree to this?" I ask, raising a brow.

"You let me collar you." He says letting his eyes drift to my neck.

Fire licks at my skin under his eyes.

Fuck me.

The server arrives at the table, plates in hand.

"Let's eat." He grins.

We finish eating the best meal I have enjoyed in a long time and relax while waiting for our coffee. I am so full; I don't even know if I will be able to drink it. I find myself fidgeting with my sweater, nervous of what's to come the rest of the afternoon and evening. I feel his eyes on me and my cheeks warm under his gaze.

"What is collaring?" I asked under my breath.

"I thought you would never ask."

He stands up and walks out to the car. He returns with a red box and places it in front of me, returning to his side of the booth. Sitting down, he looks at me with blazing intensity. This image of him is sin. I stare at him, wishing I was straddling his lap.

"Open it." He directs.

I listen. I open the box and inside is a solid silver bangle choker, with a circle in the center. The back of It is partially open, and there is a small key in the box. I looked at him questioningly, this is not what I expected.

"It's a submissive collar. The circle indicates you're mine and not open for others to play with. The key locks it, until I choose to remove it. Once you put this on, I have your consent." He leans in, seriousness in his tone. "Do you understand Olivia?"

Do I understand? I half expected a dog collar to be in the box, but this is beautiful.

"What if I change my mind?" I ask.

"Then I will unlock it, give you the key and never see you again."

He leans back, relaxed again. The thought of him leaving makes me feel empty. I want to explore myself and I want to do it with him. I pick up the key, its tiny, more like a file, and push it across the table to him. His eyes flare and his fingertips spark as he reaches for the key.

"You understand what you're accepting?" He stands and I nod. "I need to hear you say it, Olivia."

"Yes Master." I moan out.

A rumble rattles his chest as he rounds the booth to me, I lift my hair offering my neck to him. It's like my mind and body are disconnected. I am panicking on the inside, but outwardly I am submitting to this beautiful man. Running his fingers along my neck he places the collar, and with a click, locks it, placing a kiss on the side of my neck.

"You are mine now, Ma chère," danger edges the tone of his voice.

Chills consume my body.

"Let's go." he cuts coldly, tossing money onto the table.

I slide out of the booth, and he laces his hand into mine, striding through the door he turns pinning me to the wall and then his lips crash into mine. I melt into the brick behind me as his urgency and intensity burn. Our lips part and he's breathing heavily into me.

"We need to make a stop before we head to the party." He breathes inches from my lips.

"Party?"

"Oh, you will see soon enough, Ma chère. Let's go."

We drive through the city until we reach the warehouse district. I've only been through this part of town when I missed a turn. We pull up to a black brick building with a red rose on the door. The simplicity intrigues me. Parking, Marcel reaches for my hand and raises it to his lips, kissing it softly.

"Let's find something for tonight." He sounds excited.

Through the doors is a dimly lit narrow staircase, we climb the stairs as the lights change. The room opens into a boutique.

"Buy anything you want." He urges, pride filling his tone.

"What should I be looking for?" I question.

"Anything that makes you feel sexy. There is all forms of lingerie through that door, shoes to the left, jewelry in the back and racks of dresses surround us. My only request is a black silk dress, I have been dying to see that creamy skin of yours contrasted in black silk and red handprints." He nearly purrs.

Oh, my fuck.

I am not sure how to handle this side of him. Alex will kill me if I don't take advantage of this opportunity. I let my inner Alex go wild.

I explored every inch of the boutique, I set my heart on a silver strappy corset with matching thong, intentionally coordinating with my collar. Playing to Marcels request I find a slip silk black dress. The hem falls only inches under my ass and scoops low on my breast. All of me is on display for him. I find a black trench coat to add to my outfit with a pair of Louis Vuitton red bottoms to complete the look.

I step out of the dressing room to find Marcel relaxed in an oversized armchair. His gaze drifts up my body. Once our eyes lock, I slowly unbutton the coat giving him a sneak peak of the trouble underneath. He bites his lip devilishly.

The sales associate walks by and Marcel holds up his black card without question. I smirk, slowly making my way to him. I straddle him, grabbing his hands and placing them on my ass. He squeezes and growls into my neck.

"Oh, Ma chère, you have no idea what you are in for."

The associate returns, handing the card back with a bag of my change of clothes.

"Where do we go now?" I play.

"A play party."

He moves my hair from my face. Curiosity and intrigue once again cross my features. What is a play party?

Marcel stands still holding my ass.

"Ready to play?" He purrs.

Nodding I feel adrenaline and anticipation course through my veins.

We park only three blocks from my shop. Tucked away in the store fronts is a nondescript bar. I eye Marcel, he offers a dark smirk, and takes my arm. We walk to the door, and he pulls a key fob from his pocket.

Members only.

The door unlocks and we are met with a wall of bouncers. They nod to Marcel and he drops my arm lifting his and one of the men wand him, nodding again Marcel steps to the side. They repeat the process on me, but once they finish a tiny woman with a tablet approaches me.

"Welcome to 'Curated Play'. I will need to register you and your account," she nods to Marcel. "I will need your fingerprint here."

She holds a small scanner in her hand. Placing my shaking hand in hers, she scans my finger.

"Oh, honey we don't bite, unless you ask."

She winks and my center warms at her words, I blush at the feeling.

"What's your name beautiful?" She asks typing on the tablet.

"Olivia Rose."

She nods and lifts a black card and types once more. She looks up at me with a seductive grin.

"Enjoy your play time, let me know if there is anything specifically, I can help you with." She whispers leaning into my ear while handing me my black key fob.

Marcel steps in taking my arm once more, the doors hidden in the darkness open, and the energy floods the foyer.

Oh, my fucking Gods.

I have heard about private sex parties, but even in the depths of my mind I could have never pictured this. There are clusters of people gathered around beds, benches, stages and more. I raise on my toes trying to get a better view.

Each area of the expansive space is set up for different scenes of play. On the stage to the right there is a woman strapped to an X, with a ball gag. She is being whipped by a man in a full leather mask. After every lash, another woman, who is kneeling before the X, moves to lick each whelp and then licks the bound woman's pussy.

My eyes widen at the image. Marcel stands behind me as I watch the events unfold.

"What is that?" I point.

My voice barely over a whisper into his ear.

"An X-cross. Do you like it?" he pushes.

"I like watching her."

I point to the woman again licking the whelps.

"Hard limit. I do not share." He spits.

Noted.

The more I watch the hotter I am getting; I pull the tie to my jacket letting it fall open. He growls from behind me now seeing my breast on display in my choice of dress. His hands move to my shoulders pulling the jacket slowly down my arms. His breath on my neck sends chills down my spine as he plants small kisses over my shoulder.

Fuck that is intoxicating.

He turns me to face him raising his arm in the air. Seconds later a man with a red light around his neck appears.

"Please place these in my locker." Marcel commands.

The man bows his head, taking our coats and disappears back into the crowd. I stand letting my eyes dance over him. He's wearing black slacks and a black button down, that barely contain his form. My hands slowly move to his buttons. I release the first 3 letting his chest show and giving him a more relaxed look. My eyes bounce back to his as he lets a finger hook into the ring on my collar, jerking me into him, our lips nearly touching.

"You are devastating to anyone in here, but you are mine. Do you understand? I will not share you with anyone. That is my only hard limit. Now let's explore."

"Yes Master." I moan.

We make our way into another scene, he stands behind me again, with his hands gripping my hips.

In front of me, a woman is bound to a bottomless chair. Under her is a large mirror, allowing all eyes to see her open pussy.

Incredibly open.

She has what looks to be clips with chains around her thighs.

"What are those?" I ask pointing.

"Labia spreaders, they open you up and create more sensation and blood flow for oral or toy play."

"Oh!" I say breathlessly.

"Watch." He instructs.

I pull my eyes to the man circling the chair, like a predator stalking prey. He holds a flogger in one hand, a dildo in the other. The woman watches his every move. He kneels in front of her spread, spitting in his hand he rubs her open cunt. Her head rocks back and she screams "More!" My breath is shaky, and I lean into Marcel for support. The man retracts his hand and swings the flogger upward into her cunt, the force nearly knocks the chair over as it lifts on to 2 legs.

I am so fucking hot right now.

Marcels hands grip me tighter. I moan in response. The scene continues before us. The man rubs her again, and you can see her wetness dripping onto the mirror below her. He takes the dildo rubbing it against her clit that is engorged. In the next second he buries it to the hilt, and she screams. Pleasure gripping her tone. The man is fucking her hard and fast and I am grinding into Marcel. His hand slipping beneath my hem, he begins slowly tracing the edge of my thong.

"You are enjoying this, aren't you?"

"Yes Master!" I moan, needing more of his touch.

"Do you like this public display?" he growls into my ear.

"Yes."

I feel like I could climax with just his words and the scenes around us. I am so fucking aroused.

"What if I fucked you on one of these stages, with all eyes on you?"

My chest rises and falls faster at the idea of him taking me in front of all these people.

Why do I want this?

"Could we?" I ask in a whimper.

"We can do whatever the fuck we want." He growls.

I feel his cock twitch against my ass.

"Tell me exactly what you want. I need to hear you."

Fuck, do I really want this?

Yes, I do.

"I want you to fuck me, with all of these people watching. I want it NOW Master."

Who the fuck am I right now?

My words barely make it out before he's pulling me to the center stage. He swipes his card on the box at the steps. This stage is elevated, and mirrors are suspended at angles around the edges, reflecting every inch of the space. In the center there is a red leather bench. The light changes to red around us. He walks me to the bench.

"Do not move." He instructs.

I am shaking, my nerves feel raw. The lights and mirrors make the crowd fade into the background, but I can feel every set of eyes on me.

Maybe I can't do this.

Just as the thought enters my mind, Marcel appears before me, this time without his shirt, only his black slacks, no shoes. He looks fucking delicious. All thoughts of tapping out are gone. I want him, and I want him now.

"Step forward."

I obey. He steps behind me.

"Look at how fucking sexy you are. You are a fucking

masterpiece, a rare piece of art that I am the proud owner of! I am going to show all of them who you serve." He growls like the beast inside of him has been freed.

He grabs the straps of my dress and rips, dropping the fabric. The dress falls to my feet, revealing my coordinated lingerie.

"Fuck, I want to tear you apart! Get on your fucking knees!" He commands.

I fall to my knees letting them spread beneath me. He steps around me and snags my collar again arching my head to look at him.

"You are going to take my cock in that fucking mouth of yours, do not stop looking at me, understand?"

"Yes, my Master!"

My Master!? Gods I have lost my mind.

He releases his cock, and I greedily take him in, keeping my eyes locked on his. I moan at his girth and feel my pussy soaking my thong.

"FUCK! You take my cock like a good fucking whore!" He screams down at me.

FUCK ME!

I quicken my pace twisting my hands around his length as I suck the head hard, swirling my tongue around it, before I lower myself back down the shaft.

"STOP!" He commands.

I instantly release him from my grip, staring at him for direction. I have never needed this before, sex was always just fluid and something for release, but this, this is otherworldly.

He fists my collar, dragging me to my feet to stand at the end of the bench. My legs are shaking, and I fear I will cum the second he touches me. He releases my collar, only to use both of his hands to rip at my corset. He frees my breasts, they fall from their confines, and my nipples harden into peaks from my arousal. Gliding a hand over the sensitive buds he growls.

"Please, Master, please take me."

His jaw tightens as he reaches, grabbing my throat and forcing me onto the bench.

"You want me to fuck you right here?" He growls into my ear.

"Please!" I beg.

"Be a good little whore and spread your legs."

I spread them as fast as I can. He releases my neck and sits back onto the floor. I am splayed for every eye to see.

It is so fucking hot!

His hands reach my thong and rip them apart. The wet fabric now replaced with his warm mouth. I grind my pussy into his face, loosing myself into his mouth. I can feel his tongue swirling like a tornado. I'm about to come undone when he withdraws.

I sit up to see him pull a paddle from his back pocket.

Fuck!

He pulls back, slapping the paddle against my cunt. I scream, pleasure and pain ripping me apart. Again, the paddle bites my clit; I am shaking, stretching further on the bench. With a final slap I climax, pleasure breaks through me and I am writhing under the lights, my pleasure rockets higher as I feel him bury his cock into me.

"MASTER!" I scream as he rips into my pussy.

My climax rolls through me and just when I think it's over another replaces the last. I cannot fucking breathe! He thrust harder into me, burying himself deeper. Just when I think I can't take any more I feel his body go rigid, his own climax taking him.

"FUCK OLIVIA!" He yells my name, digging his hands into my hips.

We are left breathless and rocked by the erotic scene we just created.

Marcel brings me his shirt and escorts me to a private room to freshen up. He leaves me to clean up and to grab my clothes from his car, since he destroyed the dress that I came here in. I stare into the mirror of the bathroom, and I do not even know the woman that stands before me. I can't believe I did that, nor the fact that it was the most exhilarating experience of my life. I cannot wait to spill this adventure to Alex. He is going to lose his shit!

I feel renewed, like this has given me the boost I need to really live and explore myself.

This was the best night of my life.

Marcel steps into the bathroom with my clothes from earlier and my coat.

"Ready to go, Ma chère?"

"Yes, thank you for this. I never knew I needed this. This has been the best night of my life."

"You were made for this."

He closes the distance between us.

"Don't thank me yet, I'm not done with you, the nights not over."

He winks lifting my chin and kissing me intimately. I smile into him.

13

We decided to walk back to my shop to get some fresh air. I needed it. I hear my phone chiming in my bag. *Alex.*

I swipe and he is talking before I can even answer.

"Bitch, where are you at? It's late. We got a package!" Alex screams through the phone.

"Hello to you too. Wait, what are you talking about, package?"

"I mean a package, Bitch, like in a box, it's got a bow and everything! It's addressed to the both of us. If you don't get here soon, I'm going to open it without you."

"Calm your tits, I'm only two blocks away."

An eerie feeling washing over me.

"Nope, you're taking too long, you're two blocks too many. I'm opening it now."

I can hear Alex tearing open the box when suddenly a deafening sound erupts from the other end and the line goes silent. The ground trembles violently and knocks me to my knees, my phone, purse and all its contents spilling over the cracked sidewalk. My heart sinks; an all-too-familiar feeling paralyzing me.

Alex!

"What the fuck was that?" Marcel begins looking around. I can't move. I feel like time has stopped.

"Olivia!" Marcel barks at me.

I will myself out of the trance and begin stuffing all my things in my purse, in my pockets, anywhere.

Fuck it, the rest can stay.

I pick my phone up off the ground. "Alex!" I scream into the phone.

No reply. I look at the phone and the screen shows "call failed". My stomach tightens like there is a vice grip tightening on my insides.

"What if it was Alex?" I sob out.

Marcel lifts me and begins running toward the smoke now swelling up above the buildings in the distance. My pulse quickens to where my head feels like it will explode.

Please don't be Alex.

But in my heart, I already know. I can feel it breaking.

We hear sirens in the distance as we round the corner, I should be able to see my shop now, but all I can see is smoke and flames. It looks like something out of a war zone. As we get closer, we can see the rubble. My front door is next to the fire hydrant on the edge of the sidewalk. There is debris everywhere. A raging inferno has engulfed the building, its flames dancing up the sides with an insatiable hunger. My once beautiful building is now a twisted skeleton of metal, brick, and flames. It's roaring so loud I can't think. Wait, that's not the fire. Screaming. He is screaming and crying.

Alex!

"I have to get to him! This can't happen again!"

I can hear the sirens wailing in the distance, but they won't be here fast enough. The raging fire is just getting bigger.

"Alex! I'm coming!" I scream.

I turn to Marcel.

"Help me damn It!"

The look on his face is one of pity, but he raises his arms toward the sky as if he demands help from the Gods themselves. I look toward my building, my home, and watch as the fire parts, providing a clear path to where Alex lays.

"Quick, I can't hold this very long."

He doesn't have to tell me twice. I take off after Alex. I can see his silhouette laying right inside the door. There's so much smoke. I grab him under his shoulders and pull with all my might.

Dear God, where's his arm? Don't think Olivia, just move!

I can feel sweat pooling at the base of my spine, the muscles in my arms straining against my skin. Embers fly through the air, burning my flesh, the smell filling the air.

"Hurry Olivia!" Marcel yells behind me.

I feel energy pulse through my body. One more tug and Alex and I are free from the blazing inferno. I drop to my knees and reach for his face.

"Ale..."

I don't finish his name.

No!

My poor Alex. He's gone. His beautiful face is now charred beyond recognition. His left eye is missing from its socket, his right one milky and staring lifelessly. His mouth is frozen in an agonizing cry for help. Wetness drips onto his blackened lips. Tears I realize. I must be crying. I can't tell. I feel so numb, so empty. I pull what's left of Alex into my lap as I rock back and forth.

His right hand is missing, how will he ever draw his designs again?

I should've been here. Had I been here this never would've happened.

"Olivia."

I turn to look at him as he steps toward me. *POP.* Marcel stops and lifts his foot, the remnants of Alex's beautiful left eye stuck to the tread of his shoe.

I feel something in me snap.

"You Son of A Bitch!" I scream at him as I fly to my feet. "This is your fault!"

I feel the wind pick up around us, the embers from the fire swirling through the air. I watch as one singes Marcels shirt.

"Olivia, I know you are upset." Marcel starts, lifting his hands like he's placating a child.

"UPSET! Upset! Upset is something you feel when a waitress fucks up your fucking food order. I'm not fucking upset, I'm furious! I'm livid! I should've been here! Had I not been off with you like your little pet, I could've saved him!"

I feel myself losing control, chaos swirling around me. I grip the collar around my neck and with a surge of power, snatch it off and throw it at his feet.

We stand there staring at the collar, the sound of the sirens getting closer wailing through the night merge with the roar of the fire. I can't tell how far away help is, but it doesn't matter anymore.

Alex is dead.

My home is destroyed.

My life is over.

I feel myself draining.

"You need to leave Marcel." I say with what little energy I have left.

Marcel takes a tentative step towards me but stops when I gasp out loud. The sidewalk behind Marcel suddenly engulfed in flames.

I drop to my knees, a cry springing from my lips. ASC is staring me in my face, the fire bringing the letters to life.

My fault.

"I killed him." I whisper into the night.

I don't know how much time has passed. The Fire Fighters have been working the fire for some time. The smells of smoke, burnt flesh, and sulfur fill the air. I can hear Marcel talking low to a police officer. Alex is still lying on the sidewalk. I yearn to go over to him and gather him into my arms, but I don't want to look at him. My beautiful, full of life best friend is gone.

I'm shivering, I realize. Even with my jacket on, I'm cold. I look down at the tattered remains of my jacket. Multiple burn holes adorn the sleeves. I reach out to touch one and catch a glimpse of the blood on my hand. I jerk away from my sleeve and shove my hand in my pocket. I can feel a balled-up envelope inside and go to pull it out when I hear a sorrowful cry of anguish from behind me. I turn to see Marco dropping to his knees next to Alex. I rush over to him and take him into my arms.

"Oh Marco, I'm so sorry." I say soothingly as I rub his back.

I can feel his grief-stricken cries rack his body.

"Why!" he wails in my ears. "Why Alex, he was such a good person, Olivia. I love him? God, I loved him. I should never have waited so long to ask him out. I was so nervous. So afraid he didn't feel the same way about me. Why did I wait, Olivia? Why is he gone"?

I don't know what to say. I have the same questions.

Why Alex? Why not me? Why was the package addressed to both of us?

"I need to see him."

Marco says pulling away from me and reaching for the sheet. I grab his hand.

"No Marco. Don't do that. That's not Alex anymore. Don't tarnish your memory of him."

I stand up and pull Marco to his feet away from Alex.

"How did this happen?"

Marco's voice breaks on the last word, his red rimmed eyes staring into my soul.

"He called me excited about a package that got delivered. It was addressed to both of us."

"A package?" Marco questions. "I didn't deliver a package. All your deliveries come from me. That doesn't make sense."

I don't respond. I slowly shake my head, not knowing how to answer.

"What aren't you telling me Olivia?" he screams.

I can see Marcel out of the corner of my eye walking toward us, I shake my head at him, still not ready to have him near me.

"Marco..."

I start, but he isn't listening to me anymore. He's staring at the charred initials marred into the sidewalk.

"ASC. That's who the flowers were from that you freaked out

about."

I can see the anger building in his eyes, his shoulders begin to tense as he takes a step toward me.

"This was for you! YOU WERE THE ONE MEANT TO DIE!"

He screams in my face as he suddenly snatches me off the ground by my throat. My air is instantly cut off. I go limp in his hand, I have nothing to fight for, no reason to struggle.

He's right. It should've been me.

I close my eyes, excepting my fate, when I feel the air whoosh back into my lungs as my feet hit the ground. I open my eyes to see Marcel and an officer looming over Marco who is now folded up into a fetal position bawling like a newborn baby.

"Alex, oh Alex. My sweet Alex. Why? Why?"

His haunting cries echoing through the night. The last solid piece of my heart shatters into a million pieces. I turn and walk away, no longer able to bear the sight of Marco's world being destroyed because of me too.

I need to breathe. I need to get out of here. I look down at the ground and see the crumbled envelope that was in my pocket. I pick it up and turn it over. It's the invitation to the convention in New Orleans.

Should I go home?

I turn back and take one more look at the devastation behind me. There is no home here without Alex. The building is destroyed. All my work is gone. All my memories with Alex. There's nothing for me here anymore. I turn and see Marcel and everything inside me burns like the rubble behind him did moments before.

I fucking hate you.

I think to myself, even as I can feel my body yearn for him. I turn back to the invitation.

No, nothing here at all. New Orleans sounds perfect.

Part Three: Nyx Harper

14

I tell myself every year this will be the last time, yet here I am, standing in front of Lavender Lakes Mental Health. I had my mother committed when I was sixteen and since then I have made it my own personal torture to see her on the anniversary of her admission. I fucking hate coming here. Every time I see her, I'm flooded with horrific memories of my childhood.

My earliest memories are inundated with scenes of my mom screaming and blaming me for my father leaving. Apart from those times, she refused to speak about him. My mom was always manic with extreme highs and lows. The highs never lasted long, but as I got older the manic episodes just became a never-ending state of madness. She held it together long enough for me to raise myself and acquire a shit ton of trauma; that for the life of me I cannot shake and struggle with daily. Yet again, here I stand.

I make my way through security, leaving all sharp objects at the desk.

It would be a shame for her to end her life with an earring, right? I think to myself.

Rounding the corner of her hall, I can already hear her. The stagnant hall full of her screams. She's mad, but she's never like this.

I make it to her door and the nurse says,

"Ms. Elaine is out of sorts today, maybe make your stay brief." I nod.

Not a problem.

I step through the door, and she is feral. She is throwing paper and drawing nonsense on the wall in crayon.

"Hi, Lainey." I say hushed.

Her head snaps up and turns toward me. She freezes. I stopped calling her mom years before she was committed. She thinks I'm her reflection. Calling her mom only confuses her and makes her go even more batshit.

"Did you see what was sent to you? Do you see it? Can you believe it? Why, why, why?"

She doesn't make much sense. Nothing abnormal, but I do see a bouquet of blue hydrangeas wrapped in purple paper.

Who would send her flowers?

I pick up the bundle. There is no card, just a wax seal binding the paper together. The seal has the letters "ASC" embossed into it.

She screams and it is piercing. I spin around to make my escape as she charges me. Before I can stop her, she tackles me to the floor, fighting and clawing me.

"Lainey Stop!"

I struggle out of her grasp. I can feel chaos threatening to release.

"Nyx, why would you come here?"

She recognizes me.

"I fucking hate you! I should have killed you when I found out what you would be. Just like your father."

I go limp. She hasn't said my name in probably 15 years. I'm stunned. Her hands clutch my neck. She is squeezing so tight. My vision starts to blacken at the edges.

Then she's off me in a split second. My lungs burn as air roughly envelops them. The nursing staff struggle but soon have her restrained. I find my footing and I start to walk out, lungs still burning, eyes seething from the influx of mascara and chaos ever so close to penetrating my last bit of restraint. Lainey bellows out a cynical taunt after me.

"Ohhhhh Nyx, He's going to kill you..."

I turn in shock to see her wide-eyed laughing.
FUCK THIS.
I am damn near running through the hall. I'm almost convulsing with rage. The lights in the hall glow brightly, threatening to rupture, as my chaos escapes me. The tears streaming, my face a mix of anger and devastation.

What the actual fuck was that? She recognized me after all this time, why?

I'm so lost with the rant in my mind that I don't even notice the wind ripping through the hall. Her voice in my head, ringing in my ears.

FUCK THIS PLACE! Fuck Lainey Harper! Fuck it all!

I emerged from the front door and nearly fell on my face. The clouds are darkening, and the winds are howling. My hands are damn near glowing, and I don't fucking care.

Let the world burn!

I rise, ready to let chaos rip through me.

Just then I catch a glimpse of myself in a car window in front of me. I stop, chaos and storm gaining strength around me, as I stand fixated on the reflection of the woman staring back at me.

I am her reflection; my madness is only external.

Fuck. I can't do this. I have to get home.

I rush to head back toward my apartment and come to an abrupt halt when I collide with a mountain of a man. I am frozen, the wind whirling my hair like a hurricane whips clouds. Large hands grab my back to stabilize me, and I look up. I am met with the most beautiful creature I've ever seen. Instantly I still. The air goes silent and all I can smell is sandalwood, leather, and the smell of a match that's just been snuffed.

"Woah Little One, I got you."

I believe him.

His voice is low and soothing, like trying to calm a feral cat. I meet his eyes; green pools with bright gold centers. His skin has a beautiful olive tone, its depth only highlighted by his dark hair that is a beautiful mess. I'm speechless. I'm sure I look like a fucking mad woman who just escaped the mental hospital. He holds me still. He cocks an eyebrow.

"You gonna be okay, or do I need to carry you?"

"Do not pick me up." I bite out.

He smirks and lets me go slowly. Instantly I feel empty. Like he was holding me together, filling me with the pieces I'm void of. I press my hands into his abdomen, and he's rock hard under his hoodie. I step back to give us some distance and regain my control. My mind slips and now all I can think about is what else he could fill me with that's rock hard. My mouth waters and I can feel my center warm.

Get it together Nyx. For fucks sake.

My inner voice screams. I drop my hands and look up.

"I'm so sorry."

"Don't be. You look a little shaken up. Between you and the weather, I don't know which one is wilder." He offers a small grin.

"I'm Kai. Would you like to go grab a coffee to calm your nerves?"

I raise an eyebrow. I break into hysterical laughter. He looks as if he missed the joke.

"You're telling me, you want to go get coffee with a woman you just saw fall out of the doors of a mental hospital, who by all accounts looks like a psych patient?"

He smiles. Gods be damned that smile is sent straight from hell to my pussy. My eyes flutter at the intensity of his gaze. He quirks his head and with a whiskey smooth tone says,

"From where I'm standing, by all accounts," he smirks" I'm in the presence of a goddess that looks to be having a bad day and could use a latte. And if you are a psych patient you will be the most interesting person I've met in a long time."

I laugh again.

I don't laugh. This is twice now, who is this man?

I roll my eyes.

"Fine, you are speaking to my soul with the latte idea, but I need to at least stop by my apartment first."

I gesture to my face and the mess of mascara trailing down to my chin.

"Oh, I see, jumping right to asking me to come to your place. I like it!" He playfully jars.

"Not in your wildest dreams, sir." I jab.

"Maybe!" he plays.

"I'm Nyx, by the way."

His eyes blaze at the mention of my name. Fire rises in me, and the wind stirs. I bite my bottom lip trying to ground myself and not set fire to the street around us. He raises his hand and rubs the pad of his thumb across my chewed lip. The connection causes my center to slick. With a cocked brow he nearly whispers,

"So, she is a goddess," he hums "darkness becomes you Nyx, lets grab that drink."

The vibrations between us are shaking me to my core. I have never been affected like this. Normally I am the siren of men and women, but I am never the one affected. I never feel this pull.

"Yes sir." I squeaked out.

SIR... the Fuck is happening to me.

"That's a good little one." his voice dripping in sex and danger.

Oh yes, he was sent from hell to torture me! Now I'll need to not only clean my face, but also change out of these soaked panties.

We make it a few blocks in silence, the hum around us is echoing off the buildings. He is the one to break the silence.

"So, you live in the middle of downtown? Do you rent an apartment or something?"

I stop in front of Salt and Sage Apothecary; I give a presenting gesture.

"I own an apothecary and had the upstairs converted into an apartment."

He gives a questioning look. I choose not to respond. I just met this man; I don't think I need to unload all my trauma before we have one drink. I'm sure if I could read his mind, not a skill I have unfortunately, he is wondering how a woman my age, not just has a business, but owns the building and its contents. This business I have built is my external representation of self. It was funded by madness, literately.

When my mother was committed, I was allowed minor emancipation, and in turn all my mother's assets were relinquished to me. Growing up we never had much. Many nights it was cereal or ramen for dinner. Our house was small and falling apart due to neglect, much like the inside. So, when the attorney had me sign authorizing the funds from her savings account be transferred to my own, I was shocked to see the standing balance. There was over 3 million dollars just sitting there.

Elaine Harper was a damn millionaire and I lived off fucking ramen. Fucking worthless crazy cunt. Still pisses me off.

"Welcome to Salt and Sage."

I say unlocking the door. The smell of rosemary, sage, and salt fill the air. The bells hanging in the corners of the space chime as my energy bounces off them. It is the most soothing sound amid my chaos. I flick my hands and the lamps on the display tables flare to life. I feel so grounded for a change, like my chaos is contained.

For once, it feels like clay in my hand, forming to my will, unlike my normal constant battle to keep Pandora in her fucking box. I drop the keys on the counter and turn to find him awestruck by the sight of my dimly lit shop. His eyes scan the shelves lining the right wall, full of oils, candles and crystals. When his eyes come to rest on mine, I smile shyly, it's like someone is seeing me, not just the siren I am when I lure partners to my room. No, it's like *he* is seeing me.

Nyx. Go upstairs for the love of the Gods you look like a deranged clown.

"I'll be right back, stay here and please don't break anything."

I am bolting up the stairs. I wash my face and throw on a bit of fresh makeup. My hair looks like I've had my head held out a window on the express way. I laugh thinking about Kai calling me a goddess. *HA,* I'm not ugly by any stretch of the imagination, but goddess like, I'd disagree. Time feels of the essence, so I opt for a bit of glamor magic, I run a brush through my hair, it's perfect, like I spent hours doing it.

The fuck. That was easier than expected...

I stare at my reflection, my dark chestnut hair falling around my face giving life to my petite features. The light catches on my lips, and I decide to add a bit of lipstick.

Go bold.

My inner monologue urges. I reach for my favorite deep burgundy lipstick. It gives an added plump to my already full lips and for shits and gigs I grab the matching lip liner and smudge just a bit under my lower lash line. My eyes are radiating lust and temptation, and the gold is like looking at a raging fire.

Get Dressed! Fuck.

I make my way through my room leaving a trail of clothes in my wake. Stepping out of my now cold damp panties I reach in my drawer for the first pair my fingers find, lace, black and cheeky.

Fitting.

I smirk at the thought of him taking these off with his teeth... Gods I'm going to go through a lot of laundry if I keep daydreaming about this man.

I grabbed a pair of sheer black tights and a black skirt.

Fuck it. All black goddess of darkness tonight.

I throw on a black cami and my boots, I opt for the high heal boots. Kai is at least 6'3 and I'm, well, not even 5'1. I take one last look in the mirror, I look far less like the mad woman running from the crazy house and much more Nyx, in control always.

Don't tell your chaos that.

I roll my eyes at my own thoughts.

I make my way down the stairs, and I feel his eyes before I even look up. I glance up from under my full lashes. He is rising from my cozy chair in the reading nook at the front of the shop.

"Fuck me." he blurts out.

"If you're lucky." I wink.

My inner self is giving me a standing ovation.

We got this.

I see the heat rise in his face, then fire burst in his eyes at the thought. He clears his throat nervously and steps in close. I step in to close the space between us. Initially to show him I'm not that weak girl he found on the street, but also to feel the fullness of his presence. He looks down at me, I meet his blazing gaze.

"I'm going to need something stronger than a coffee now." he nearly whispers.

"I'd like that."

He reaches up slowly letting his finger leave trails of fire up my arm, my skin burning from his touch. He reaches my jaw line and strokes it with the most intimate touch. My center clenches at how he touches me so delicately. In stark contrast he grabs my chin with his thumb and fore finger, notching my head higher to look at him. I had been so enthralled watching his finger trace my arm that I'd broken eye contact, in that split second, he commanded my attention back to his eyes.

A muffled growl rumbles in his chest and my control breaks, my head drops back slightly, my lips parted, and the smallest whimper escapes. The candles on the counter behind us combust and fire rages on the wicks. My center echoes the heat of the flames.

What the actual fuck Nyx... Are you about to orgasm?

The intensity of his gaze breaks to stare now at the inferno raging on my counter. I step back hating to break the connection but needing to regain my composure.

What composure, you nearly climaxed from his touch and growl, are you kidding me right now!!

I pivot and rush to the counter to extinguish the flames of the candles, my own flame still consuming me internally.

"Sorry about that, they have a mind of their own I guess." I offer the only explanation I can.

"How about we find a bar before the whole place comes alive." he says nervously.

"Perfect." I say dryly making my way to the front door.

15

We find our way to the bar; I offer up my go to place when I'm wanting to escape and have some privacy. It is a nondescript bar, hidden away in an alley off Main. Pour is the type of bar that only locals come to. There are no frills or flashy social media presence. It's a bar for those who want a well-made drink and unique bar food. The food is anything but mediocre.

The owner, Morgan, lived abroad for decades and when he finally came back to the states, he opened Pour, and made it a melting pot of his adventures around the world. The walls are lined with black and white photos from his travels. The floor is not overcrowded with tables, most of the seating is cozy booths with perfect dim lighting. The moody atmosphere is my soul's happy place. Morgan, nods to me as we walk in.

"Nyx, your booth is open in the back. Where is Mia?"

He gives Kai a once over and throws me a questioning look.

"Oh, she's around, I'm sure. Getting into trouble no doubt." I banter back.

We make it to my reserved booth in the far-left corner. I sit with my back to the wall allowing the perfect vantage point to people watch and to keep his attention focused on me.

I am the one in control.

"Who's Mia, your sister?" He immediately inquires. I smirk.

"No, far from it. She is my ex-girlfriend turned roommate and friend." He waits for more with inquisitive eyes.

"We dated for about 2 years, but we fell into a pattern of

convenience not passion. I care for her dearly, but not as a partner, as a friend."

"She is okay with you seeing other people?" he pushes.

"I don't see other people, I have my fun yes, but it is no strings attached. We lead separate lives and enjoy having a safe space together." He concedes.

"You have a private booth at this hidden gem?"

"You, Sir, are full of questions huh."

I pull my attention to Morgan bringing me my usual spiced whiskey, Calabrian chili feta dip and perfectly toasted bread.

"What can I get you?" Morgan asks while placing my usual in front of us.

"I'll have a Whiskey on the rocks as well."

Morgan nods and moments later is back with the glass.

"Nyx, let me know if you need anything."

He offers a sweet smile. Morgan is a middle-aged man, that still could pull any woman he wanted. His salt and pepper hair falls just long enough for him to brush back. His deep blue eyes are always kind to me and give me a comfort I don't always have. Kai coughs violently.

"What the fuck is that! Damn that's spicy." I try to hide my amusement.

"I enjoy the heat." I say dragging the bread through the dip.

"I see that. I need water, how are you drinking spiced whiskey and eating that dip from the pits of hell?" he coughs out raising his hand to flag down Morgan.

Morgan without words brings over the water with a smirk.

"She got you with the heat huh." Kai rolls his eyes and chugs down the water.

"I'll bring over some pretzels." Morgan offers as he heads to the kitchen.

I trace the rim of my glass with my middle finger, clockwise, letting it dip into the glass. I have done this too many times to admit, but I always get such a power rush from beginning to siren. My other hand drifts up to my lips, allowing me to chew ever so slightly on my nail. At this point my 'victim' is normally watching my hand on the glass, but not Kai.

"If you need something in your mouth, I'd be glad to offer a few replacements for your fingernail."

He says looking over his whiskey glass tipped to his mouth.

Let's play asshole.

I lick my lips and lean back.

"You are confident, huh?" I wink.

He laughs, the sound that comes from him is delicious. Every fiber of my being reacts to him.

"Little One, you are sin; you drip seductively with it. Carving out every desire I could possibly want, but I do not entertain brats. You will not get what you want from me without letting go of that control you are so desperately trying to hold on to. I will not play that game with you. I want you to show me you, the side of you that no one sees, Little One."

I try to maintain my position, I feel my eyes flare, but falter at his words.

I am not a brat, but I always get my way.

I lean in challenging him.

"What makes you think this is a game?"

He mirrors my position at the table, his lips mere inches from my own.

"Is it not? Power play is a game. You have been fighting to regain your power over me after I offered to pick you up off the street. Taking me to your storefront to compose yourself and coming down the stairs looking like you are the Queen of men damned straight to hell for catching your eye. Then bringing me to your spot, having me order while you are catered to by a man who would give his soul for a second of your attention. You are playing on the guise that I am a weak man, that I can't handle a woman like you," he inches closer "but Little One you are mistaken. I am the one that has control, and you need to let go. I can help you with that."

My breath catches and I cannot stop my gaze from dropping to his lips. I have never been so turned on by someone challenging my control. I have never been this alive with chaos. The glass in my hand shatters as chaos surges through me, but for the first time it isn't threatening to bring this building to rubble.

I want him.

The light above us flickers as if to agree with my thoughts.

"Now, Little One let's go."

I smirk at his command. He slides out of the booth, throwing a hundred-dollar bill on the table, nodding at Morgan. I slowly move out of my safe space. He catches my hand and electricity sparks between us. He withdraws looking at his hand and leaning into my ear,

"We will also need to talk about this later."

We made our way around the block to my storefront; the lights were still off so Mia hadn't returned. The rushing of blood in my ears is making it hard to maintain my control. Kai is walking in front of me.

Thank the Gods.

Why can't I read minds! Fuck that would make things so much easier.

"Open the door Nyx." He booms at me.

Who the fuck does he think he's talking to?

"Excuse me?" I bite out.

"I said open the door Nyx. Do not make me ask again."

Mmm why do I like this?

I unlock the door and we step in. I flicked my hand toward the lights on the displays again. I manage the one on the right, but he catches my hand before I can ignite the left one. He snatches me forward and I collide into his chest. Sliding his hand up to the nape of my neck, fisting my hair, and arching my neck back.

"That's enough of that Little one. I will show you what power is, and you will feel more powerful than you ever thought possible, but you have to let me show you. I know we just met but you can trust me. I will push you to your breaking point, but

I will not harm you. Do you understand?"

"Yes, sir." I whimper.

He takes my hand and leads me to my apartment. Once inside he coldly asks.

"Which room?"

I appreciate his knowledge of Mia at this point. I'd hate to be mid, whatever is about to happen and her walk in, the horror.

I nod to the door on the right and follow him in. My room has a full wall of floor to ceiling windows that are clad with impressive deep burgundy curtains that run their length. The curtains are open in the center allowing the light from the street to filter in, illuminating my king size bed. The frame is black wrought iron with an elaborate headboard adorned with moon phases. I just got it in, from one of my favorite new vendors, Rose and Ember. The rest of my room has scattered stacks of books and candles atop them. In the corner there is an antique gold full length mirror, it was the only thing I saved from my childhood home. Everything is oversized in this room, and it makes me feel even smaller with the massive man standing in front of you.

"Stand in front of the mirror. Do not move. Do not speak. I am going to light these candles" he gestures all around the room.

"I can..." I start to say, but he clips my words with a look, arching his eyebrow.

"I have no doubt."

It takes what feels like forever for him to light the candles. All while I'm standing here, feeling very exposed for someone who is fully dressed. He finally walks over to my bed and sits back and watches me for a beat.

"Undress." he states blankly.

What... this is not how I do things.

"Get out of your head. Take your clothes off now."

I comply. I start with my boots.

Oh, how I regret not putting on a bra tonight.

My tights, skirt and shirt follow. I'm standing in-front of a mirror facing, honestly the most attractive man I've ever seen in nothing but my panties.

Normally, I would have him kneeling between my thighs, but this is not normal. My entire body flushes with heat. I'm so exposed.

Get it together Nyx you're a goddess!

I tell myself. I stiffen my spine, chest out, locking my eyes on him.

"That's a good girl."

He growls moving to stand in front of me. My mouth parts and legs nearly give from the weight in which that comment hits me.

Good girl, why is that so intoxicating?

My breathing has picked up tremendously since he closed our distance. My nipples are hardened into tight little peaks that are now grazing his hoodie.

Gods, I want him to take that off.

"Let go Little One, you will enjoy this so much more if you set yourself free and relinquish your control to me."

Or ill burn the whole damn building to the ground buddy...

Without hesitation he grabs my waist, picking me up, I wrap my legs around his waist, he buries his face into my neck and just his breath has me letting out an enthusiastic cry to the Gods.

"Oh my fucking Gods".

I feel him smile into my neck and mummer.

"Cry to the Gods all you want, but this is my altar, and I will be the only one worshiping you; my dark goddess" He purrs into me. A moan escapes me.

"That's my girl."

His girl what!! I'm no one's girl. But why do I feel like I want to be his.

He throws me onto my bed. Leaning forward I try to pull him atop me, but he's unmovable.

"NO." he commands.

My hand retreats like a child that has just been scolded for touching something breakable. I eye him questioning. He removes his hoodie taking his shirt with him.

Fuck me!

His body is mouthwatering. He has a slim build, but his shoulders and chest are broad and carved of stone. His body is adorned with beautiful black and grey tattoo work, I can't make out what they are in this light, but I plan to explore all of them in time.

"Lay back and do not touch me."

But I want to...

I want to stomp my foot and protest. Maybe I am a brat after all, but I do as he says. He kneels between my splayed legs. My pussy has its own heartbeat at this point beating faster than my own. He places his large hands on my thighs and runs them up and down. My head rocks back at his touch.

"Let go Nyx. Let me have you."

His hand traces up my hips to my breast. They are not big by any means, but they sit firmly at attention to his touch. My hands move to him without thinking. He retracts instantly.

"I said No touching" he growls.

I can't even find my words before he flips me to my stomach, arching my hips into the air. My ass on full display. I try to object, but his hand is in my hair, pressing my face into the bed. He leans over to my cheek.

"That was your last warning. Keep your hands on the headboard and face down. Let go Nyx."

I do as he says, his voice making my thighs shake. I have never given a third of this control to anyone before. I am out of my element and shaking at the thought of letting go. He trails his hands down my spine and round my curves. He growls as he slides my panties to my knees.

"Gods be damned, that is the most beautiful pussy I have ever seen."

In an instant he brings me to his face and licks my slit all the way to my ass. I release a needy moan, rocking myself back into him for more, when a harsh smack hits my ass. I squeak.

"I said let go."

I relax back not knowing If I want to let go or keep being a brat, because that was earth shattering in the best way possible. He laps at my pussy again and again. I feel my need dripping down my thighs.

This is torture.

As if hearing my thoughts, he pushes two fingers into me; I curl around him. He growls at the grip I've placed on his fingers, and he deepens his fingers down perfectly stroking my G spot. My body relaxes into the bed, stretching my arms forward grabbing the headboard. I feel my orgasm growing closer and closer.

"That's it Little One, fucking cum for me" he whispers.

I arch my back, perking my ass up higher. He runs his free hand up my back slowly, all while he's fucking my pussy at the most torturous rhythmic pace with his other. He reaches my neck fisting my hair and jerks me back into him, my back melting into his stone chest. The hand that had been caressing my G spot retracts. The emptiness in my pussy aches, gripping greedily, wanting his touch to resume. His left fist is full of my hair, he pulls my head to expose my neck and leans into my ear.

"I want you to free yourself from control Nyx. Do this for me. Let me have you, all of you."

He trails a mixture of kisses and nips down my neck to my shoulder. The act, sensual and overwhelming. My legs quake from need. His free hand now gliding down my stomach. He spreads my lips and pushes his fingers into me once more.

"You are dripping for me my Little One."

I feel his hard length twitch against my ass, suddenly aware of just how hard he is beneath his jeans.

FUUUUCK... let go Nyx, what's the worst that can happen?

I nod to myself agreeing. I let go. I relax into him. He responds immediately as if sensing my acceptance and releases my hair. I drop my head back into him, letting him take me. He takes control; using his left hand to hold my throat, putting the most balanced pressure on my neck. His hand that had been lazily playing in my soaking wet pussy now finds purpose. He dips his fingers back into me and out. He retracts to rub the wetness over my swollen bud. He has avoided my clit thus far, and the sudden attention to it has me weak. He circles it with methodical precision, drawing moans from my throat.

"Kai please." I beg.

"Say it again!" He growls almost feral.

"Kai…. I need you please!"

I cry out breathless. His chest rumbles and he rubs my clit with pressure that sends me to my peak.

"Cum Little One, let me have all your power."

He growls into my ear as he tightens his grip on my neck, my vision darkens, he could kill me right now and I'd go willingly. I fall over the edge; he releases my neck. I break into an earth-shattering orgasm; flooding oxygen into my system and ecstasy into my veins. I am overcome.

"Fuck Kai!" I cry out, my lungs burning.

I inhale deeply and melt into him, and I release everything, all of me, all control, all restraint, all fear, everything; all that is left is this moment. I feel whole. He tightly wraps his arms around me.

"Come back to me."

I snap back to reality and the flames of the candles are blazing, threatening to engulf the room. I breathe out slowly, all the candles extinguish and the light from the street goes black. Kai is still holding me like he is afraid to let go.

Now who won't let go.

"Kai?" I whisper.

"Yes, Little One?"

He is raggedly breathing like he is trying to control himself now.

"Thank you."

We lie silently for a while, taking in what just happened. He's laid back, his long body nearly making it to the end of my bed. I have my head on his chest, with his arm wrapped around me; listening to his heart that has found its rhythm again. I would swear there is a muffled hum coming from him, but that's probably just me. We hear Mia come in, bitching about the power being out all over the city.

Shit.

I snicker when I hear her trip over the ottoman. Rolling over onto my stomach I start to fidget with my rings. Only moonlight illuminates the room now. Streaks flow in, highlighting just how good Kai looks in nothing but jeans, he looks like a fucking god with how the moonlight bounces off him. I try to speak but can't find words. I trace a tattoo on his arm. The thought of what else I want him to do to me surges through my body and an arch of electricity sparks across the tattoo.

Shit.

"Please do not try to convince me that was just static." he pushes.

I have no explanation. I fidget with my rings again trying to find a way out of the conversation I feel brewing.

"Or that this apartment is so drafty, that it blew out all of these candles at once, the candles downstairs, that nearly set the place on fire, don't just have a mind of their own. I am not going to sit here and ignore what's happening. It's time to talk."

Fuck... Fuck... Fuck...

I have never told anyone what I can do. I own an apothecary sure, primarily normal people come in here searching for what they think will give them power, but there is no chaos in them. I do have men and women come in that request privacy and special orders, but I have never offered up information about myself. I'm sure they can feel my power as much as I can feel theirs, but still, it's unspoken. Hell, I never even told Mia. Why do

I want to tell him?

"I can't." I sigh.

"Why not?" he pushes.

"Because I've never told anyone, and if I tell you…" I trail off.

"If you tell me what Nyx? What could possibly be worse than letting go of your control?"

He turns his body towards me, propping up on his elbow, running his fingers along my spine.

"If I tell you and you freak the fuck out then what, you go around telling everyone how crazy I am and how I almost set fire to my room with you in it; that I'm just like my mother and need to be locked up." my voice cracks.

Don't you dare fucking cry Nyx.

"Shhhh, Little One," he hushes. "No matter what it is, I'm right here."

I drop my head into my hand, fighting the urge to cry.

Why do I want to share this with him?

The hairs on his arm rise as I lift my head. I twist my wrist and the candles in the room ignite. Light floods the room and I sit up, placing a pillow in my lap for some failed attempt at a wall.

"That's fucking beautiful." he says looking around the room.

"I am chaos."

I murmur twisting my hand again opening the window. He shakes his head sitting up. I'm still looking at my hands wrapped around my pillow, defeated.

"Look at me," Kai urges.

I meet his gaze and a tear slips from my lid.

Fucking traitor.

I look toward the windows not wanting to let another fall. He moves in closer and takes my hands in his. I look at them, how mine looks so fragile, how easily he could crush them, yet he's so gentle.

"Look at me Nyx, I'm not going anywhere. I'm right here; that was fucking beautiful. You are not chaos, you are a Goddess."

I look at him with surprise and the feeling of every nerve in my body being exposed. I look at his lips, and I just want to kiss him. I never kiss. It's my rule. Kissing is too intimate for a siren, but I want him. Siren or not I need him.

16

I wake to light drifting in through the windows. I roll over, expecting to still see Kai lying next to me, but he's gone. Disappointment sets in. We talked all night. I told him about my magic and what I can do and how I typically lose control. We talked about what had happened earlier that day with Lainey and he just listened. I felt like I'd known him my whole life. Though we didn't talk much about him, other than that he moved around a lot as a teen, he spent most of his childhood in New Orleans. Which explains that hint of a southern accent that slips through.

I pull the cover over my head, wishing this empty feeling to disappear. I grab my phone and text Jinny; she works in the shop with me. I let her know I may not be in today. Mental health day.

More like mentally fucked day.

I smell breakfast cooking; it smells so good! Mia does love a good breakfast, but she never cooks.

"Who the fuck are you?!" Mia yells out slamming her bedroom door. I sit straight up.

WHAT? He's in my kitchen... FUCK ...

I grab my panties and the black t-shirt off the bed.

Well, this isn't my shirt...

I bound through my bedroom door to see Kai turning to Mia, shirtless offering her a cup of coffee.

Oh, my fucking Gods he's still here.

A smile blushes over my face and I can't help but bite my lip.

"I'm Kai, you must be Mia." he says, turning to meet my gaze, smiling with a raised eyebrow at the sight of me in his shirt.

Mia shoots me a concerned look; One full of confusion and, I swear, hurt.

"Nyx?" Mia questions.

"Uh, yeah. Uh Mia this is Kai. He stayed and is now making breakfast." I state the obvious.

No shit.

"Are you serious right now, Nyx?" Mia grabs her bag and heads for the door.

"Mia, we will talk later." I call to her. She slams the door.

"Well, that's not how I wanted *your* morning to start Little One."

Kai says handing me a cup of coffee. "But seeing you in my shirt like that, is how I want start all of my days!"

I look up at him with a smirk sipping my coffee.

"I thought you left."

"Now why would I do that?"

"I thought you said you and Mia were just friends now."

"We are." I snip.

"Well from where I'm standing, she was not okay seeing someone stay over."

Fuck, he's right.

"She was just surprised, I'm sure, to see you. She knows no one stays the night, and for you to not only have stayed but to be making breakfast, that seems more than just a one-night stand."

He nods as if to see my point.

"Hungry?"

"I am starving" I smile.

Breakfast was delicious, and so was the view. The image of Kai shirtless, standing in front of my stove, will live rent free in my mind long after he is gone. He's cleaning up and I'm standing at the bar, just watching him work. I never have anyone cook or clean for me, so it's nice having someone willingly do it.

"If you keep eye fucking me like that, I'll have to show you what it's actually like." Kai flirts, turning to stand in front of me. My eyes trail over every inch of him.

"I need to shower and get ready to head down to the shop."

I need a break from this, and he doesn't need to know I'm taking a mental health day.

I try to turn and walk towards my room, but he snags my waist, stopping me. I turn back.

"I think you should take the day off," he smirks.

"I think I need to go shower." I snip.

He is lifting me to the island before I can even protest.

"Come on Little One, you know you want to stay."

He says sin dripping from his lips, I'm sitting almost eye level with him now. His large arms firmly pressed into the granite. I stare up at him unamused.

"I don't like to be picked up."

"Little One, you don't even know what you like with me."

He moves into me, spreading my legs further. We are inches apart and he keeps looking at my lips, I know what he's about to do before he moves.

Stop him.

I ignore the bitch in my head; I want him. It's like he knows this is a hard limit for me. He moves slowly, raising his hand to my chin, looking at my lips and then at my eyes.

"You are more than I could have ever dreamed of," his lips so close to mine.

I move without thinking, leaning further into him. Our lips touch and electricity rises in the air.

Oh, my fuck, what have I done? I can't stop.

The need in our kiss is palpable. I feel every fiber of my being coming undone. The light from the windows is growing dark and I release the kiss to take a breath. As I do, lightning cracks across the sky, like the Gods themselves are shocked by my actions. Thunder shakes my entire apartment. I lean back into him as he smiles into my kiss.

"That's you, isn't it?" He whispers.

"Yes sir." I smile back into him.

Just as the sound of rain pours from the sky. His chest rumbles at my confession. He is kissing me again with more urgency than before. I am arching my body into him wanting to feel more of him. I am losing myself in his kiss. He picks me up from the counter, wrapping my legs around him and I feel his cock throbbing beneath me. My pussy aches in response. Another crack of lightning through the sky. Just as the front door slams open.

FUCK.

Our attention turns towards Mia, standing in the doorway soaking wet.

"You have got to be kidding me Nyx." She scoffs. Kai sets me down.

"Oh my god, let me get you a towel."

Way to go Nyx, break your first rule and now Mia is standing here soaking wet while you were tongue fucking said breaker of the rules.

"I am so sorry Mia," I say handing her the towel.

"Why are you sorry, for letting some guy stay the night, for lying to Jenny that you needed a mental health day or for the fact that I just walked in on you KISSING him?"

I stare blankly.

Kai was right. She is not okay with this.

"Seriously Nyx, what the fuck are you doing?"

Kai grabs his hoodie off the couch and walks to where I'm standing leaning in,

"I am going to let you handle this, I am sorry. My number is on the fridge, text me, see you Little One," he says hushed, kissing me on the cheek.

Shit. FUCK.

He walks past Mia with hands raised as a sign of defeat, with one last glance he smiles at me.

Stay... My thoughts cry... *Snap out of this shit Nyx.*

As if all the air in the room comes slamming back into me with force I focus on Mia.

"We need to talk!" She snaps.

"Who is he?" Mia stands gesturing at the door.

"His name is Kai."

I sigh walking over to the couch, grabbing a pillow to create my imaginary wall between us.

"You kissed him." Mia says nearly crying. "In two years, Nyx you never kissed me like that for fucks sake. How long have you been seeing him?"

I feel ashamed of her words.

"I kissed you all the time Mia, you know that." I snip.

"Sure, you did Nyx, you kissed my forehead, my cheek, my body, my pussy, sure. Never once in two fucking years did you ever kiss me like that. Not once."

Tears breaking from her eyes.

She's right.

I brace myself for more. She is telling the truth, and it digs deep into me.

"Fuck Nyx, why? Why him and not Me?"

Ice runs through my veins.

"Mia, I'm sorry. I had no idea you would be so affected by this. I thought we agreed to just be friends." She laughs.

"We agreed? Ha. No Nyx, that was all you. I wanted to be with you. I wanted to be the one that brought the light out of you, but you would not let that happen. YOU pulled away. YOU created the rip in our relationship."

She paces the floor shaking her head. I cannot move. I feel like all the air that I found is gone again.

"How long?"

I know exactly what she is asking, but I do not want to admit it aloud.

"How long what, Mia?"

"How long have you been seeing him?"

I stay quiet. I cannot answer her. If I tell her I just met him yesterday, it will break her.

What the fuck have I have done.

"Not long." I mutter out.

"Of course, do you even know his last name?" She snarks out. "What does he do for a living? For fucks sake do you even know what food he likes?"

She's right again; I do not know any of this. I have let this man into my life, let him see me, released myself to him and told him about my chaos. This is not me. I would have never done this before him.

So why now, why him?

I try to find the words but fall short. I drop my head into my hands. Regret racking my body.

"Fucking fantastic Nyx. I bet you told him about your power too." My head snaps up.

"What did you just say?"

It comes out a lot harsher than I expect.

"I don't know what the hell to call it, the shit that happens around you. Do not treat me like an idiot, candles don't fucking light themselves Nyx."

I'm in shock at this point. "Tell me I'm wrong, then. Tell me you didn't give him more of you than you ever gave me."

"Mia, please understand I had no intention of ever hurting you. I..."

"You what Nyx, you're sorry? Because you damn sure didn't love me. I'm done Nyx. I'm done with thinking you will see me how I see you, and I'm not going to wait around here for you to realize who I was to you."

She grabs her bag; tears stream down her face and makes her way to the door. She looks back at me and what little strength I had left breaks.

"I don't even know who you are now, Nyx."

The door slams following her words. My tears break free. I am sobbing so hard I can barely breathe.

What have I done?

Mia's words cut me to my core, but the pain I have caused her cannot compare. Every word she said was the truth; not one thing did she have twisted. I hurt her, I have caused her unimaginable pain and never thought twice about my actions or our relationship. I told Kai that Mia and I grew comfortable in the relationship and there was no passion. I was the cause of that; I did not let her in, I did not try to open myself to her.

How could I be so blind and self-centered? So arrogant to think that it was her and not me.

A mixture of fury and sadness evade my body, books fly from the shelves as I cry harder into my hands. I am a fucking mess. I find my footing and make my way through the apartment to my room.

Where is my phone?

I find my phone still lying in the bed. I swipe till I find Mia's name and send the call. It rings and then forwards to voicemail. My fingers are swiping across the phone.

Me
Please come back, I need to explain.

Mia
Fuck off Nyx. I don't need anything from you now.

I want to scream or cry, or both. My energy is null. I can barely keep my eyes open now that they are swollen from my tears.

You did this.

Maybe I do need that fucking mental health day after all. I crawl into bed pulling the covers over me, but all that I am met with is the smell of Kai in my bed. I sigh wanting to grab his number off the fridge, but knowing I need to get control of myself. My body gives into sleep.

I wake to my phone vibrating on my nightstand. I focus my eyes and the sun is setting.

How long was I out?

I see Jinny's name on my phone.

"Hey Jinny, what's going on?"

"Hey girl, there is a guy down here that says he knows you and wants me to let him up to your apartment."

"No." I blurt. I need the space to collect myself. "Tell him I'm not feeling well, and I'll talk to him later."

"Yeah girl, sure thing. I'm about to close for the night too. I will make sure everything is locked up for you."

"Thanks Jinny."

The line clicks. My body is pulling me to get out of bed and run downstairs to wrap myself in him, but I can't. I cannot give myself to someone that I know nothing about. I need a fucking shower, maybe I can wash away the regret that is weighing on me. I check my phone one last time for anything from Mia but find nothing. I turn on the water to let it warm and my mind snags back to Kai's number on the fridge.

Do not fucking do it.

I roll my eyes knowing I don't need to engage him, but I need to tell him something, so he does not keep coming to the shop.

Keep telling yourself that.

Running through the apartment I swipe the number from the fridge and hurry back. I would hate for Mia to walk in on the scene of me running through the living room naked with Kai's number in my hand. Grabbing my phone, I make my way back to the bathroom. Steam is pluming from the shower; I grab a scoop of my shower salt and throw it into the bottom of the tub. The smell of eucalyptus and lemon fills the air. Inhaling the scent, I typed out a quick message to Kai. It takes 4 times for me to finally send the text.

Me
I need some space.

I sit staring at my phone waiting for his reply. I set my phone down and finally decide to get in the shower when my phone chimed.

Fuck. Do I give it a minute or reply now. Read it now.
I snatch my phone.

Kai
I'm guessing your talk with Mia didn't go so well. Want me to bring you some dinner?

What is with this man feeding me? No, I do not want him here. What if Mia were to come back and find him here again? No. Not happening. I set my phone down not wanting to reply now. I need space. I step into the shower letting the hot water melt away all that is binding me. The steam mixed with the scents from my shower salt relaxes every inch of my body. I could stand here forever. My phone chimes. I stick my face into the water.

Maybe I'll drown and not have to deal with any of this mess. I could never get away that easily.

I turn the shower off and decide to face my problems. Another chime.

Wrapping myself in a towel I grab my phone eager to see who texted me.

Mia
I'm going to my sisters. I just grabbed a few of my things. I'll let you know when I need to get the rest. There is no need to talk, I think enough was said today.

Sighing I reply.

Me
I understand. For what it's worth, I am truly sorry for not seeing any of it sooner. It was never my intention to hurt you, Mia.

Mia
I know. It's just time for me to move on. Be careful Nyxi.

Tears well in my eyes, threatening to overtake me again. She hasn't called me that in forever. At this point I will myself to respond to her, but I have no response. I take a deep breath needing to calm myself.

I've done this more in the last 24 hours than I have in years. I flip to the next message.

Kai
Little One? Are you okay?

Me
I need some space, Kai. I don't even know who you are, and I've let you into my life and chaos has ensued.

Kai
Yeah, I get that, but I can let you into my life. I want to occupy the space you are in. Nyx you can push all you want, but I'm not running.

Why do I want him to come over? I can't. I need to regain my control. He's breaking down my walls faster than I can rebuild, and this is not a comfortable space for me.

Kai
If you want to know me, let me show you who I am. Just give me a chance Nyx.

"No". I say to myself slamming my hand on the counter looking in the mirror. Puffy eyes and wet hair, what a sight I am.
Get your shit together.
I pull myself up. I'm going out.

17

I find myself walking in the doors of Absinthe. It is a trendy club where everyone is there to find their own pleasure. I'm met with a bouncer that's the size of a bear, I run my finger across my lower lip, he looks at me smirking.

"Right this way."

He says lifting the velvet rope into the VIP section. I do not normally use chaos like this, but I need to feel in control. The VIP section is not my normal ground to find a good time, but I want to people watch and find just the right person to distract me. I catch a glimpse of myself in the floor to ceiling mirrors. I look like bad decisions in the making, but I am controlling them.

About fucking time.

I am in black skinny jeans, with sheer black long sleeves. The only pop of color is my burgundy bra peeking through and my lips. The first thought that came to mind when putting my outfit together was a black widow. I flag the server down needing something warm to internalize the heat I feel on my skin. I am humming with anticipation. I love to siren; it is such a power rush and gives me a hold of my power. The server returns with my usual, cinnamon whiskey.

"This is on the blonde at the bar."

She says pointing to the bombshell at the end of the bar. I nod, raising my glass to her. I throw my head back letting the whiskey set fire inside me.

Let's play.

I head towards the bar feeling all eyes following me. I make my way up to the blonde. I reach her and offer my hand; she takes it, and we head to the dance floor. The beat slows; I raise my arms letting the electricity in my body flow, my hips are swaying to the beat, and I let my spell spill from my lips.

> *"In whispered words and candlelight's gleam,*
> *I weave a spell, a desire's dream,*
> *Their heart entwined, enchanted deep.*
> *With every word, their thoughts I steep,*
> *Drawn to me, their longing grows.*
> *In passion's dance our connection flows.*
> *By magic's might, their heart's afire,*
> *Enchanted now, by my desire."*

The blonde reacts immediately grabbing my waist and matching my movements beat for beat. I'm losing myself in the feeling of control and her lips on my neck. I close my eyes and all I see is Kai. My eyes snap open and my pulse quickens. I move closer to the blonde her hands moving over my body. I shake my head trying to get the image of Kai out of my head.

I eye the waitress, holding up my hand I gesture for her to bring me two more shots. I turn and grind my body into the blonde, the scent of vanilla and cinnamon swirl around me. I let my spell spill again, stretching my siren song and the music picks up. The power is intoxicating.

The waitress brings my drinks. I throw them back one after another. The warmth fills my body and I hum with satisfaction. I feel it again; I feel my soul calling out for him. I continue to dance, but my hands are warming.

I'm in control, what is happening?

I look at my hands and they are almost glowing. I shove them in my hair forcing myself to focus on the blonde and music. Again. I feel my soul call out for Kai. I can't shake it. My soul is splitting, and this man is going to drag me to hell.

"Little one?"

That was not my own thought. It was Kai's voice in my head.

That's it, I am going crazy.

I need to get some air. I unwind my spell and break connection with the blonde. Confusion crosses her beautiful face as she turns back for the bar. I make my way to the front of the club; my lungs are stinging with the need for air. The doors open and the cool night air bites my skin as I draw in a deep breath.

"Little one?"

I spin to find Kai standing in front of the bear sized bouncer, worry etched into his expression.

Why in the hell is he here?

"Kai why are you here? Did you follow me?"

Kai's expression turns serious walking towards me.

"You called me here. Nyx I was at home. I heard your voice calling me."

What the actual fuck is he talking about.

"Nyx are you okay, why am I here?"

I have no answer to why he is here or why he heard my voice.

"Can we get out of here?" I ask feeling like I'm in a daydream.

"Yeah, I'm parked over here."

He places his hand on my lower back and electricity flows back through my body. If it weren't for the concern on his face, I would fuck him where he stands. We get to his all-black SUV, complete with blacked out windows.

"Nyx, what did you do?"

He commands, opening the passenger door.

That's a good question.

He closes the door as I slide in. Out the window, I notice he's wearing a black tee, flannel pajama pants and slides.

"What the hell are you wearing?" I ask as he sits back into the driver's seat.

"Well, I was sitting on my couch watching the game and then I heard your voice calling me."

My eyes widen.

"The next thing I know I'm parking in front of this club and arguing with the bouncer to let me in."

"So, you weren't following me?"

"Nyx, I have no idea how I ended up here. What is going on?" He looks scared.

"I don't know." I say looking at my hands.

"How was I hearing your voice calling me, drawing me here?"

"I don't know Kai, this has never happened before."

"What were you doing in there?"

"Dancing." I say dryly.

"With whom?" jealousy dripping from his tone.

"A girl, I needed a distraction from all this" I gestured around us.

"Then why am I here? Nyx what the fuck happened in there? Were you using your chaos?"

"Yes. I needed control. I came here to find someone to distract me, and when I set my eyes on a girl at the bar, I began to draw her in with my chaos, but I have no idea how you heard my voice."

I think back to seeing his face and my soul calling for him. There is no way I summoned him. No way that's possible. I have never done that before.

None of this should be possible.

"What are you not telling me Nyx? You're holding back."

"It's not possible."

I say aloud, contemplating my soul summoning him from across the city. Reality hitting me hard, it's the only explanation.

"My soul summoned you, Kai."

He stares at me with concern and intrigue. I begin to ramble.

"I was dancing and losing myself in my siren and I closed my eyes and saw you. My soul cried out for you, even though my thoughts were telling me to stop. I heard your voice, Kai. I do not know what this is. I do not even know your last name, or what you do for work or even your favorite food. None of this makes sense."

The wind howls around the car as I feel chaos reaching out.

"Reighn, CRNA and pasta" he blurts out knocking me out of my own head.

"What?" I look at him like he has two heads. The wind stops.

"My last name is Reighn. I am a traveling CRNA, and I love pasta. You said you didn't know those things about me. Well now you do."

I laugh, Gods do I laugh hysterically. I cannot stop. I am laughing so hard he begins to laugh making light of this fucking weird conversation.

"Can I drive you home?" he asks, still chuckling at how bizarre this all is.

"Yes sir." His chest rumbles at my consent. I love that sound.

You need to control yourself.

We are walking up the stairs to my apartment and I can feel the tension between us. I open the door, only to be reminded of the shit show of a morning I had. Books lay scattered around the apartment.

"What happened in here?" Kai eyes the mess.

"Well Mia was upset, and we had it out." I admit.

"I see that."

"Kai, do you want to stay?" I say stepping towards him.

Why are you asking him to stay?

"Little One, I would love to stay, but I have to be at the hospital at 5am. It starts my 24-hour shift. If I stay, I won't be worth anything. Can I rain check the invitation?"

I'm floored. He's telling me no.

Brat.

Is he responsible or did I just scare the fuck out of him by summoning him?

"Oh, is this because of earlier?" I say looking at my hands. He steps in lifting my chin.

"Nyx, I am not going to lie, being drug out of my house in my pajamas and slides was not the highlight of my night, but I was worried about you. I did not know what was happening and I thought something was wrong, but do not for one second think me not staying has anything to do with you. I know you need your space and I have a long 24 hours ahead of me. It is late; get some sleep and text me in the morning Little One."

I smile at his words of assurance. I raise on my toes to close our distance.

Do not kiss him.

Against my better judgment I want to kiss him. He drops my chin and lifts me with one arm.

"I hate being picked up" I protest.

"I know." He's smiling crushing his lips into mine.

I melt, my body and soul hum with contentment. My brain screams in frustration. His hands grab my ass, and he rumbles into my lips. I feel like I will lose all control with this man. He strides to the island and sets me on top. My hands are in his hair, and I am pulling him on top of me. He growls as my hand reaches for his cock.

"Not like this." He pulls back with a growl.

BUT I NEED THIS.

I want to scream at him. I lay on the island breathless. This man's kiss destroys me to my core. My pussy has soaked my panties, and my nipples are digging into my bra. Every nerve in my body smoldering from his touch. I run my hand through my hair staring at the ceiling, willing myself to regain control.

"Nyx?" He muses.

I sit up looking at the man who will be my undoing. He is a perfect disaster, his hair a mess from my hands, and his rock-hard cock on full display in his blue flannel pants.

I fucking love this view.

"This is not the space, Little One. I want to give you what you need, even if it leaves me in a cold shower. I do not want our first time together being in the same head space as this morning. As much as I want to stretch that tight pussy of yours, I want you to be ready. You asked for space. I will give you 24 hours." He winks.

Gods be damned where did this man come from?

"Kai, you are tearing me apart."

"Not yet." He plays.

He kisses my forehead, holding his lips to me for several seconds, my heart skips at the sweetness. It's like he's contemplating something, I just don't know what.

"I'll lock up."

He turns towards the door. He opens the door looking back at me shaking his head at me still sitting on the counter. It looks like he is kicking his own ass for stopping us.

"Night, my Little One" he says shutting the door.

I fall back onto the counter covering my face.

What am I going to do with this man?

I'm opening the shop when Jinny comes through the front door looking moody as ever. She wears her signature black tights, shorts, and Doc Martin's, but today she's wearing a bright orange sweater.

"Feeling festive in September?" I play. She rolls her eyes putting her bag behind the counter.

"Maybe, I love the season."

"Well, it's giving pumpkin patch for sure!" I tease.

"Oh, I forgot to tell you!! You will never guess who came into the store yesterday. Elizabeth James."

"What! The author, No way! What was she doing here?"

"She was in town, and she stopped in to browse and ended up placing an order for onyx, she wants to use it to promote her new book!"

"Are you serious! That's fucking amazing, why didn't you come get me?"

"Things seemed a little on edge and I didn't want to bother you."

"Oh, yeah." I trail off.

"Hey, is everything okay with you and Mia, she seemed really upset and stormed out. Does that have anything to do with the ridiculously large man that came down before her?" She changes the tone of the conversation.

"Yes, there was a misunderstanding on my end, and I messed up. She will be at her sisters for a while." I clarify.

"I see. So, who is the guy?" She pushes.

"If we are going to gossip about my love life, let's at least do it while refilling the herbs." I offer looking to the wall of gallon jars behind the counter. She nods.

We spent the better part of 3 hours talking about Kai, Mia and me. I hate talking about my life with Jinny, but honestly, she's the only person I have to vent to at this point.

"So, are you going to keep seeing him?"

"I don't really know. He is giving me some space to think, but I don't really know where to go from here."

"Well, if you want my advice," she says waiting for me to object, "I think you should go ahead and fuck already, get it out of your system and then you can move on to the next!"

I stand there with my mouth open in shock. "Jinny!" I scold.

She shrugs knowing she's right.

The door chimes, I turn to see our delivery guy with a matte black box tied with a crimson bow.

"Miss Harper?"

I nod, not really knowing where this came from. He sets the box on the counter and has me sign for receipt. Jinny is nearly bouncing waiting for him to leave.

"What's that!" She squeaks.

I pull the bow and open the box.

Inside is a note.

> *My Little One,*
>
> *I'm taking you away for the weekend. I have a special night planned and I want to take this off of you. Be ready by 2. It's a bit of a drive. We will get ready in the suite.*
>
> *Kai*

I flip the card in my hand smirking.

What happened to giving me space?

I glance at Jinny tapping her foot impatiently.

"What's in the box already!" Jinny whines. I unfold the black tissue paper.

It is like he knows me.

I laugh to myself. Inside I find a deep burgundy satin dress, *it*'s beautiful, my soul sings. It's full length with what appears to be slit to the hip. Jinny swoons.

"Oh Nyx, that is stunning!"

I notice there is more in the box, laying the dress on the counter I remove what I'm guessing is black lingerie from the box as well. It is not your typical lacy bits of fabric most men would buy. It is strappy and leather. It is a thigh harness and leather corset.

Oh, My Gods.

There is another note.

> *I see you found my favorite part. I want to show your rough edges even in such a silky dress.*
>
> *See you soon.*

My center tightens. Oh, this is going to be fun.
Looking up from the note I catch Jinny's stare.
"I guess that means you are seeing him again after all."
"I guess so." I admit working the note card in my hand.

18

I'm packing my bags, and I feel him before I hear him knock at the door. It's like my body feels his presence.

He is early.

"It's open."

I call. My back is to my bedroom door, I feel his eyes tracing my body.

"Enjoying the view?" I play.

"You have no idea; I like this travel look you have going on." he points to my overly casual outfit of denim shorts and a crop t-shirt.

I throw the last few items in my bag, then turn to finally look him over. To my surprise he is in scrubs.

The Gods sent him to destroy every part of me.

The sight of him in something as normal as scrubs tightens my core. If he were to come into my hospital room covered in tattoos, muscles barely contained in the fabric of his scrubs and that face. They would have to get the crash cart. It is unnatural to look that good.

"Are you enjoying the view?" he retorts.

"Maybe." I add.

He walks over to the bed and grabs my bags. Careful not to touch me.

Is this him giving me space? I don't like it.

"Let's go, it's a drive to Seattle and we still have to get changed."

Seattle! That is a drive!

The drive to Seattle is beautiful this time of year. The cool breeze through the sunroof with the overcast sky makes my dark little soul buzz with joy. We drive in comfortable silence most of the ride. It's an odd feeling to be able to sit in silence with someone yet feel completely at ease. He turns on his play list, letting the music fill the space between us. I know this song. He rolls the windows down as if knowing the energy will be too much to fill the SUV. 'Just Pretend' by Bad Omens swirls around me. My soul sings.

His hand that had been holding the gear shift reaches for me; wrapping his hand around mine he brings it to his lips, kissing so softly. The beat drops and he sings the chorus like his life depends on it. Closing my eyes, I drop my head back letting the words wash over me, hairs raise on my arms, and its not my chaos, its him. I look back at him as the chorus plays again and I sing out with him. The energy in the space between us is electric and my center is pooling. I feel like something has just shifted in me. I want this man more than I have ever wanted another soul.

You are not falling for him.

Pulling up to the hotel I want to get into the room as fast as possible. I want to devour him. We make our way into the elevator, and he taps the key fob against the sensor.

Fancy.

The doors close and his hands are in my hair, flanking either side of my face. I rise on my toes to close our distance. My heart is pounding, and my breathing has gone uneven. His expression looks reckless.

"Nyx, I need you to let me have you. I cannot give you space, I need to have you, all of you. If you let me take you, you are mine. There is no turning back. This is your only chance to run. Do you understand!"

He demands. Danger sparks the intensity in his emerald eyes.

"Do you understand!?" He growls.

He looks like there is a beast threatening to break through what's left of his reserve. His breathing goes rigid, His jaw clenches at my delayed response. My core goes tight.

Here we go.

The doors open to the suite.

"Take me Kai."

He releases a feral growl dropping my hair and picking me up under my ass. Our lips collide into sparks. Literal sparks. I bite his bottom lip.

"Sorry" I whisper through my teeth. He smiles against me.

He's striding through the suite. He stops at the bed, our kissing is desperate, my thighs tighten around his waist and my need rocks my hips. His hand fist in my hair, jerking my head back breaking our connection, I whimper at the loss. He nuzzles my neck.

"Safe words," he kisses my neck.

"Yellow, to push intensity."

He continues and nips my neck.

"Orange, to maintain."

He trails my neck to my collar bone.

"Red, to stop."

He bites down hard. I feel my skin break, I let out the neediest sound I've ever heard slip through my lips.

"That's my good girl!"

Holy hell.

He takes both hands and shoves me off him. I go flying onto the bed. I take a second to take him in, he looks like a different person, a demon, full of desire. I prop back on my elbows and my legs fall apart, offering myself to him. He grabs my ankle dragging me to the edge of the bed. I pull my shirt over my head exposing my breast. He shakes his head and tsks.

"You are a fucking Goddess Nyx."

He is ripping at my shorts; the button goes flying across the room. He steps into my spread thighs, leaning in to trace my body with his fingers. My skin tightens at his touch.

"I want to mark this perfect skin."

He traces my breast; leaning in, he bites down again on my collar bone. I moan again in response, arching my hips to find his body.

"Please Kai."

I beg, unsure of what I'm begging for. I reach for him, pulling his shirt up. He straights and pulls his shirt off, he kicks his shoes off and releases the tie on his scrubs. I sit up admiring the sight of this fucking God or demon of a man. His pants drop off his hip slightly. The image soaks my panties.

"Can I?"

I ask looking at the bulge in his pants. He nods as if to give me permission. I slide off the bed dropping to my knees, releasing his cock from its confines. My mouth waters, I wrap my hand around his rock-hard cock. It is the thickest cock I have ever seen. I don't even know if I can fit him in my mouth. I trail my tongue from the base to the tip with a slow swirl. He rumbles with pleasure. I allow the spit pooling in my mouth to spill out running down his length. Looking up at him letting the spit trail from his cock to my lips.

"Fuck Nyx!"

He hums his approval. I smirk feeling my vixen come out to play. I take him into my mouth, allowing my hands to swirl as I suck and bob on him. He grows harder in my mouth. My eyes widen at the fullness, I push him to the back of my throat and tears pool in my lids. He rumbles louder.

"Not yet."

He commands. He reaches down grabbing me by my throat. I whimper biting my lip.

I love this, letting him command me.

Laying me back on the bed he pauses with his hand still around my neck.

"If you don't slow down, I'm going to lose control," he warns.

"Let go Kai." I tease.

His grip tightens.

"You are going to destroy me."

I moan in response. He rips my panties to the side and lines his cock with my slit.

"You are dripping for me Nyx, good girl." he praises. I dig my nails into his arm.

"Please Kai, take me."

"FUCK!" He growls through his teeth as he buries his cock into my center.

"KAI!" I scream as I feel myself rip to take all of him.

He releases my throat and wraps his hand around the back of my neck, using it as leverage to drive me down harder against his thrust. I am so full of him; I can barely breathe. My nails now trail down his back leaving deep tears in his skin. He growls as I dig deeper into his back.

"Nyx, more. Yellow."

He encourages, slamming into me again, harder this time. I cry out with a mix of pleasure and pain. I find his shoulder above me and bite in. I need something to buffer this overwhelming sensation. He picks up pace, growling. He reaches between us, finding my throbbing clit. He circles the bud and electricity arcs through my body.

"Good fucking girl."

My orgasm is threatening to take me, and his words are pushing me closer. I need this, his pace, the weight of his body on me, his thick cock stretching me to my limits. I need all of him.

"I have an IUD," I blurt out.

Nyx you slut.

My inner self scolds. His chest rumbles.

"Cum for me Nyx, now!"

He circles my clit adding more pressure and I come undone.

"OH MY GODS, KAI!"

I scream as my orgasm rips through me. The lights surge threatening to rupture. My pussy grips around his cock begging him to let go as my orgasm rolls again.

I am still cumming!

"Fuck! Nyx!" He growls out as he pours into me, my pussy milking him.

My body gives out and I am left breathless laying under him. He slides out of me with a moan. He rolls to his side, wrapping me in his arms.

He holds me, letting the aftershocks of our orgasms slow. I have never felt more drained and yet full of power. My hands glow as I trace the spartan helmet on his chest.

"Nyx?" He whispers.

"Yeah?" I match his volume.

"Can I keep you?"

I sit up to look at him, his face full of concern, deep in his own thoughts. He looks at me and his eyes are wanting.

"For now."

I play trying to lighten the mood.

"Don't we need to get ready?"

I say moving away to get off the bed. He catches my wrist and pulls me into him. Meeting me with a deep kiss. I melt into him. He breaks our kiss, looking at me, and caressing my cheek, I lean into his touch, and he smiles.

"Please let me keep you." He says kissing my forehead.

"We need to get ready."

He concedes.

Our bags must have been brought up while we were... occupied.

Well, that's embarrassing.

The suite is massive, I swear it is the size of my apartment. I am pinning my hair up when Kai walks in fully dressed.

Close your mouth.

He looks like a god, or a devil, he is in an all-black suit, that is tailored to perfection. My mouth waters and my pussy tightens. He stands in the doorway adjusting his cufflinks. I bite my lip drinking him in. He smirks at my expression.

"I am going to head down to the party to meet up with Jon. Come down when you're ready Little One."

"Yes sir."

I nod while pinning my hair in to a falling updo.

He tsks, shaking his head.

"You are going to be trouble tonight. See you in a few."

He strides away still shaking his head.

I take my time getting ready. I may be giving him my control in the bedroom, but I control everything else. I opt for light make up, with just enough make up on my eyes to make them radiate the energy in me and a glossed lip, nothing to outshine the dress. The dress is perfect. It hugs my curves and leaves little to the imagination. I forgo the panties at this point, why ruin a perfect dress with panty lines. I look over the leather straps of the corset. Its less fashion more BDSM and I am loving the juxtaposition of the deep burgundy satin and the harsh black leather. I tighten the straps, accenting the curves of my waist. I slip my leg through the thigh harness.

This is fucking hot.

The split in the dress opens perfectly exposing the leather binding my thigh. I take one last look in the mirror admiring the image staring back at me, the curls falling from the relaxed updo, the fire of the dress and the cold leather. It looks like I am going to rule all mankind.

Maybe just Kai.

I make my way out of the elevator bay, not really knowing where to go. I feel the energy coming from behind me and look to the desk to my right, the clerks behind the counter are staring at me like I have two heads. I laugh to myself at the awkwardness of the moment. I point to the hall behind me, as if asking if that is where the party is. Their heads all bob mindlessly.

I'll take this as a good sign of my appearance for the night.

I laugh to myself at the thought.

I find myself at the top of stairs that lead into a ballroom. I stand at the top until I feel Kai's energy in the room. I let out a sigh knowing I'm in the right place. I straighten myself and inhale deeply. My body warms and my chaos is humming, not on the verge of exploding, but wanting to play. This feeling is intoxicating.

Descending the stairs, I see the room is lively and full of small cocktail tables. To the right of me is the bar and Kai.

Time to play.

I call out to him, well my soul does. I am testing myself honestly to see if I can repeat what happened at the club. Kai is mid drink of his whiskey.

"Kai, turn around."

My soul whispers devilishly to him. He slowly moves his drink from his lips, pivoting around to find me. His eyes blaze and his jaw tightens. This man is fucking stunning in t-shirt and jeans, but in an all-black suit, Gods be damned, he is my personal devil.

The man he was talking with at the bar follows Kai's gaze, dropping his glass when his eyes set on me. The glass shatters causing the slightest of disturbances, but Kai moves to the bottom of the stairs never breaking eye contact.

"What's wrong Kai, second guessing my outfit choice?"

My soul toys with him.

Where has this bit of chaos been, I fucking love it.

His jaw clenches further and I can see his fist tightly bound to his sides. I descend the stairs at a painfully slow pace, allowing all eyes to follow me to Kai. Kai waits so patiently at the bottom. I finally reach him and immediately he pulls me in and kisses me with painful urgency. I hear the glasses on the bar rattle at the burst of energy the connection causes. I break our kiss and smile against his lips.

"People are staring, Kai. Want me to really give them a show?" I tease.

"I see you plan is to be a brat this evening."

He scolds me, pulling away from our kiss and taking my hand tightly in his.

"Oh Kai, I think everyone knows I'm all yours tonight," my soul plays with his mind.

"You would be surprised."

He says aloud, then snaps his head around at me realizing I didn't say anything again.

"You have got to stop that, I'm going to look crazy talking to myself," he plays.

"But I love it, it's a new shiny power I didn't even know I could do, and I can only do it with you."

"I get that Little One, but I can't communicate back the same way, now can I? So in public settings, I look crazy listening to your voice in my head."

"Fine," I scoff rolling my eyes.

"There's that brat again," He growls. "I'll be taking care of that later."

My center tightens at the threat.

We reach the bar, and he orders me my spiced whiskey and a double for him.

"So now your drinking spiced whiskey, too?"

I play. He rolls his eyes and gestures for another.

"I need the burn to keep me from taking you where you fucking stand."

He grits out tightening his jaw. He looks fucking devilish, and I want to take him straight to hell! I grab his belt and pull him into me, his eyes ignite with desire as I bite into my lip. A man clears his throat, breaking the moment.

"I hope I'm not interrupting, Kai who is this vixen of a woman you have been hiding?"

Kai is slow to move away from me, he rubs the pad of his thumb across my bottom lip before slowly turning to greet the man. His voice heavy with an Irish accent.

"Jon."

Kai nods to him in a smooth as glass voice, like his cock isn't rock hard and barely confined by his pants.

"This is Nyx Harper, my partner."

Partner? Interesting choice of label. Why was I half expecting him to say girlfriend.

I quickly chase my thoughts, casting a seductive smile at Jon extending my hand.

Jon stumbles on his words at my smile.

"Jon Murphy, what project are you working on with this lad?" He pushes, shaking my hand slowly.

"Romantic partner, Jon" Kai snaps with a clenched jaw.

"Oh, I see now, no labels ay, must be new and not official." Jon jabs.

"Play nice boys, no need to start a bar fight. I would hate for your blood to stain my dress."

I raise my brow looking directly at Jon, desire sparking in his dark eyes.

"Ha!" Jon laughs "You think Kai over here would fight me over you, lass?"

Kai stiffens and clenches his fist.

"I got this babe."

His head snapping to me at the mental intrusion. I wink at him.

"Oh, Mr. Murphy on the contrary."

I say condescending, taking his glass from his hand, tracing the rim counterclockwise with my forefinger.

"I am far more dangerous than he is."

Jon's face is turning deep red, but not from embarrassment. I cease the movement of my finger and he sucks in air greedily. Shock scorches his reddened face.

Kai wraps my hand in his with a small squeeze.

I guess he approved of my fun.

"Jon, do you need some water? You look a little worse for wear." Kai smirks, turning to me, "Miss Harper, would you like to get out of here?"

"I'd love that."

Kai ushers me through the crowd with his hand firmly planted in the small of my back. We make it back to the elevator bay and the energy is vibrating off us. Just as the doors open Jon calls out to Kai.

For fucks sake Jon.

Jon meets us at the elevator with a vindictive smile etched

into his expression.

"Kai, I wanted to see if we could share your newfound toy. She is fucking outstanding, and we could all have a damn good time."

Don't be a brat, don't be a brat.. Fuck it. This should be fun.

I slowly walk towards Jon, letting my hips sway slowly. Placing my hand on Jon's chest, I slowly round him letting my hand glide over his arms and shoulders. He is well built under his tailored suit. When I let my eye spring to Kai he is seething.

Game on.

"I think that is a fucking fantastic idea, don't you Kai?"

I say leaning my head on Jon's arm. Jon puffs his chest thinking he is really getting laid tonight. He moves his arm I'd just laid my head on, reaching back he grabs my ass. Kai smashes his fist into the elevator call button again.

He's very angry, I like him angry.

I smirk at him winking.

"Over my dead fucking body! Get your fucking hands off of her." Kai demands closing the distance between us.

"Come on Kai, why do you get to be the only one to have fun?"

Jon berates Kai by smacking my ass harder. Kai meets Jon eye to eye, fisting Jon's shirt as he slams him into the wall.

"If you ever put your hand on her again, I will cut your limp dick off and make you choke on it."

Kai's voice booms through the hall, he is seething. Jon just stares at him with a smirk.

"You won't always be around Kai, we both know that."

Jon smiles at Kai. Kai shoves him harder into the wall and releases him.

He grabs my wrist, and the elevator door opens. He snatches me into the elevator and his jaw is clenched, threatening to break his perfectly chiseled face, he swipes the key fob; the doors close.

Fuck.

19

Kai releases my wrist, smashing the emergency stop button. I back myself into the far wall, he's very angry. His energy is dangerous and chaotic; any second he is going to find his own chaos to release. In a single step he turns and rips me from my feet, holding me by the throat against the wall, just at his eye level.

"What the fuck was that Nyx." he yells.

I can't answer, his grip only tightens at my silence.

"Fucking answer, me Nyx." He commands, slamming my head into the wall.

My nails claw at his arm. He relaxes his grip just enough for me to gasp out.

"Fun."

Like a wrecking ball his free fist hits inches from my face into the wall beside me.

Red Flag. Fucking hot red flag.

"You are mine; do you fucking understand me. No one fucking touches you but me. I will kill anyone who tries to put their hands on my Goddess. Do you fucking understand me?"

Oh yes sir, I do.

He again eases the pressure so I can speak.

"Yellow."

His eyes go wild at my use of his safe words. His eyes flash with heated desire, replacing the anger. He places me down onto my feet, backing away he release the stop button. He shakes his head glaring at me.

"You're a fucking brat." he spits.

No, I'm your brat.

I step to where he leans. I draw back my hand slapping him across the face. My ring catching his bottom lip.

"Correction Kai, I'm your fucking Brat." I smirk.

Blood runs down his chin from his split lip. I reach up swiping my finger along his lip, bringing it to my own. His eyes are locked on my every movement now. I lick the blood from my finger. The doors chime.

"Yellow" he growls lifting me into his arms.

I wrap my legs around him squeezing my thighs together adding an additional power struggle between us. Our lips are crashing together, a mixture of whiskey and iron. The taste of his blood on my tongue is consuming me. It has ignited a new fire within me that is burning hotter than I knew possible.

Hell Fire.

We crashed into the room he had gotten ready in earlier. The room is dark, and I hear him kicking off his shoes. He stops walking and breaks our ravenous kissing. I lean back and his face is darkened with shadows.

"Nyx, light the candles." he whispers.

Fire ignites around the room, blue flames rage. He sets me to my feet and looks around at the creation.

Fucking Hell Fire...

I look around the room in shock. I close my eyes and ease the fire down. The fire retreats. I open my eyes and he stands in front of me holding two pieces of black fabric. I eye the material in his hand unable to decern what it is. I arch a brow.

"You are all mine Nyx. I'm going to push all your limits tonight and I'm going to enjoy every inch of you. I will take all of your control. Do you understand."

The brat in me responds playfully.

"Yes, daddy."

In an instant his face changes from desire to danger. His hands are around my throat.

"RED!" He barks. His hand shaking. "Don't every fucking call me that! I am not your fucking father!"

Red flag...

"Yes sir, I understand." I squeaked out.

"Get on your knees Nyx." he grinds out through his teeth releasing me. I listen.

I rest on my knees while he walks around the room. He pulls out a black duffle from the closet and tosses it on the bed. He comes to stand in front of me.

"I want your mouth around my cock."

My imagination runs wild as I reach for his belt, but he retracts.

"You are to wear this until I take it off."

He pulls a black satin mask from his back pocket. I nod. He places the mask over my eyes, and I feel him step back into me. I reach for his belt making quick work of it and his pants. I move closer to him, freeing his cock. I wrap both of my hands around his length. Just as I try to take him in my mouth my head snaps back as Kai fists my hair. A moan escapes my lips.

"Nyx you're so greedy, I want you to enjoy every inch of my cock with your tongue." He releases my head and I smirk.

Ok, let's play.

I release my hand from the base of his cock, and l flatten my tongue against the base. Slowly licking my way to the tip. He lets out a stifled groan. I repeat this again, but on my last sweep I suck his balls into my mouth and stroke his cock.

"Fuck Nyx!"

He grinds out fisting my hair again making me release him. Out of nowhere he lands a slap against my face.

Did he just hit me.

"You don't know how to listen do you, check in?"

Check in, what's the fuck does that mean?

"Nyx, safe word now!"

He growls slapping me in the face again. Iron springs from my lower lip this time. I feel the flames of the candles rage around us.

"Yellow" I spit, letting my chaos settle.

"Thats a good fucking girl!" he praises. "Stand up."

I comply, biting my bloodied lip. The next thing I know he's picking me up and tossing me over his shoulder.

This feels unnecessary.

I squeak and he tosses me onto the bed. I am still in complete darkness, and I despise it, but it makes all my senses tingle with energy. I hear him moving around the bed, then unzipping the duffle bag. My curiosity runs wild. My breathing picks up; anticipation is drumming as loud as my heart.

I feel his hand on my wrist, then the sensation of cool leather wrapping around it. There is a click, and he secures my wrist and ankles to restraints. My pussy throbs at the tension between us. I can feel my dress is hitched at my hips exposing my pussy to him. I strain my ears trying to visualize what he is doing. I feel his energy humming louder than ever and my body is aching for his touch. This lack of connection is making me crazy. I have never been someone who craves another, but with Kai, I need him.

That scares me more than anything.

The bed moves in response to his weight and then the blind come off my eyes. In the candlelight, he is kneeling between my spread thighs with only his half-buttoned pants. My breath catches as I see that he has on a mask.

Fuck me.

It is a black skull ski mask, and I have never been more turned on. He is just looming over me, not saying a word and the intensity is making me needy. I catch a glint in his right hand, the light catches it again, it's a fucking knife.

Red flag, red flag, maybe?

He sees my eyes trail, and a low rumble escapes him.

"Nyx do not move, do not speak. You are all mine, and I will kill anyone who ever tries to touch you again."

My pulse races as he lowers the knife to the apex of my thighs. The cold blade brushes across my slit and I still. The flames around us swell.

"Shhh Nyx, I will take care of you."

I remain still and his blade lifts my dress further up my hips. The fabric rips against the blade and he continues to slice through the dress, until all that's left is what's beneath the corset and across my chest. He is panting as hard as I am.

He's enjoying this.

He cuts through the straps on my shoulders and then drags the tip across my collar bone. The sensation causing my center to tighten and pool beneath me.

"You are fucking beautiful."

He growls out, ripping what was left of my dress off of me, leaving just the corset and thigh straps.

"You are MY Goddess, and no one will ever see you in that dress again." he murmurs. "I'm going to push you Nyx. Give all of yourself to me. I need all of you."

"Please," I beg.

What am I even begging for?

"Safe words?" He asks again, trailing the knife now over the mound of my breast.

"Yellow, Orange, Red."

I manage out breathless. He hasn't even touched me and my body is threatening orgasm.

"So if I do this," he questions nicking my breast with the knife, "where are you?" All I can manage is a feral moan while pulling against the restraints. "I need a check in Nyx." He warns.

"Yellow, fucking yellow!" *Who am I?*

"Good fucking girl, Nyx!" he damn near moans out.

The knife trails down my body, then back up to my collarbone, I hiss as he deepens the pressure. I feel the warmth pool and begin to run down my skin. I am vibrating and pulling at the restraints, I need to touch him.

"Please Kai," I'm begging again.

His eyes through the mask are on fire, the sight alone is intoxicating. He is toying with me, making me beg for his touch, giving him all control.

"*Kai I fucking need you now.*"

His head cocks to the side. The next second the blade cuts

my inner thigh and I scream out. He removes his mask and is snarling with desire. I feel the blood dripping from my thigh. I cannot take another second of this torture. The binds release to my will and I am wrapping myself around him.

"Fuck me Now, Kai."

Our lips crash into each other, I bite down on his bottom lip until I taste copper. I release at his growl and he's kissing and nipping my neck. He bites right into the cut from the knife. I drop my head back at the euphoria. With a free hand I feel him release his cock from his pants and without warning, plunges himself into me. I cry out at the force and stretch of his cock.

"Your pussy is so greedy Nyx!" He moans.

I feel my center tighten around him. Our movements are reckless. There is no sense of savoring this moment, we need each other. It feels like he is tearing me apart. My world is shattering.

"Look how well you take me. Fuck Nyx you are milking me." He moans shakily. "Good Girl!"

I break.

"Kai!!!!"

His name screams from my lips as I grind into him riding out the orgasm that has my vision going dark.

"Fuck Nyx!"

He growls spilling into me as he lays me back onto the bed, driving himself deeper into me.

The aftershocks finally release us from their hold, and we are left laying together in silence. He traces every inch of my body with his fingers; when his hand reaches my check he locks eyes with me, there is so much energy radiating from his green eyes. I never want this to end.

"What are you thinking about?"

I love this little silent communication I can have with him. Shaking his head at my voice whispering to his mind.

"You, my Little One. I have never tasted a sin as sweet as you."

My heart skips, and I feel like tears could fall at any moment.

What is happening to me, why do I need him so much?

"Nyx, I would walk through every hell for this moment with you. You are the moon in the darkness, calling me home and I am falling in love with you."

He whispers and vulnerability flares through his eyes. The air leaves my lungs, and darkness falls over the room.

"Orange."

20

Three weeks have passed since our trip to Seattle, and I cannot get enough of him. If he is not at the hospital, I am in his arms. I am in love with this man, yet I cannot bring myself to tell him. It scares the shit out of me how much he feels like home. I feel safe with him, and he brings out so much of me that I have never shared with anyone. I find myself consumed by him in every way.

Lately I feel like he is generating his own energy, he tries to downplay it, but I can feel something in him changing. I have also found it extremely hard not to call to him while he is away. It has gotten way too easy and comfortable for me to speak to his mind. Telepathy is a practice I have never even attempted, yet with him it just happens.

Get out of your own head.

My own thoughts are snapping me back to reality. Jinny is opening our newest shipments, and I am supposed to be looking at purchase orders, but I cannot stop the image of Kai's face playing in my mind.

"I miss you."

I call to him. He's on the last 6 of his 24 and it's torture for me.

The door chimes and Jinny greets the mail carrier.

"Nyx, you have mail." she calls over.

She hands me the mail and most of it is normal everyday junk mail, but there is a letter addressed to me.

Well kind of?

Scrolled across a heavily weighted envelope is:

JESSICA WRIGHT

Nyx St. Claire

St. Claire?

It has an energy I can't place. I pop the seal and find it's an invitation.

> **I.S.A.O**
>
> **INTERNATIONAL SOCIETY OF ALCHEMY & OCCULT**
>
> Location: 82305 Tulane Avenue, New Orleans, LA 70112
>
> Date: **October 28, 2023 – October 30, 2023**
>
> On Behalf of The International Society of Alchemy & Occult, we would officially like to invite you to attend and participate in our convention. The conference will be held In New Orleans at Humanity Hospital. Although vacant since Hurricane Katrina, the realtor has agreed to open the doors to allow our conference. The setting is perfect for all factions.
>
> The purpose of the 3-day conference is to bring together researchers from around the world who are interested in exploring the links between the supernatural, phenomena, wicca, and many more factions. We plan to touch on all magical practices.
>
> Should you require more information on our convention, please visit our conference website at www.secretsocietyDDCL.com. Thank you. We look forward to seeing you at the conference.
>
> Sincerely,
>
> **THE INTERNATIONAL SOCIETY of ALCHEMY & OCCULT**
>
> *Thomas Woodwind*
> (Conference Coordinator)

I have gotten many invitations to these things, but I never go. This one just feels different. My phone chimes, breaking my train of thought.

Kai
Little One, you are very distracting when you play in my head. I miss you too.

I smile at my phone, and it chimes again.

Kai
I'll see you tonight. I made reservations for 8. See you soon, my Little One.

Me
Can't wait babe.

I have never loved anyone before, but Kai makes me want to give him all of me. In the short time I've known him, he has challenged me mentally and physically. Around Kai my chaos is controlled, and I feel free for the first time in my life. I am actually happy. The front door swings open and a cold wind whips through the store. It has been raining all day, but it is not a storm, and this is not a natural wind. I rush to the door to shut it and the chimes in the corners ring out. There is an energy vibrating off them and it's dark. I keep protections in the shop but have never seen them react. I struggle with the door, fighting the wind. The wind gusts and flower petals bounce off the threshold, stopping in their tracks.

Why are there spelled flowers trying to enter my store?

I managed to close the door. There is an eerie calm that falls over the street. The wind dissipates, leaving nothing but tiny flower petals littering the ground. *Hydrangeas?*

"Hey Jinny, let's call it for the day."

"You are amazing! I have a date with my couch and spooky movies!"

"That sounds like something I can get down with myself! Be careful getting home with all this rain."

"Have a good night, Nyx. Oh, and it's not my business, but happiness looks great on you." She winks grabbing her bag.

I smile, knowing she is not wrong.

I'm lining my lips when I feel him behind me. He tries so hard to sneak up on me, but I always feel him.

"Hey there, I'm almost ready."

I smile over my shoulder. He steps in closer, wrapping his arms around my waist, nuzzling my neck.

"I have missed you, Little One."

Chills flood my body; his touch makes me weak. I sink back into him dropping my head back to look up at him.

"We could always stay in?" I muse.

"Little One I want to take you out. Though the idea of staying locked in this apartment forever is very tempting." he whispers tracing my cheek.

"Oh, come on Kai, you know you love having me all to yourself." I play turning to face him.

"Little One, I love more than that." he says kissing my forehead.

"We are going to be late." I blush placing my hands on his chest.

The restaurant is stunningly romantic. It has that old world luxury feel. The gold and crystal chandeliers make the room sparkle with elegance. I look to Kai, who looks very proud of his choice.

"Kai this place is beautiful."

"Wait until you try the food, The chef and I went to college together and he is a James Beard Award winner. His food is inspired."

I lace my hand into his as he leads us to our table. It's nestled in the corner, near the piano.

"Good evening, Mr. Reighn, I will let the chef know you here. Would you like me to bring a bottle from our signature selection."

"Yes, that would be perfect." Kai nods to the server.

"Mr. Reighn, you are full of surprises."

I play noting the way people seem to want to serve him.

"Ms. Harper, you have no idea."

A server returns with a bottle of wine and a glacette; another with plates of beef carpaccio and a third with our glasses.

"Only one glass for her." Kai tells the server and sees my questioning glance.

"I'm on call, but you should enjoy yourself."

I nod and my eyes widen as the plates are placed in front of us. I love beef carpaccio, and this looks delicious.

We eat and make small talk through the buzz of servers switching out the different courses, five to be exact. I never eat this much, but the food is perfection. The servers clear our final course and bring us over coffee.

"Kai this night is amazing." I smile while taking a sip of my coffee.

"Little One, I want all of your nights to be perfect. I got you something." he says reaching into his pocket. My heart stalls. He brings out a black box.

Too big for a ring box, thank the Gods.

"I wanted to get you something that brings you as much balance and happiness as you bring me." Opening the box my heart skips.

"Kai, it's beautiful."

Tears filling my eyes as I remove the black metal bangle from the box.

It is delicate but strong. In the center is a piece of moonstone, in the shape of a crescent and on the inside, there is 'Forever Mine, Little One.' Kai kneels next to me taking the bracelet and placing it around my wrist.

"Nyx, I have never felt this way for anyone in my life. You are my dark queen that I want to forever worship. You have brought out a side a me I never thought existed. You are my constant. I love you Nyx Harper, in this life and the next, you will forever be mine."

I reach for his face, searching his eyes for anything that tells me this isn't real, but all I see is love and home.

"Kai, I love you."

I whisper to his mind.

He wraps me in his arms, holding onto me as if he lets go I'll disappear into thin air. I feel every eye in the restaurant on us.

"Babe, everyone is staring."

"Let them, Little One."

"Let's go home, my love."

Words I have never spoken to anyone crash into Kai. He releases me, gazing into my eyes awestruck by the moment. Shaking his head with a smile he takes my hand leading me out. Kai nods at the waiter.

"My card is on file, let Brian know the meal was exquisite."

The server nods, "It is our pleasure to serve you both, Mr. Reighn."

21

We make it back to my apartment, and I swear this may be the best night of my life. I never thought I would ever find someone I would ever need in my life, much less fall in love with, but with Kai, everything is different. He grounds me, his energy makes me thrive and I don't have to pretend with him. He sees me, all of me, even the darkness; he embraces it, and does not try to bring a light out in me like everyone else. He is content with who I am.

I am so in love with this man.

I curl up on the couch, kicking my boots off and swirling my wrist to light the candles throughout the space. Kai grabs the chunky knit throw from the back of the couch and wraps it around me. He sits back, pulling me into his chest, I melt into him, closing my eyes.

This is my home.

"Nyx?"

"Yes, love?"

"I need to talk to you about something." his tone turning serious. I sit up to examine his expression.

"Is everything okay?"

He sighs, and a heaviness falls over him.

"Kai?"

I ask, feeling uneasy. He meets my gaze, regret filling his green eyes. Just then candles surge, we scan the room as they threaten to engulf it. Kai looks to me, questioning if it's my doing, I shake my head knowing this isn't me. The balcony doors burst open;

wind floods the room extinguishing the flames. The air stills, but it's ice cold. Darkness takes over the room and I feel the hairs on my body rise.

"Nyx, what is happening."

"It's not me."

Kai phone rings, breaking the silence. He swipes it quickly, listens, then stands.

"I have to go Little One, there is a trauma. I will come right back. Lock the doors and do not leave."

I nod, feeling just as uneasy as he looks. Kissing the top of my head, he pauses, not wanting to leave. He reaches the door and turns back to me.

"Hey," I call to him. "I love you, hurry back to me."

Kai smiles then drops his head, closing the door.

I light the candles as I close the doors. I have never felt a cold like the wind that just ripped through my apartment. The energy was off, a dark and overwhelming feeling of distress. I am making my way back towards the kitchen as I hear my phone ring. I see the caller ID and my heart stops.

Lavender Lakes.

Minutes later I am rushing through the doors of Lavendar Lakes. The nurse on the phone said there was an accident, but only stated I needed to get there right away. I am running through the halls until I am met with a team of nurses standing with their heads held low.

"Where is she?" I bark out. Lainey's charge nurse steps forward slowly.

"Ms. Harper you may want to take a seat."

"I said, where is my mother?" my voice booming through the halls. The air feels thick and dark.

"Ms. Harper, there was an incident. Ms. Lainey has been taken to the hospital."

"What kind of incident? What are you not telling me?"

One of the male nurses glances down the hall towards Lainey's room. I am moving before I realize it.

"Ms. Harper, you can't go in there!"

Her words are futile. My feet are moving of their own accord. The air grips my lungs, and I can feel chaos flooding the halls. I reach her door and I am stopped in my tracks. My eyes widen, taking in the gruesome scene laid out in this room. The smell of iron and copper invades my senses, blood, so much blood.

What the fuck happened in here?

Blood is spattered across every surface, congealed in some spots and still fresh in others. On the far wall there is crude writing, like that of a child's, written in blood.

Lainey.

I drop to my knees reading her words to me.

He's here. Run. Run Nyx. He will kill you.

Tears fall from my eyes, I cannot breathe, all I can do is scream. The lights surge as my heart breaks into pieces.

"Ms. Harper, please you cannot be in here!"

My head snaps up at the realization that, they said she was taken to the hospital, she is alive, right?

"What hospital?" I bark out, standing to face the nurse.

"Mercy General."

I try to stand, but my knees are weak, even with the chaos pulsating through me. I reach out to use the door frame for support when I notice something shiny under the edge of the door. I bend down to find a single gold cufflink covered in drying blood. A shock shoots through my hand, images strobe through my mind. I see my mother's face; a look of torment plastered across her features. The vision causes me to release the cufflink and the connection breaks.

No, no, no mom!

I fall forward and begin searching frantically to find it. I grab it and will it to show me more. Rolling it in my fingers I see it, the initials **ASC** engraved into the gold.

Who the Fuck is ASC?

My thoughts are interrupted as the images overtake me once more. Mom! She is struggling with someone. All I see is their arms with Lainey pulling and screaming,

"Leave her alone, damn it!"

The cuff link flies off of his jacket sleeve at her last attempt to pull him toward her. I see a dark silhouette walk away; a loud sadistic rumble of laughter follows. Lainey looks at the cufflink and cries.

"This is all my fault baby, maybe if I'm gone, the threat stops here, I'm so sorry Nyx. I love you."

And with those words she digs the cufflink into her wrist. The sound is sickening, as she slices upwards, the crimson blood welling from her skin and dripping to the floor. She finishes at the crook of her elbow, her hand shaking. She grabs the cuff link in her other hand, struggling to hold the slick metal in her hand. She rubs it against her shirt, bright red smears against the white cotton. Sweat beads at her brow, color draining from her lips as she presses them firmly together. Her face twists as she takes in a deep breath and presses the cuff link into her skin on her other wrist. She makes it to her forearm before her strength gives out. Screaming in agony, she falls to her knees and begins crawling as sobs escape her. She makes it to the wall, running her fingers through her blood and begins writing.

I jolt back to reality spinning on the charge nurse.

"How the fuck did something like this end up in her room?" I demand.

The nurse stumbles to find the words as she takes the cufflink from my hand.

"I am so sorry Ms. Harper. I have no idea how this was missed. Her visitor was searched before he was allowed in. "

"Visitor! Who was here?"

"I do not know Ms. Harper. He only signed ASC to the logbook, I assumed he was a friend."

I have to get out of here. I snatch the cufflink from her hand. This is not over, and I need to go to my mother.

Running through the emergency room lobby I search for someone to help me find her.

"May I help you?" an older lady behind the desk asks.

"My mother, Elaine Harper, she was brought in from Lavender Lake, can you tell me where she is?"

"Oh, honey she has been taken into surgery, why don't we find you a coffee and I can take you to the surgery waiting room."

"Just take me to the room please."

She nods and I follow her through the halls.

"Honey, I'll let them know you are here, they will be out to update you soon, I'm sure." She offers a sweet smile.

I sit for what feels like an eternity before someone finally emerges from the suite.

My heart stops. The surgeon walks out, dropping his head and taking off his surgery cap.

No, no, no. Please Gods say this isn't happening.

I stand to meet him.

"Ms. Harper. I am sorry, we did everything we could, but the damage was too extensive, and she lost too much blood. I am so sorry."

My world stops. None of this makes sense. My chaos is vibrating, but shock has set in, and I stand unable to move.

"Ms. Harper, I think you need to sit down."

His words are muffled in my head, Through the muffled sounds I hear Kai's voice break through.

"Nyx!"

Kai is running down the hall towards me. He pulls his cap off throwing it to the floor. I collapse to the floor screaming from a pain unimaginable, images of her slicing into her wrists burn my mind. Kai reaches me falling to the floor, wrapping me in him. My body convulses as reality hits me that she is gone. My mind races, how can she be gone, she has not been my mother in years, but this is breaking my heart in half.

"Little One, I am so sorry. I am right here baby, let it out, I am right here."

I scream again letting go of chaos that was ripping through me, electricity surges from my body. Kai holds me tighter, not even retreating from my burst. I do not know how long it has been, but there are no tears left to cry.

"Let me take you home Little One."

I nod, unable to speak.

Kai carries me up the stairs to my apartment in silence. I feel empty, shock must still have its claws in me, because I am numb. Setting me on the couch he wraps me in a blanket.

"I'm going to get you some hot tea Little One."

I curl up staring blankly, turning the cufflink that I have been squeezing this whole time. Kai returns moments later with a cup.

"How did you know I was there?" asking as I take the cup from his hands.

"I was scrubbed in when they brought her into the surgical suite, so I didn't look at her chart, but when I saw her face, I knew. The resemblance between the two of you is uncanny. After everything," He trails off pulling me into him. "The surgeon said he needed to go let her daughter know and I knew it was you. I am so sorry Nyx; words cannot express the sorrow I feel for you." Shaking my head.

"How?"

I ask, hoping the vision I saw of her was not real.

"How what, Little One?" his tone low.

"How did she do it?"

"Nyx, I don't think…"

The lights surge and the balcony doors begin to shake. I turn my eyes to him, feeling the fire burning in my gaze.

"Nyx, I know you are in shock, but I am not your enemy. Nyx.

Your eyes, there are flames in them. Please try to calm down, babe, please." Fear edging into his tone.

"Tell me." I demand again.

I need to know if I'm going crazy.

He drops my gaze to look at his hands.

"She slit her wrist, both arms from her hands to the bends of her elbows. Nyx, I don't understand how she was able to do that."

The fire in me loses strength. I look at my hand and hold up the cufflink, his words confirming the vision.

"With this."

I hand the link to him. He takes it from my hands rolling it between his fingers. Rage penetrates his expression.

"Someone came to visit her, there was an argument, a tussle, and she took it." I shake my head, the vision is still fresh, yet distorted. "The last time I saw those initials she gave me the same warning."

"What warning, Nyx, what are you talking about?"

"The day you met me, I had been to see her. There was a bouquet of hydrangeas with a wax seal that had these initials embossed in it. Her warning that day was 'he's going to kill you' and tonight she gave me another warning to 'run.'"

Kai stares at me in disbelief. I feel darkness creeping up my spine as I narrow my eyes on the cufflink.

I close my eyes and the darkness takes the room. It's not mine. The balcony doors burst open and the wind howls through my apartment again.

I am not in the fucking mood.

The obsidian and quarts around my apartment glow, nearly splintering from the pressure.

Is this what I need to run from

I rise to my feet letting chaos warm my body, I have had about enough of whatever or whomever is fucking with me. My head drops back, and I let chaos rip through the room. A thick fog flows from my hands rising around me and Kai. I push harder and the wind bounces off the fog barrier preventing it from reaching us. Kai stands placing his hands on my shoulders. I swear it is like he is trying to let me use his energy. I have felt more and more energy from Kai over the last few weeks, maybe it's just his love, but I need all the help I can get in this moment. I focus on his hands on me, and I let power flood the room. The fog presses further and then the balcony doors slam. The air goes still.

"Nyx?"

I open my eyes and the room is clear, and the only darkness is my own. I look around the room and papers are everywhere.

"I have got to clean this up." I say pulling away from his grasp.

"Nyx, we can do that later, what the fuck just happened?"

"I don't know, I assume it's what Lainey was warning me about."

Mom.

My eyes burn trying to fight back tears. I sit on the floor trying to pick up all the scattered papers. Kai kneels next to me grabbing my hands.

"Nyx, stop. Now is not the time to worry about papers on the floor."

Just then the invitation to the ISAO falls into my lap.

Lainey said run, let's run.

"I need to pack." I abruptly stand making my way to my room.

"Nyx, fucking stop for two seconds. Your mother just died, and you are wanting to pack. You're still in shock, you need to sit down."

"No Kai, If I stay here, I will end up like her. I need to go."

"Go where, Nyx? You don't even know what you're running from."

"New Orleans. There is a convention and I need to go; I cannot stay here and wait to end up like my mom. She told me 'He is coming', well, good luck finding me if I'm not here! Kai, come with me?"

"Nyx." His tone changes.

"Please Kai, let's go away. I need to breathe."

"I don't think you should go. Stay here with me. We can take care of the arrangements for Lainey and then go somewhere else. Please."

His tone is pleading and his eyes worried. I am pacing through my room tossing clothes and toiletries into my bag as he stands in the doorway.

"Her arrangements have been made since she was committed, there is nothing for me to do. I'm leaving. I've felt drawn to the letter from the moment I received it. This is what I need to do. Please Kai, I need you there with me." His face falls.

"I can't go to New Orleans with you, Nyx." I grab my phone booking tickets on the next flight out.

"Kai, I bought you a ticket, just come with me. I need you right now. Please."

"I'm sorry, Nyx I cannot go with you to New Orleans. Stay here, we can change the tickets to anywhere else in the world, please Little One, just stay here with me."

I sigh standing at the door with my bag. He moves to stand in front of me, I reach for his face pulling him in to kiss me.

"*I love you.*"

I open the door hoping he will just agree and come with me, but he doesn't.

"I am going, maybe you will change your mind, I'll text you my hotel information."

I turn and walk out of the door without another word.

"*I'm running mom, I'm running.*"

Part Four: New Orleans

22

Libby James

I step off the plane and I am met with the October air of the bayou. It is definitely not as cold here as it is in Seattle. The drive to my hotel is mesmerizing. Through the different neighborhoods, the culture and diversity of the city are on full display. I never thought this city would feel so magical. As we sit in traffic, I laugh to myself thinking the drive through the French Quarter was going to be easy and I could just check into my hotel within an hour of leaving the airport, but no such luck. The streets are alive here. Crowds fill the sidewalk and spill into the streets. Oddly, I don't hate it; the amount of culture and history packed into every corner is breathtaking. From street shows, art, and music; there seems to be something for everyone here. I think I may be in love with the city.

Who knew? This is just the distraction I needed.

After making it to the hotel and checking in, I make my way to my room. I truly cannot get over how beautiful it is here. The balcony overlooks the quarter, and I feel so at home in a city I've never been to. I can feel the energies of others like me mixed with regular people and the mixture is overwhelming.

This feels like home.

I look at the clock on the wall opposite the queen-sized bed. It reads 6:35pm. As much as I want to find answers to who 'ASC' is, and prepare myself for the convention tomorrow, I need to unwind. I pull my phone from my back pocket and decided to check in with Finn.

Me
Hey! I just wanted to let you know that I made it. It is beautiful, I wish you were here.

FINN
Me too. Duty calls though. Have you some fun love. I hope you have the trip of your lifetime and find all the answers you desire.

Me
I love you, Finn O'Brien.

FINN
You have no idea of the love I have for you Lib. Now, go and enjoy!

    I don't waste time unpacking my things. I begin rummaging through the clothes trying to decide what to wear. I brought a rather flashy dress, so I might as well wear it. Something about this city calls to my powers and I don't fight it. I slip on the dress, and it fits like a glove, every curve accentuated by the gold fabric. I eye myself in the mirror and I decide to let my magic go free. Swirling my wrist, the lights surge and my hair spins around me, curls falling into place. With another twist my face is beautifully highlighted with makeup. I stand in awe of how easily my glamor flowed through my hands.
That will do.
I grab my bag and head toward the elevator.

    Stepping out of my building and onto the sidewalk on Royal Street, I take in the beautiful sight. People are everywhere, but I feel a unique hum beckoning me. There's something about my magic here that feels different, stronger even. I walk, enjoying the night air and different sounds and smells coming from the quarter.

There is a magnetic pull, gripping me with no reprieve. I find myself following it blindly. I finally glance down as I get to an intersection; written on the sidewalk is the street name 'Bourbon'.

Isn't that the party street? Fuck it, let's have some fun!

I stroll through the hordes of people and there again it hums. The sound is deafening, even over all the excitement that is going on around me; the hum is literally vibrating. I find myself in a daze staring at the entrance of another hotel.

I enter without much thought, just the urgency to get where my magic is taking me. To the left I see a set of wooden doors and a sign that says Burlesque/Jazz Night. I pay the cover charge and enter. It is a quaint room, soft jazz plays in background as beautiful woman dance, performing classic burlesque. I would be mesmerized by them if it weren't for that damn pull. I don't know how I know, but something, or *someone* is here, and this is where I am meant to be.

My eyes are drawn to two females sitting at the bar; It's them. There is energy radiating from them, and I am captivated by it. I follow the beacon of energy. As if by some trance, they both turn to me as I make my way to them, a shocked expression on their faces that I can't help to think that they are mirroring from my own. The petite beauty speaks first.

Nyx Harper

What the fuck!

In front of me stands another witch, she is strikingly beautiful and from the expression on her face she is just as shocked as us. I decided to calm her nerves.

"There you are!"

I tease like we've been waiting on her. Confusion further etches into her expression.

"I'm kidding, this is weird as fuck, we know. So, quick rundown, I'm Nyx Harper, this is Olivia Rose."

I gestured to the two of us. Olivia offers an awkward wave.

"We have no idea why we ended up in this bar, but one thing is for sure we are a little freaked the fuck out! Turns out we are both witches and from the looks of it, so are you. So, please tell me you know why we are standing here looking lost."

She stands there with bewilderment on her face.

"I need a drink."

She shakes her head and grabs a seat next to me. Olivia and I look on, waiting for her introduction as she orders from the bartender.

"I'll take two of whatever they have, and another round for them. I'm Elizabeth James, Libby..." I cut her off mid-sentence.

"You're THE Elizabeth James?"

I gush. The bartender places the drinks in front of us and she throws back the shot of spiced whiskey and then downs the hurricane.

"What the hell are y'all drinking?" she coughs and shakes her head. "Yes, I take it you have read my books, you can call me Libby."

"Hell yes, I have! You were also just in my shop a few weeks ago and placed an order."

"I received an order from you as well Libby, I hate to break it to you, but you will not be getting that order from Rose and Ember." Olivia trails off, her voice cracking on the last word.

"Wait, you own Rose and Ember?" I turn facing Olivia inquisitively.

"Yes, well I did, I mean." Olivia replies, not understanding the significance.

"I own Salt and Sage! I ordered a headboard from you and Libby just placed an order from me. I shipped it out a few days ago."

The words flood from my lips as I shake my head trying to understand.

"Why are you both in New Orleans?" I ask, feeling their response before their words become audible.

"A convention, very last-minute decision." Libby admits.

"Same." Olivia looks down at her hands again.

"Yeah, I only flew down this afternoon. I was trying to check in, but I couldn't pull myself from this bar."

I look at them and my eyes cannot stop looking at their aura. Normally, I see other witch's auras in varying intensities and hues, but theirs, matches my own; deep burgundy. I have never seen someone match my own.

"Well, this seems oddly coincidental." I add.

"I got the invitation weeks ago, but I almost didn't even consider this due to the last name on my invite, but with everything in my life; I just needed to come here for answers." Libby admits.

I reach into my bag, pulling out my invitation. Tapping it against my hand, debating on if I should acknowledge the fact that my last name was incorrect too. Olivia speaks before I can, pulling a crumpled letter from her pocket.

"Yeah, I felt the same, I assumed there was a mishap in the mail room or something, but my invitation was addressed to Olivia St. Claire."

I shake my head; my disbelief quickly changes to shock when Libby displays the same last name on her envelope. I raise mine to show the same.

"I am going to need several more drinks and food. How about we move to a booth before diving into this magical shit show." They slowly nod, agreeing.

We moved to a private booth and before I know it, we are all gossiping and giggling like schoolgirls. The conversations just flow from us, and I feel the strange sense of home. Only with Kai have I ever felt safe and at home. My mind slips to my mother, feeling guilt over her never being my safe place. I don't know why I would ever feel guilty for someone I couldn't fix, but I do, and this connection with them only highlights my grief. I hide it in my laughter and snarky comments, but I am hurting.

"*Kai, I miss you.*"

I call to him. No response. I feel an empty ache in my core.

"Hello, earth to Nyx!"

Libby snaps her fingers in front of my face to catch my attention. I turn and smile at her.

"Sorry, I must have drifted off for a moment. I need to eat something." Olivia pushes the alligator sausage my way.

"You look like your mouth is missing a piece of meat, try filling it with this," she says with a laugh.

I can see she's struggling; trying to hide her pain behind her smile. I wonder what her story is, but she's not saying. I imagine I could flick my wrist and knock her over, she looks like she hasn't slept in days. I don't know why, but I feel very protective of her.

"So, we all got these invitations, and they all have the same incorrect last name on them. What the hell is it supposed to mean?" Libby asks.

I shake my head as I take a bite of the sausage.

My Gods this shit is delicious.

I run my tongue across my lips, relishing in the flavor.

"I have no clue, but it can just add to the weird shit that's been happening lately." I mumble, my mouth stuffed with sausage.

"Did you eat any of this Libby, it's fucking delicious."

"Not yet, I was letting you have your fill before I tried any." Libby and Olivia turn and look at each other before they bust out in laughter.

"Did I miss something?"

I ask. They continue to laugh until tears start streaming out of Olivia's eyes.

"Jesus, I needed that, apparently you did too." Olivia cries out. I look at the sausage on my fork and turn and look at Olivia.

"You nasty Bitch." I drop my fork and join in the laughter.

"Can I get you ladies anything else?" the waitress interrupts us.

"Yes, another round, and two more sausages, please?" Olivia says before she starts laughing manically again.

"Girl, you have issues." Libby states, her face turning all serious. "What do you mean weird shit?"

She turns to me and asks. The energy at the table changes quickly. Olivia sits back up, nervously twisting her hands.

"Just that, weird shit."

I say empathetically. Libby's phone buzzes on the table. She picks it up and a smile crosses her lips.

"Someone special?" I ask.

Libby looks up at me and her smile brightens.

"Yeah, yeah it is. It's my boyfriend Finn. We haven't been together long, but Gods damn, he gets me, ya know? Like I feel like he sees me more than I've ever seen myself. I've always hidden in my writing, but with him I don't have to. It's been a wild ride, but he makes me feel safe. He told me he loves me. No one's ever said that to me. I mean my mother did, but I never got to hear her say it, at least not physically. She died right after I was born. Jesus sorry, I'm rambling."

She quickly stops speaking, looking back down at her phone.

"My mom's dead too."

Why the fuck did I just tell them that?

"Same."

Olivia says as she knocks back another drink.

"I guess that's another thing we have in common."

"So, we are all female business owners, our mothers are all dead, we are all witches, and we got an invite to the same convention with the same last name. That's a little bit more in common than I'm comfortable with. Anything else?" I ask.

"Do you want our life story?" Libby asks.

"I don't think they have enough alcohol in here for all that."

I say with amusement. A thought crosses my mind.

"Does ASC mean anything to either one of you?"

Olivia's eyes fly to mine, a fire burning behind them. I hear Libby set her glass down, but I can't pull myself away from Olivia, something fierce in her eyes holding me in place.

"I take it they do mean something to you."

"Death." I barely hear her whisper the words.

"Same." Libby says.

Mom.

"For me too."

We sit there in silence, the realization that this isn't a coincidence hitting us all at once.

Who the fuck is ASC?

I make one more attempt to reach out to Kai.

"Kai, I need you. I'm scared."

Silence is the only response.

Fuck.

23

Olivia Rose

I wake in a cold sweat for the third time tonight, my heart about to beat out of my chest. I turn and look at the clock. 3:49am. Ugh. These nightmares are going to be the death of me. I reach for the glass of water on the bedside table and take a drink. I know they are nightmares. Alex would never say to me the things he said to me in my dreams.

"Why Bitch? Why did you let me die? Was being Marcel's pet that much more important than me? I thought I was family?"

My mother chiming in.

"She killed her own mother; do you really think you mattered more to her than me? She loves no one and only cares about herself and her power."

I shiver as the last nightmare plays through my head. I loved my mom, but Alex...Alex was my person, the other half to my broken soul. He put me back together when I thought nothing could. Now... Now I don't know how to function without him. I'd gladly give up being a Witch if I could have him back.

Tears are now streaming down my face.

Damn It! I'm tired of fucking crying.

I know I will never be able to go back to sleep, so I kick off the covers and get up. I go into the bathroom and splash water on my face and look in the mirror. I look like hell. My face is pale, my blue eyes almost green from all the crying, the red whites of my eyes making them stand out, my hair an unruly curly mess. I grab a hair tie off the sink and throw my hair into a messy bun. I need to clear my head.

Quickly I rush back into the room and throw on my Nirvana t-shirt and a pair of black leggings. My hot pink sneakers I left in my car from the last time Alex, and I went to the gym are beside the bed. I try not to think about it and slip them on my feet. I shove my phone and the hotel key into my crossbody bag and am out the door before I can stop myself. I pass the hotel gym, slowing down for only a moment before I decide I need the night air to clear my head.

I step out onto Royal Street and take a deep breath. I can smell the beignets from across the street, the sugary smell makes my stomach churn. I need to move. My feet are moving before my brain even registers. My body slowly responds, the muscle memory taking over.

Breathe into your nose, out your mouth. Pump your arms.

I pick up the speed, the street signs flying passed me like I know where I am going. I can feel the sweat trailing down my back.

The humid bayou air is getting thicker as the sun rises above the buildings in front of me.

Close everything else out but your breathing. One, two, three breathe. One, two, three breathe. One, two, Alex.

My steps falter and I catch myself before I fall, balancing my run back out.

Damn it Olivia, focus!

I slow down and begin to look around. The sun has risen above the houses in front of me.

I know this area. How long was I running?

I look at my watch. 9:45am. My body knew where I needed to be this morning. Alex's words replay in my head *'confront your past, so you can live in the present'*. Easier said than done. Oh, Alex, that would be fine if only you were here. This isn't the 'present' that I want to live in.

This is for you Bitch!

Tears well into my eyes for the second time this morning. The thought of Alex instantly brings the distorted image of his lifeless burnt body to the forefront of my memory. I fight to not think of him dead and lifeless and instead bring his laughter into my mind. I swear I can still hear his voice. Give me strength Alex.

I got you O.

I continue walking around the bend until my feet bring me to a stop.

I'm doing this for you Alex.

I lift my eyes determined not to let him down.

You already did that Olivia.

My breath hitches as I take in the sight. In the place my home once was, stands a fire station. Fucking fitting. The glass doors are gleaming, Station 22 written boldly above the doors. Orange and yellow mums surround the flagpole by the walkway. There's a bench beside it. I don't know why, but I feel drawn to sit there. I walk over and lower myself to the bench and sit there and stare, memories of my childhood swarming in my head. I welcome them like a long-lost friend and remember happier times.

I don't know how I recognize him, but I do. The sun is high above the building now, glaring into my eyes, but the captain who pulled me out of my window that night 6 years ago walks out of the bay door and looks my way. He immediately starts closing the distance between us.

"Firefly." he says with an expression of shock plastered across his face.

I did hear him correctly.

"You remember me?"

Is all I can manage in a low whisper.

"How can I forget? It happened right here almost six years ago. It was the worst fire I had ever seen. It was like the fires from the pits of hell themselves came to devour your home. And you, how could I forget a face like yours?"

Under normal circumstances I would be all over this. Sure, this guy is old enough to be my father from the looks of it, but he isn't unattractive by any stretch of the imagination. A true silver fox, perfectly manicured beard, and each muscle prominent under his uniform. And those sea green eyes, my god, just as beautiful and kind as they were on that horrible night years ago.

I wonder how Marcel would fend against this mountain of a man. Fuck him.

I smirk at the idea. But this isn't under normal circumstances. A flood of guilt wrecking me all over again, the smirk washing from my face.

I'm sorry Mom. I'm sorry Alex.

Tears burn at the back of my eyes.

"I need to get out of here."

I choke out, cutting off the sob ripping from my chest before it has life.

"Oh my goodness, miss. I'm so sorry. That was so very inconsiderate of me." He says as heat fills his face; sorrow etched across his features. "Where do you need to go? Please allow me to take you."

I don't know why I feel comfortable with the idea of him taking me anywhere, but I do.

"I need to go to *Humanity Hospital,* please."

"Miss, Humanity Hospital was shut down after Katrina." He stated as if I wasn't aware of it. "If you need medical attention, we can check you out here and get you to the closest hospital."

Great Olivia. He thinks you're fucking crazy.

"No, I don't need medical attention. There is a convention there today that I am to make an appearance at."

I sigh looking down at my watch to check the time. It's 1:45.

How the hell has half the day disappeared?

I suppose getting there early isn't a terrible idea. I just have to get away from here, my oxygen supply counts on it.

He looks at me skeptically.

"Come on. I'll have you there in no time."

I should probably go back to the hotel and change but, shit, I don't have the energy. Fuck it. Who gives a shit what I look like.

The ride over was filled with the sound of his rambling; how he pushed for a station to be built where the most memorable event in his career took place and how the city of New Orleans has multiple stations now due to the influx of travelers and residence. He's recently been promoted to Chief, and he feels it's his duty to protect his district. Station 22 is his home. I listen to him with fawning interest, making the appropriate "mmhms" and "yup" where necessary.

Any other time I'd enjoy this ride, his voice is calming and oddly seductive, but Gods could he shut up.

I couldn't be happier when we pulled to a stop.

"Thanks for the ride."

I say as I rush to exit the truck, closing the door on his.

"Anytime Firefly".

I take a deep breath and head up the steps. I'm early, but from the looks of it, I'm not the only one. Libby and Nyx are already at the front entrance waiting for me, no doubt. They are looking at me as though I have two heads. I'm sure I look a little worse for wear but still. It's not that bad. Nyx is the first to pipe up.

"What the fuck are you wearing? Did you sleep at all last night?" She laughs sarcastically.

I'm not up for this.

"Clothes." I snap out.

"Bitch come here."

She says as she points to the ground in front of her. Skeptically I step forward. Nyx lifts her hands and I feel her powers wrap around me.

"There," she says.

"What the fuck kind of magic did you just do?"

"It's called glamour bitch, are you even a witch?"

She asks lifting her phone and turning her front facing camera toward me. It takes me a moment to drink in the sight; my hair is no longer a mess, and my face looks as though I stepped right off of the runway.

What the fuck? Alex will shit himself when I tell him this is possible.

I smile and hand the phone back to Nyx.

"Shall we go in?"

Libby asks from beside us. They join me as we walk through the door. A sign with an arrow that says, **'ISAO CONFERENCE 3:00 PM'**, stands as we enter the building. The hospital looks exactly like what you would expect out of a building condemned after a hurricane. A pungent stench of mold clings to my senses. The girl's eyes meet mine and I know they are feeling the same as I am, a nervous energy radiating off them; I assume I mirror their looks of concern. An off-energy buzzes all around me. The signs point us to a descending stairwell through a door labeled basement.

"Well, isn't this cozy?" Nyx plays.

Who is this bitch?

"Did y'all know that during Katrina the basement was actually the morgue? It is said that all of the bodies were washed away and never recovered. It's said that they haunt the halls of this very hospital today."

Libby rambles, worry etched in her voice.

Great, word vomit. This one must talk when she is nervous.

"Well, they're dead, so what's the worst that can happen?" Nyx says mockingly.

"That's enough, Alex." I yell.

"What?"

Nyx turns to me, a look of bewilderment on her face. Grief instantly slaps me in the face.

Shit. Shit. Shit. What the actual fuck? How could I have forgotten, even for a moment.

"Never mind."

Why does this tiny person remind me so much of him?

Another wave of guilt and regret wrecks me.

I gear up to make an explanation, but the current situation draws all of our attention to the present. We come to a metal door with a small window and a silver tattered plate hanging to the left of it reading MORGUE.

We stand there, not moving, an energy pulsating behind the door. It feels familiar, but I can't place where I recognize it from. I shake my head. I feel like my brain is in a fog. Maybe I shouldn't have come today, I'm not in a good headspace right now.

Fuck it.

I push past Libby and Nyx, and sigh.

"Let's fucking get this over with, shall we?"

The door squeals loudly, as if its hinges are screaming for release. The room is pitch black. I find the wall behind me and start feeling for a light switch. When I flip the switch, every fiber of my body tells me to retreat.

Run.

The floor is all but washed away, dirt replacing what it once was. On the far wall, a crimson curtain hangs from the ceiling to a stage. Right in front of the stage are four rusted metal fold out chairs. Libby pipes up first.

"Has anyone else noticed that we're the only ones here?" She says stating the obvious.

"Doesn't look like they were expecting a large audience either." I say, gesturing to the four chairs.

"Fuck This!"

Nyx snarks. We all silently agree and turn toward the door. CLICK. The door locks loudly just as the lights go dim and we hear the curtains lift. Slowly, we all turn our attention to the stage and the silhouette of a man standing in the center; the spotlight above him casting an eerie shadow across his face.

His eyes, I know those eyes! Marcel?

24

"Don't leave so soon, we're just getting started, ladies." His voice etched with danger and warning.

"Please take a seat Olivia. Elizabeth. Nyx." He says gesturing to the chairs.

Definitely not Marcel, he's much older.

I don't know why, but my feet start moving in the direction of the chairs, as if being pulled. I look over and see Libby and Nyx matching my steps with concern etched across their faces. We all take a seat.

This is bad. I feel it. Run, Olivia.

I attempt to stand but I am paralyzed where I sit.

"I am Augustus St. Claire, and I want to tell the three of you a few stories that will be sure to keep your attention."

He begins as he lifts his arms, building an illusion for us to watch. I've never seen magic like this, but it grips my soul, and I can't look away. I feel myself being sucked into his illusion, like I'm standing there watching it all unfold. His voice cuts through the images.

"It was a cold spring night almost 28 years ago. The club was dimly lit. Smoke wafted in the air like a drunken elixir. My glass was cold in my hand, almost drained of the bourbon. I sat in the booth wondering why I was even there, looking down into my now empty glass. All I wanted was to fucking go home and relax, but something called for me to go there that fateful night. The music started and the sound of the most angelic voice broke through."

Why is he staring into my eyes as he shows us this?

"All I could focus on was her piercing blue eyes and flaming red hair. It was like we were the only two in that room. Her singing called to me." He says almost fondly of the memory.

Mom. He's talking about mom.

"She filled an emptiness inside me I didn't know existed. We were inseparable. She made me feel alive in a way I didn't think possible again." His voice turning to ice, "Until you. I could feel it right away, the evil and darkness that you possessed. I told her multiple times to get rid of you, but she wouldn't. I wasn't strong enough to do what I needed to do then. It is funny what love will keep you from achieving. You took someone I loved away from me, and I vowed I would take everything away from you before ridding the world of the abomination that is you."

Is he serious? Maybe I do deserve to lose my life. Seems fitting. Why should I live when mom and Alex aren't here? I am the cause of that. I am an abomination.

"Taking away from you was the fun part. I remember watching her in the kitchen as she cooked for your birthday. Delilah was still beautiful but not the woman I fell for. You tainted her. She was merely a shell of what she once was. A flip of the wrist and you were out. She tried to reason with me, begged me not to hurt you. The fear in her eyes when she realized you weren't the only one I planned on hurting that night. I relished hearing her scream as the fire burned her alive. I stood over her and made sure she knew choosing you over me was what killed her. Even with her last breath, she begged me not to hurt you." Augustus shakes his head in disgust. "You were supposed to die with her that night. You were supposed to burn for what you did, but somehow you escaped."

"What? It was you?" I whisper.

This motherfucker killed her? Not me! All this time…

Tears well in my eyes, I cannot breathe, my body is shaking with emotion. I faintly feel Libby interlace her fingers in mine. I am thankful for the warmth of her touch. My breathing slows.

Mom really loved me.

I think shockingly to myself.

A cruel smirk splays across his face.

"I truly thought that her death would be too much for you and you would break, but I was wrong. You managed to rise from the ashes and start anew. You built yourself a new life and developed a successful business utilizing your magic. I watched you, and I waited. Finally, a new opportunity started to show itself to me. A smart girl like you, I'm sure you figured out what it was?" He asks. I do not answer.

I'm sure this is what shock feels like.

"Someone new to love." Just then his body distorts and standing before us is Marcel with his hand upon Odin's head.

What? What is happening? Marcel? Odin?

"Ahh Ma Chère, cat got your tongue? But I wasn't enough to break through walls, was I?"

A wave of confusion fills me.

How can this be?

I want to say it aloud, but I can't say a word. It was Marcels eyes. I open my mouth, but nothing comes out. Disgust at the thought of every encounter with Marcel rushes to the forefront of my brain.

I'm about to vomit.

He shifts back and continues.

"See, I am a powerful Warlock, an illusionist, a shifter. I can distort an image, make you see what I want you to see, very few witches have that ability, not to mention I have been letting this play out for quite some time now."

He says as his eyes land on Libby beside me. Her hand tightens. I hear a faint whisper escape her lips.

"Not Finn."

"But I underestimated you, Olivia, I thought you would be searching for someone to give you confidence and free you from your own insecurities, but I made the mistake in thinking Marcel would be your undoing. You didn't fall in love with him like I planned; his dog maybe, but your heart already belonged to someone else. Someone already helped you put all your pieces back together. So, I had to pivot, and when you played right into my hand, his death was a masterpiece."

I feel bile building in the back of my throat. I know what he is going to say before the words come out of his lips. ASC, Augustus St. Claire, burning into the sidewalk outside our home flashes before me.

"Watching you drag his body from the fire, hearing your screams as your soul shattered."

With that, he waves his arm and the scene outside our home unfolds. My screams for Alex echo through the room.

I can't breathe.

Tears are streaming down my face. Libby squeezes my hand harder. I hear Nyx's quick intake of breath.

"It's exactly what I needed to break you."

He is beaming with pride, the joy pouring out of him is disgusting. I can't feel anything now. My mind is shutting down, I squeeze my eyes shut, not wanting to see the scene playing before us, but am instead met with flashes of that night. Marcel taking me on the stage for all to see, the fire, Alex's lifeless body, Marco blaming me.

Please stop.

I try to say the words, but they won't come out. I can't do this, I have to get out of here, I need to run!

Get up Olivia!

I can't move. My body isn't listening to me. My breathing is coming out faster and faster.

I'm so sorry Alex. You didn't deserve this.

My body feels numb except for the vice grip of grief squeezing my lungs. The sound of him talking is slowly fading, being replaced by a shrill ringing.

"Now look at you, you are nothing Olivia! You have nothing! You will never be anything again. I did this to you. I took everything from you."

He smiles, flashing his teeth. I break at his last words, my brain screams.

He's right. I am nothing!

The room goes silent.

Libby James

Olivia is lost in her mind, catatonic even. I squeeze her hand trying to bring her back to us, but with his words and the horrific display of darkness, I can't blame her for imploding. I don't know how she's been functioning. He killed her mother, her best friend and her spirit. I can still hear her screams echoing in the room. His laughter cuts through and makes my bones ache. This man is evil.

"You are a fucking monster!"

Nyx spits at him, pulling from the force that binds us to our seats.

"Now, now, Little One, wait your turn."

He lifts his hand and she's firmly planted back in her seat, terror etched into her expression.

"You are strong, aren't you Little One?" He pushes, turning his gaze back to me.

"Now for you my illusionist, Elizabeth, your skill is impressive, but you have never explored your ability; good for me, not for you, nor your mother."

My heart sinks. Images fill the air as they had before.

"I met my darling Daya in her most vulnerable. Her energy pulled me right into that cancer institute, of all places, directly to her curtain drawn room. She was so small and fragile."

Mom.

Tears slip my lids. It's my first time ever seeing my mother outside of the image from Agatha, right before her death. I wish I could have time to memorize every detail of her beautiful face, but Augustus continues to spew his venom.

"Even hooked up to all those machines she exuded so much

strength... until you took up residence in her womb. A fucking abomination. You were killing her from the inside out."

Images of her skin greying, her body betraying her as her womb expanded, flood the room. I can't breathe, the air from my lungs is being pulled from them.

I am so sorry Mom.

"I refused to stand by and watch as your darkness consumed her. Being that you're here today and she isn't, is a clear indication that my premonitions about you were true."

Fuck you.

My stomach is in my throat at his words. How could anyone love this man.

"Unlike your sister
" He looks to Olivia, who is still staring blankly.

She's drowning in her own thoughts.

More tears threaten my lids as he gears up to tell me more.

"You need love. You needed to be loved unconditionally. Your desire to have someone to call home was easy to play into."

He raises his hands to his face, dropping it to reveal Finn.

This cannot be real.

My thoughts trail. Tears fall as Finn's voice rings out through the room. The amulet on my neck scorching my skin underneath, but I'm too pissed to scream, as the numbness sets in.

"What's wrong Love, have I struck a chord?"

His face changes back to the personification of evil. I close my eyes and shake my head. Willing the images of me and Finn to stop.

I let him see me. He is my father. I feel sick.

"Let us not forget that bitch, Agatha, my baby sister. Luckily, she let her guard down long enough to let me in, then I laid wreckage to her precious little coven. She almost gave me away. If I wouldn't have stolen her last breath, she would have ruined everything."

I shudder at his words, remembering the look on her face when she saw him next to me. Images flash of their faces, choking on their own blood as he slit their throats.

"You played your part so well for me Love, burning the evidence of the crime and then taking me back to your place, to let Finn console you all night long." His voice drips with sickness.

"You sick fuck!"

I spit, tears betraying my anger. His laughter again fills the room and I feel ill.

I have been fucking my father.

The realization crushes me. He not only destroyed my soul, but he has killed so many innocent people, and manipulated so many lives.

Because of me.

Fuck this, I have lived through worse. He did this as a sick twisted game. I will not be his fucking pawn. He will not destroy me. I push on the binds, to no avail. How are we going to get out of this? I look to Olivia, she's so far gone, how will I reach her? My eyes bounce to Nyx, who looks like she is about to break free at any moment, her hands are glowing and rage flares. Her eyes find mine, all I see is panic.

Me too sis.

Nyx Harper

I am fighting against the binds, thrashing my body trying to break free, but I am failing. The pressure around me is suffocating.

"Kai! Help me!"

I call to him; I don't know what else to do. I feel my chaos raging through me, but I am bound and unable to break through. I lock eyes with Libby, her silence cries to me.

I'm scared too.

I want to comfort her, and Olivia, poor girl, she's so broken. I feel his eyes on me, I turn my gaze to him letting rage be the only emotion he sees in me, I'll be fucking dammed if he knows I'm scared.

"Oh, Little One," his words dig deep as my mind begs him not to be Kai.

Please let him not have fucked all of his daughters.

"You are a force. If only your mother's mind could have had your strength. I visit her, you know, and every time I see her, I fall for her all over again."

The images appear again to torment us, I fucking hate this man and his sick fucking game. Images of him and my mother flood the room, she was so perfect.

"Lainey has always been my north star, from the moment I met her, she changed me. She was so young, her eyes had life and joy."

My throat burns as I push the sadness down.

I am so sorry mom.

"I was a different person with her. She showed me what it truly meant to love, her innocence was refreshing, and I needed her. I was drawn to her purity. She made me want to be good and pure like her, and then you happened, draining her light and filling it with darkness. My sweet, beautiful Lainey was consumed by your darkness. Her mind was no match for you. Maybe once I destroy you, she will find her light again, and I can take her from that place."

My eyes snap to Libby.

He thinks she is still alive?

She nods as if realizing the same thing.

"Now how will I destroy you Nyx? You needed someone to release you from your control, but it couldn't be me. Balancing the guise of Marcel and Finn was difficult enough."

Relief hits me that HE wasn't Kai.

"So, I had to recruit some help, that wasn't easy either."

My heart stops at his words.

"Son, come on out and take a bow."

Son. I let my brother fuck me.

He gestures to the curtain. Kai emerges, sorrow etched into his face.

"You fucking bastard!" I scream to his mind.

"Kairos here did not make my plan easy; he did not want to be a participant in my orchestrated chaos. I had to bind his powers to encourage him to fall in line."

Augustus lifts his hand, illuminated fibers appear around Kai, some were already frayed barely holding together.

"Nyx, my dear you were so close to releasing his bind, I never anticipated you would be able to scratch at it like that."

My mind flares to the hum I heard from Kai, and how I was able to hear him call back to me that first time in the club. Tears sting my eyes. Kai looks to me, longing, his expression defeated. He let this happen, binds or not he manipulated me.

None of it was real.

Rage consumes me, I feel the binds around me weakening. I look to Libby, glancing at the invisible barrier. She pushes against it, nodding at the weakness.

"Thank you, Kairos, for being her undoing son."

The fibers fall to the ground. Immediately I hear Kai's voice in my head.

"Baby please understand! I tried to tell you!"

Kai pleads to me. Tears fall from my eyes and chaos overwhelms me, wind howls around me, my hair spirals and I breathe out. In an instant I am bounding towards Kai, my body consumed with my chaos as it takes over. My arm lifts, Kai flies into the back wall, my hand squeezes the air, as Kai claws at the invisible restraint at his throat.

"I fucking hate you!"

"Baby please, I love you!"

He bounds back to me. Hearing his voice in my head, is fracturing my heart. All this time he was setting this up. All the nights I spent with him, all the time I let him take my control. I fucking love him and he did this! Augustus's words replay in my head, 'Thank you, Kairos, for being her undoing son'. I feel my chaos rise with my emotions.

"None of this was real! Son! Who has the control now brother?"

A scream from somewhere deep inside me escapes my lips and all I can see is Kai in my grips.

I am going to kill him.

The wind roars around me, the ground shakes threatening to give beneath us all. I hear a humming, like he is trying to communicate with me, but my chaos is crushing the sound.

"Nyx!"

I hear Libby scream, cutting through my chaos, I turn feeling my gaze burn into her.

"He is not the enemy, yet. Don't do this."

I contemplate crushing his windpipe, but she's right. He is just a pawn, a fucking worthless pawn. I drop my reach, watching him crumble to the ground unconscious.

Augustus is trying to make his way through the room to Libby. My hands rise and fire burst from the earth surrounding him. The fires rage blue.

Hell Fire.

Time feels frozen. Libby makes it to my side; in a haste her words flood me.

"WE will make him pay for it all. He thinks your mom is alive, that's our upper hand. How did she die?" she pushes.

"She slit her wrist after his last visit, the night before I flew down." Her eyes softened at my admission. "With this. She grabbed it off his jacket in a struggle his last visit." I hand her the gold cufflink.

"Snap Olivia out of it, you can't hold him on your own."

I nod. Shock hits me as she closes her eyes and transforms into my mother.

"Nyx, if he gets out of that bind, we will not leave this place. Hurry!" She pushes me to Olivia.

Augustus fights against my bind, Libby is right, I need Olivia to push through. I reach her side and she is blank. I scream her name, shaking her.

Nothing.

"Olivia! Bitch we need you!" Her eyes stare blankly ahead.
Shit, how the hell am I going to bring her back to us?
"Fuck!"

I scream at her again as I feel him overpowering me, fire retreating, the color turning to red, as I focus on her. Somewhere in the back of my mind I hear a voice say one simple word. 'O'.

"Gods damn it O! I fucking need you!" Her eyes snap to clarity.

"Alex?" She asks, sorrow filling her tone.

"O we don't have time, we have to stop him, please!" she nods as if finally realizing the urgency in my voice.

"I don't know how." She says with shame in her voice.

"Just think fire, think about what he has done to you; let it consume your chaos and then let it flow, O, you can do this." I push her. Her hands glow red.

"That's it O, now focus on him!"

I join her concentration and the fire burns blue again. Libby stands at the edge of the ring. I nod and she steps through the fire.

My chaos finding new strength.

I have to keep them safe.

25

Libby James

I feel every bit of rage and pain that Nyx and Olivia have endured.

Use it Lib. Fuck me. Bad happens to me, I'm used to it, but not to them. They're my family now.

Letting chaos guide me, I step through the fires of hell and direct my anger to the man responsible for this all. The winds howl and the ground is shaking.

He has to believe me.

"Lainey, what... What are you doing here?" He asks, a softness to his tone.

"I'm so proud of you Auggie, you did it!" I praise.

"Oh, my Lainey, I have missed you so much. I have not seen you this bright in so long."

"Auggie, you did it. You have brought them to their knees. Look at them, look at how you have destroyed them." I gush.

"That's all I've ever wanted to hear. With the world rid of their darkness, your light will return my love and we can finally be together. It was always you." A smile plays on his lips.

Fucking piece of shit.

I kneel before him, mirroring his stature, and I put my hands on either side of his face. His face leans into my embrace.

"Oh, my sweet Auggie ... but don't you see what you have done?"

I hold up the gold cufflink. A display of panic wreaks his movements as he reaches for it. I pull away just out of his reach, and I dig the cufflink into my wrist and up my arm. Blood gushes from the depths of the crude incision painting my white cotton gown. I scream out in agony.

"Auggie you are the reason I bleed." I scream slicing into my other arm.

"Lainey! Please stop! What have you done!" He cries as my blood pours out and onto the ground.

"You did this to me, but guess what I am already gone!" I say as I shift before his eyes.

Checkmate.

He's distracted, as he screams in disbelief. I back out of the fire, locking my eyes on his until I've made my way out and I laugh. I fucking laugh.

Nyx Harper

Libby joins me and Olivia, Augustus is screaming from inside the hell fire.

"We have to do something; this will not hold him." Libby yells over the roar of the fire.

I nod, all I can think of is draining him of everything he is. Chaos rips at my core and the need to let it go is breaking me from the inside. I glance at Kai; he's still laying lifeless where I dropped him.

Let him die.

"Libby! Olivia!" I yell, grabbing their attention. "Let all your chaos and grief flow through you, we are going to need it! Repeat after me!" They nod, and I begin to cast.

"I call back my power, once lost, now found,
I break the chains that tightly bound,

Influence that sought to take my light,
Is banished now, with all its might.
I reject you and your force,
My strength renewed, my own life's course,
I strip you of your dark domain,
No harm from you shall touch my name,
I am the undoing of your hold,
With this spell, your story's told.
All power that you once possessed,
Now flows within my heart and chest,
My wrath has all but just begun,
And so, with this, you are undone."

The spell falls from my lips, as my sister's begin to recite it back.

Sisters, that's going to take getting used to.

Again, I repeat along with them, the spell comes to life, conviction and intention consume the words. I look to Olivia and tears stream down her face, but its not from sorrow, it's pure rage. I feel my own match hers.

The spell fills the room as Augustus screams falling to his knees, his energy draining from his body, flowing through the fire; feeding us and the wrath we are bringing upon him.

"You will never be free of me! I will be ever present. I will haunt your memories, your daydreams and nightmares. This I promise you all!" he screams.

Olivia steps forward and a surge of energy bounds from her, crashing through the room. The walls shake and the ceiling begins to crumble. I step to her grabbing her hand. My winds swirl around us and our hands are bright red. Chaos consuming the space around us. I look to Kai once more, now standing staring at the scene unfolding; tears burn from my eyes. My focus breaks as Libby screams my name.

"NYX!"

Libby screams panic wrapping her tone. I drop Olivia's hand and clarity finds me. The room is crumbling and the fire is consuming all.

I lost control.

My winds recede, but the fire is growing, it's not me. *Olivia.*

"We have to get out of here Lib. Olivia is lost in her chaos." I reach for Olivia and scream for her.

"Olivia!"

She steps closer to the ring that contains Augustus. I grab both of her hands and pull her back, flames blaze in her eyes. I have never seen this before. She is consumed. She snatches her hands back, then shoves them into me, the force sends me flying across the room. Everything goes black.

"Little One, you have to get up. NOW!"

Kai's voice screams in my mind. I try to move, but everything hurts. I hear his voice again as I try to open my eyes.

"Please Little One, you must get out of here. Get up Nyx!"

My eyes flutter open. Libby is kneeling above, shaking me.

"Nyx! Oh, my fucking Gods!" she cries.

"We have to stop her, or we are all going to die."

I cough out. Libby helps me to my feet.

"I will hold back the fire, you get Olivia."

Libby squeezes my hand and runs to Olivia. The room is filled with smoke and the walls are falling around us. I pushed the fire back from us and the door. My hands are shaking, and my head is pounding. My focus faltering as my strength gives.

"You're not alone Little One, I got this. You and your sisters get out of here!"

Kai's voice cuts through the chaos once again. I look to him standing focused on the fire. He nods to me. I rush to Libby who is shaking Olivia violently.

"She's not hearing me!" Libby cries harder.

"O, snap out of it!"

I scream, as my hand slaps across her face. The flames in her eyes extinguish instantly. She stands looking at me in shock.

"Gods damn it O! We have to get out of here!"

I scream at her again as the ceiling over the stage collapses. She nods.

"RUN!" Kai screams at us.

Libby and I drag Olivia through the halls, fire engulfing everything. Lights cut through the smoke. *Firefighters!*

They usher us out the front doors. The entire building is ablaze. The whole scene is utter chaos. Smoke fills the air, making the evening sky pitch black.

How long were we in there?

As we are being led down the stairs, I see O collapse.

"O!" I yell.

"Don't worry Miss. The Chief's got her." The firefighter pulling me down the stairs says.

"Let's get you checked out."

He tells me as I am loaded into the back of an ambulance and given oxygen from the EMT.

"We have another one!" I hear a firefighter yell. I look up to see Kai being helped into the ambulance that Libby is being treated in. His eyes meet mine.

"*Little One please let me explain.*" He pleads to me.

"Can you shut the doors please?" I ask the medic who is tending to the cut on my forehead.

"*Fuck you.*"

Tears streaking my face through soot and blood. I hold his gaze as the doors close, using the last of my chaos to close the veil, breaking our communication.

Olivia Rose

There is a frenzy of activity, but it all feels like its in slow motion. I stare at my shaking hands.

I almost killed everyone.

My thoughts consume me, breaking what's left of my soul. My attention pulls to the deafening roar echoing through the air. The once towering structure begins its descent into chaos. The ground trembles beneath the weight of impending destruction, embers surge into the air as the building falls into itself. An energy not of fire or destruction cuts through the air and I feel my hands tremble even harder.

I did this.

"Trouble seems to follow you."

I hear a voice break through my thoughts. The fire Chief stands before me, for the first time I see his name on his turnouts. *Proctor.*

"I am so sorry." I apologize, tears fall from my eyes.

"Why are you sorry?" he steps in closer, pulling the blanket tighter around me.

"This is all my fault." I cry harder.

"How could this be your fault?"

I feel hands on me, but it's not him. I look up through the tears and see Libby standing next to me.

"Olivia, we could never have predicted this would happen. This is no one's fault, but the conventions for having organized this event in such a dilapidated location." Libby's words rush out.

"What exactly happened?" Chief Proctor asks.

"I couldn't stop..." I start to explain, but Libby cuts me off.

"O, no one could have stopped it, it was an accident."

Her eyes bore through me. I feel her squeeze my hand urging me to shut up. Chief Proctor eyes us, wanting to push further into my words, but concedes. I look up to him once more. His sea green eyes never waver from mine.

"Thank you, Chief Proctor, for saving me. Again."

My words breaking at the end. He reaches his hand out, squeezing my shoulder.

"Firefly, don't thank me. It's my job but take my card in case you think of a real reason this keeps following you, or if you just want a friendly face to talk too."

He looks to the rubble inferno behind us.

"And it's Rhiley." He winks...

Firefly? Why does he keep calling me that?

My mind catches on the name as I turn his card over in my fingers, his cellphone number written on the back. A weak smile finds my lips and I nod. He squeezes my shoulder one more time before he takes his leave and Libby steps into my eye line.

"Olivia, are you kidding me right now! You can't tell anyone what actually happened in there, especially the fire chief!"

I cringe at her words, knowing she is right, but how long can I lie when this shit keeps happening to me?!

"I'm sorry Libby, I wasn't thinking."

Her face softens and then her eyes light up, excitement filling her face.

"Firefly! How adorable is that! I think he has a thing for you! He's a little older but damn he's fine! And those shoulders! He carried you down them stairs like you were a feather! The two of you would be adorable together! You should call him!" Libby word vomits all over me.

"Libby, this is not the time."

I snip, blushing slightly. She smirks but concedes and sits next to me as we watch the fire retreat.

I hope that motherfucker burned for what he did to mom and Alex.

I look at Libby, and then over at the ambulance with Nyx inside.

And for what he did to them too. My sisters.

A Few Weeks Later

26

Libby James

It's been almost two months since the collapse of the Humanity Hospital. In this time, we decided to take a reprieve to collect ourselves. Finding a gracious property manager that has allowed us an open-ended lease has given us the opportunity to take a mental break. We all needed this time to get to know each other and try to heal from our individual traumas.

Coming to a mutual agreement, we all have come to the conclusions that we need a fresh start. Olivia has made it very clear that she wants to stay in New Orleans. Although her past trauma is ever present here, so is the connection to her mother; plus, she doesn't think she can live in Washington without Alex. Fortunately, we all love it here; the energy of the city feeds our souls with something that we never knew we needed. With the powers siphoned from Augustus, the three of us are finding that our powers are stronger than ever, not that O will use hers yet, but we are working on that.

Olivia has nothing left to tie her to La Conner. The investigation into the explosion sits open, but she's not needed. She's been cleared of any wrongdoing. The police are focusing their attention on the only unaccounted for person, Marcel. Luckily for O, that hasn't held up the insurance claim. All her insurance paperwork has been done via email and a local lawyer and she received her lump sum payment yesterday. Nyx and I, on the other hand, have some loose ends to tie up in Sequim and Bainbridge.

Getting off of the plane we hop in our uber and head to Sequim first. Nyx needs to sign the paperwork to get the ball rolling on moving Salt & Sage to New Orleans and to explain the plan to Jinny what the future of Salt & Sage will be. O and I take the time to walk Main Street. I recognize the alley leading to Pour; shaking my head at the memories now scarred into my mind.

"Hey, witches, wait up!" Nyx calls strolling down the sidewalk. She makes it to us still standing at the alley way.

"How did that go?" I ask.

"Surprisingly well, with a little coercion and severance pay, she took it like a champ. I think she had suspicions since she's been running the place for the last six weeks. The moving trucks will be here within the next few weeks, and she agreed to help out in the following months with the transition."

"Can we grab something to eat?" Olivia asks, looking down to Pour.

"Yeah, I'm starving, and this is my favorite place in Sequim." Nyx turns down the alley way.

Great let's just dive right into the memories.

The bar is just as I remembered it that night. Morgan's eyes widen and land on Nyx.

"I wondered if I was ever going to see you again! Where have you been?" he asks.

"If I told you, you wouldn't believe me!" she smiles, but it doesn't reach her eyes.

Morgan glances at me, recognition plays over his features, but he says nothing.

Thank the Gods.

"Your booth is open; I'll bring over some appetizers!"

"Thanks Morgan." She calls to him, leading us to a booth in the back corner.

"You have a reserved table?" I play. Nyx drops her eyes fidgeting with her black bangle.

"I said it was my favor spot, didn't I?" I can hear the pain in her voice, but I let it go.

"These photos are breathtaking." Olivia interjects.

"Thank you, I took them myself." Morgan winks, placing three plates on the table.

"Oh, this one is spicy, Nyx forgets to mention that to anyone who accompanies her." He shoots Nyx a wink.

"Morgan, these are my sisters. Libby and Olivia." Nyx adds as if clarifying something unsaid.

"Sisters? Libby, you didn't tell me you were Nyx's sister last time you were here." He laughs. "A beauty like yours, I can see the resemblance. Let me know if you need anything else." He smiles, his eyes snagging on Olivia as he makes his way to the bar.

"Damn O, Morgan just eye fucked the hell out of you." Nyx jabs at Olivia.

"That would be a nice distraction." O raises her brow, as she shoves bread into her mouth.

"OH, my Gods that is so good and spicy!" Olivia swoons over the food.

"Libby you've been here before?" Nyx asks me as she takes a bite.

"Once, when I came to your shop." I quickly dive into the food, I feel like I haven't eaten in days, and look for a way to change the subject.

Thankfully Morgan brings out several more plates for us and provides a distraction.

"Is he always like this?" O asks.

"Yeah, Morgan loves to feed people. He is a great guy." Nyx adds.

"Well, I could get used to looking at him." O chimes in as her eyes follow him to the bar.

Morgan pours four tumblers with an amber liquid and walks over with a round of whiskey.

"Ladies, I couldn't let you all leave without trying my house spiced whiskey, it's a favorite of Nyx's." Morgan offers a sweet smile. We all grab a glass, tipping it to each other, along with Morgan. The whiskey hits my lips and fire erupts within me.

Damn that's good.

I notice Nyx hasn't taken a sip of hers, her expression is pained. She brings the glass to her lips and a tear falls from her eye.

"Thanks Morgan, I'll take the check." She offers.

"Nonsense, It's on the house. You girls should come around more often. This was a nice surprise." Morgan winks at Olivia.

"Thank you, Morgan." I say. Nyx just looks back to her wrists fidgeting again with her bracelet.

"Can we get out of here; the memories of this place are haunting. I want to leave Washington and never look back." Her voice trailing off. She is hurting but keeps trying to hold it back.

"You read my mind." I concede.

"I'm going to find the restroom really quick. I'll meet you both outside." Olivia offers.

Nyx and I head for the exit and step out of the bar. Still seeing the pain in Nyx's eyes, I decide to attempt to get her to talk. She is hurting, and I desperately want to help her.

"Hey Nyx, you know you can talk to me, right? I am here for you." I say delicately. She offers a weak smile.

"I'm Fine."

Sister, you are far from 'fine.'

Olivia Rose

Grabbing my bag, I find a pen and jot down my number on the napkin in front of me.

If he is going to keep staring, then he better call.

I walk to the bar where Morgan is pouring a drink and clear my throat.

"Hey once you're done there, can I speak to you privately for a moment?" I offer him my best smile. "Um, sure. He concedes with a questioning look on his face.

Without a further word, I head down the corridor leading to the restroom and wait right outside. Morgan rounds the corner and catches my eye.

Showtime.

I begin walking toward him and he pauses. I do not slow my pace, in fact I all but tackle him; pinning him to the wall where he stands. He looks at me with bewildered amusement. Pressing my body into his, I lift and begin kissing him deep and rough. It takes him a moment to catch up but when he does the sensation shoots straight to my pussy.

Well fuck! She still works!

I feel his hands reach up and tangle into my hair, pulling me in to deepen the kiss further.

Gods yes, this is exactly what I needed.

Pulling back, we are both panting, as I reach into my pocket and pull out the napkin, shoving it hard into his chest.

"Maybe next time you see me, you can do more than eye fuck me." I bite. Leaving him speechless, I turn and head out of Pour. The Gods know if it weren't for my sisters waiting outside, I would've fucked him right there.

Libby James

The drive to Bainbridge is quiet. This place once felt like home, now it's pulled from my nightmares. A dark cloud falls over the car and we seem content in the silence. No one says a word until we get out of the car and stand in front of *Grimoire.*

"It's cozy." O says with a smile. I just nod and head for the door.

We walk into *Grimoire* and immediately I notice the color drain from Nyx's face, as she catches sight of MK; sitting on the counter laughing, lost in conversation with Tink. MK's face falls as soon as she sees us.

"What are you doing here?" Nyx asks, her tone soft like nothing I have heard from her before.

"Oh, you've met MK?" I smile.

"Yes, we know each other. That's Mia." Nyx says almost inaudible.

"I'm Tink, MK's girlfriend, and you are?" she says as she hops on the counter next to Mia and grabs her hand possessively.

"It's Nyx. Nyxi are you okay?" Mia's tone is soothing and full of questions.

"Can we go talk somewhere privately?" Nyx asks Mia pleadingly.

"MK are you fucking kidding me right now? Do you really give two shits if she is ok?" Tinks volume raises.

"I know exactly who the fuck you are. You need to leave now! And no, you most definitely cannot go talk somewhere." Tink is yelling now.

"Ya'll just hold on a damn minute." I say as my brain puts together the pieces here. I turn my attention to Nyx.

"Are you ok?" I ask. Tink all but jumps at me.

"What the hell do you mean is *She* ok? Does she have all of you under some spell? Because obviously she's a witch just like you. Do you have any idea what that bitch did to MK? What is she doing here anyways? Why are you with her?" My brain catches up and I'm quickly realizing the shitshow that this day is becoming.

Great, I'm in the middle of a fucking girl fight.

"She's my sister Tink, and I would appreciate it if everyone would just calm down here so we can all talk rationally."

"Sister? You don't have siblings Lib. You were in foster care, remember?" She talks down to me as if she is scolding a child.

Who the fuck does she think she is?

"Well, it turns out she has two." That's when everyone turns their attention to Olivia who has been silent this whole time.

"It's Olivia. I suggest you change your tone, or you will be choking on your teeth if you continue coming at Nyx like that; I'm not in the mood for this shit." O bites with ice etched on her threat.

Tink stares at O, temper brewing in her features, but something in O's stance makes her think twice before speaking. She turns to me instead.

"So, what is this about, I thought you said you were on an extended vacation and needed time to clear your mind since ASC was no longer a threat?" Tink questions with a lifted brow and her tone more even now.

"Well, yes, um we need to talk Tink. Let's go to my office."

"No, I'm good, whatever you need to say can be said right here in front of MK and your *family*." Her last word comes out with hints of hate and disdain directed at O.

I see the fire in O's eyes as she steps in front of Nyx.

Fuck is she really going to choose now to finally use her powers again?

I see Nyx mumble something to O and her face softens.

Thank the Gods.

I look at Tink, one hand gripping MK's, the other balled into a fist.

This is not going as I planned at all.

"Fine." I sigh. "The last few weeks I've done a lot of soul searching, trying to figure out what's best for me, my business, you, them." I say quickly. "I'm moving to New Orleans with them, Tink, I would love it if you would do the honors of running Grimoire here." I say with excitement.

"I will visit you and will still be running things, just from a different location. I know how much you love this place."

I spit out quickly. A painful expression plasters Tink's face.

"You're leaving me? For Her? What about Finn, where does he fall into this shit?" She gestures to Nyx.

"It's *them!* And I am not leaving you. I'm just moving Tink, and he wasn't who I thought he was."

Pain making my last worse come out cracked.

"It's the same fucking thing Libby! You want me to stay here and do your grunt work while you run off with THEM and do your witchy shit." Tink screams at me.

"Fuck this! I don't need you or this store. If 'they' mean more to you than I do and you just met them, then good fucking riddance!" She yells. She grabs Mia's hand, and they head for the door. Mia pulls away from Tink.

"Nyx, what happened? Did he hurt you?"

Mia's eyes full of pain and concern over seeing Nyx. It is obvious she can see Nyx is hurting. Tink snatches Mia's hand again, this time with anger.

"Why the fuck do you care if she got fucked over by him, she chose him over you. Fuck her MK, and these other witches. They only care about themselves."

Locking eyes with Nyx, Mia turns with a silent apology plastered on her face as the bell chimes.

"Well, that went over fucking swell." Nyx says sarcastically.

"Looks like I'll need to find a new hire to take over *Grimoire* here." I say with a sigh.

I'm not wrong, am I? I mean, they are my family, after all.

I feel a deep need to protect them and that's what I intend to do. Olivia is still hurting; she wears her heart on her sleeve, and I hurt for her. The way she protects Nyx, it's clear she feels a strong bond with her. Unlike her though, Nyx suffers in silence, hiding behind her sass and sarcasm. This is where I am needed; Tink will be ok. I'll give her time to cool off and then I'll try to call her.

I look around the bookstore, my gaze pausing on the chair. I feel the vomit burning at the back of my throat.

"Maybe selling it is the better solution." I say shaking my head. Nyx and Olivia step to each side of me and grab my hands.

"We got this," they say simultaneously.

"Thanks." I tell them, squeezing their hands.

It's all going to be okay. I have a family now to lean on and protect.

27
Christmas Morning

It's odd for a witch to be this obsessed with Christmas, but I cannot help myself; of all the holidays to choose from, this is my favorite. The house is decked from top to bottom in Christmas décor. There is an eight-foot tree beside the fireplace, a rarity in New Orleans, in the living room. There isn't a bare branch to be seen, but 'our first Christmas '23' is front and center. Stockings are hung from the mantle, with candles and garland decorating above. The smell of cinnamon and pine permeates the air. I even wrapped the banister in garland and lights.

Okay, I may have gone overboard.

I'm practically vibrating waiting on Nyx and O to wake up. I look at the clock on the stove 5:45am. *Damn are they going to sleep all day?*

I begin to think back, reminiscing on how we got here while I wait on the sleeping beauties.

All three of us have been through so much these last two months. The only bright side is finding each other. I feel so protective over them. Maybe Tink is right, I did choose them over her, but they are my blood. I am the older sister, it's my job to keep them safe and I couldn't do that in Washington if they were living here. Plus, this city calls me in a way I've never felt in Washington. I texted her 'Merry Christmas' this morning, but she just left me on read. I'm just going to have to let her be mad for a while. She will come around.

I see Nyx coming into herself so much more and my heart swells with pride. Kai still tries to reach out, and I can tell that bothers her but hopefully he will let her live in peace soon. A lot of her time right now is wrapped up in the relocation of Salt and Sage. She convinced all of us to buy three connected buildings. Salt and Sage on one corner, Grimoire in the center, and Rose and Ember on the other. We discussed combining our stores into one but decided we all needed to keep that part of us separate. Our lives can't be consumed by each other, we need to lead separate lives. That's easier for them than it is for me. Just yesterday Nyx came home from the grocery store talking about a woman she met while shopping. They are going to check out a new Hot Yoga studio next week. She invited me and O, but O said she'd rather run, and honestly, fuck that. People are drawn to her though. She has that aura about her.

Olivia does too, but she is still struggling badly. I hear her call out at night for Alex. She is still overcome with nightmares about his death. I tried once to go in and console her, but that ended badly. She seems to be drawn to Nyx and finds comfort in her witty sarcasm. They couldn't be more opposites, but they somehow balance each other quite nicely. Nyx and I have been trying to teach Olivia how to cast, her knowledge is very limited, but it has been a slow process. She never explored her powers like we did growing up, and she carries fear around with her thanks to Augustus. She hasn't used her powers since she brought the hospital down, but she will get there; it will just take time. Filling her stock at the store is going to take some time too. She apparently intends to do it all in a forge, whatever the hell that means. I am curious to watch though.

Chief Proctor came by last week to check on her. She was a little startled that he knows where she lives, but he won her over quickly with that killer smile and quick wit. They sat on the front steps and chatted for almost an hour. Nyx and I kept peeking out the windows at them. The man might be older, but he is fine as fuck. She swears he was only doing his job, but Nyx and I know that man has his sights set on her, she just doesn't see it yet.

I hear footsteps and they bring me back to reality. I look at the clock, 5:55am. I cannot contain my excitement. Nyx stands at the bottom of the staircase rubbing her eyes as a yawn escapes her lips, her hair a tangled mess.

"What the fuck Lib? Are you trying to wake the neighbors? It's not even 6am."

"Oh no, I was making coffee and listening to a little Christmas music, was I being too loud?" I say smiling innocently. I hand her a cup of coffee. As soon as she goes to take her first sip, I can no longer contain my excitement.

"Merry Christmas Bitch!" I belt out, throwing my arms around her and nearly scolding the both of us. She almost drops her cup but recovers. Looking at me shaking her head, she is trying to convince me that she's not dealing with my shit today, but she is fooling no one. I see the smile she's trying to hide, playing on her lips.

Wait until she sees, she's going to shit!

I walk to the bottom of the stairs and yell up.

"OOOOOOOOOO! Wake up! It's Christmas." I've never had a family and I've always wanted to do that. We hear a commotion upstairs like she fell out of bed. *Oops.*

She emerges from her room at the top of the staircase, her hair a tousled mess, and slowly descends the stairs.

"Come on beautiful, I got a surprise for y'all!" I say enthusiastically. She groans.

"Lib, I haven't even had my coffee yet, what the fuck is wrong with you?"

"Well hurry up, bitch, it's Christmas morning! Nyx is finishing hers. Go grab you a cup and then I want y'all in the living room pronto."

"I have you a cup poured on the bar." Nyx says as she rounds the corner to join us. "Don't fight the Christmas magic."

Just then I hear heavy steps descending the stairs. *Tell me this isn't real. This bitch.*

Morgan flushes, with his head held low, hair disheveled, as he buttons his shirt while coming down the stairs. Nyx literally has to pick her jaw up from the floor. Once he is at the bottom, he kisses O on the cheek.

"Call me. I had a great time." And then tips his head to Nyx and me. "Nyx." "Libby." walking straight out of the front door without another word.

"Oh, my Gods, you fucked my bartender?" Nyx says to break the ice.

Real subtle Nyx.

O smirks.

"Well in all fairness, he fucked me. Multiple times. He came down for a little birthday rendezvous."

Laughter and squeals burst from all three of us!

"But Morgan? He's like old. I mean, yeah, he's fine as fuck, but he's old." I play.

"He's hot O, I do not blame you. Was he any good?" Nyx raises her coffee cup as if to 'cheers' O, with a devilish smirk.

"Oh, my Gods Nyx! Seriously?" I say shaking my head at the two of them.

"Wait you said birthday?!" My brain is catching up to what she just said. *Your word vomit is becoming a problem Lib.*

"Yep, a Christmas witch, Christmas Eve actually, but close enough." O responds. I roll my eyes.

Of course, she is.

"Why didn't you tell us?" Nyx pushes.

"Honestly, it didn't come up, I don't know your birthdays either!" O says as she drags her hands through her messy hair.

"January twelfth." Nyx states.

"February sixth. Problem solved. You're forgiven. Now go get your coffee. And what kind of cake do you like?" I bubble with excitement.

"I don't like cake." She says matter-of-factly as she pushes past me and heads in the direction of the kitchen.

"Who the fuck doesn't like cake?" Nyx asks.

"Apparently our Christmas Witch." I say with a laugh.

"Nyx go with her; I'll be right back." I rush up the stairs to get their presents and head to the living room to set up.

O walks into the room first.

"Where is Nyx?" I ask impatiently, tapping my Christmas slippers.

"She said she'd just be a second." Just then Nyx rounds the corner holding a muffin in one hand.

This bitch, what is she doing?

O and I look at her with so many questions.

"What?" Nyx looks confused by our expressions.

"Nyx, why are you holding a muffin?"

"Well, O doesn't do cake; she can't open presents until she blows out a candle and makes a wish."

"This is a Christmas present, not a birthday present!" I say impatiently.

They are killing me! I'm ready to open these myself if they don't hurry up.

"Where's the candle?" O asks sarcastically.

"Yeah well, we don't have any fucking birthday candles, so I'll improvise.'

Nyx places her hand, palm side up above the muffin. A single flame ignites from her hand, and she smiles up at O.

"Blow it out bitch and make a wish!" Nyx laughs.

"So, this is what we are doing. Where's my birthday song?" She looks at us with the most serious look on her face. Nyx glances at me like 'are you going to sing?' I shake my head at her.

O breaks out into a smile, "Fuck it!" she laughs, closing her eyes as if to make a wish and blows out the flame. Laughter erupts once more, and the house feels like home.

I can't help but smile. I stand beside the two huge boxes and gesture for them to come over.

"Nyx the black one is yours."

"Of course it is because of my soul, right?" She jabs as she hands the muffin to Olivia. A small giggle escapes her as she rushes to the box and quickly pulls the lid off. Nyx squeals as she lifts out the little black kitten and pulls it to her chest. Reading the name tag aloud, she laughs.

"Salem, Isn't that fitting." It's in this moment that I noticed true joy spill out of my little dark sister. She laughs pulling me from my thoughts.

"Lib, you got me a hairless pussy, it's like you know me!" as she snuggles her face into the bald little cat.

"O, it looks like Morgan isn't the only one who got a little pussy for Christmas!" Nyx cackles as she settles on the floor to snuggle Salem and watch O open her gift.

"Well... um ... Okay then!" I say. "Your turn O!"

O stuffs the last of the muffin into her mouth as she walks over to the emerald-green box with the massive red bow atop it. She lifts the lid slowly and peers down. I see multiple emotions dance across her face as she stares into the box. Carefully she lifts the mastiff puppy up into the air like it's a ticking timebomb. For a moment I think I may have read the situation wrong and made a mistake.

Fuck Lib, what were you thinking?

Just as I am about to apologize, she looks at the nametag 'Odin 2.0'. The truest smile I have ever seen forms as tears fall from her eyes.

"Lib, he's perfect. He's real." she says as she sobs and buries her face into his fur. Odin 2.0 licks at Olivia frantically as he tries to consume every muffin crumb, he can find. I pull both girls, and our new pets, into my embrace and that's when I realize that this is what it was always meant to be about.

I finally have my family.

"Merry Christmas," I tell them.

Our moment is broken with the sound of the doorbell; I pull away.

"I'll get it. Y'all can play with our new family members." I say to them as they sit on the floor laughing as Salem and Odin 2.0 sniff at each other. I walk to the front door and open it, but no one is there. *Hmm that's odd.*

Just as I am about to close the door I see it, a cream-colored blank envelope. My blood runs cold. Picking it up, I turn it over in my hand and my fear becomes reality. It has a wax sealed with the letters ASC embossed.

There's no fucking way!?

I look around again to see if anyone is close by, but I don't see anyone.

"Lib, who is it?" O yells from the living room.

I quickly fold the envelope up and shove it into my pocket as I close the door and walk back to the living room.

I will not let that bastard ruin Christmas; he's taken enough from us.

"No one, must've realized they had the wrong house." I say with a smile.

"Who's ready to open the rest of the presents?" Nyx reaches for a present under the tree.

The rest of the morning is filled with laughter and fun.

This is what it feels like to be part of a family,

I think to myself.

This is what I am protecting.

I continue to join in the Christmas festivities and pretend like the envelope in my pocket isn't a lie I am keeping from my sisters. As they are laughing and playing with Salem and Odin 2.0 I slip into the kitchen and pull the envelope out of my pocket. I quickly open it and pull the card out.

MERRY CHRISTMAS

ENJOY IT WHILE IT LAST.

I'LL BE SEEING YOU.

DAD

The fuck he will. Without a second though I shred the envelope and card and tossing it in the trash. I look into the living room at my two baby sisters.

I will protect you both if it's the last thing I do.

Sneak peek into The St. Claire Series: Sinful Scars ...

Kai Reighn

A click draws me from my rambling thoughts. My dark queen stands on the balcony, the bayou wind sends her hair swirling with the scent of her favorite amber oil, and it blooms through the night air. I watch her from the patio next door, cloaked in my shadow.

When I found out her and her sisters were staying in town, I had to be near her anyway I could, even if that meant forcefully persuading the former occupants of this house to leave. Now, I sit watching her lean against the railing, wearing my t-shirt. She can try to convince her sister's she's fine and that she is over me, but she is lying. She craves me and her in that shirt confirms it; she will be mine again. The veil lifts, her mind and soul open to me. I pause letting her feel just how close I am.

"*I know you are out here.*" She calls to me, but I wait. If I just start calling to her, the veil will seal once more. I just want to feel her a bit longer.

"*Is that why you are wearing my shirt?*" I ask trying to get a smile out of her before she shuts me out again.

"*Leave me alone you sick fuck!*" her voice screaming in my head.

"*Just let me explain, Little One, there is more to the story, please!*" I beg.

"*You betrayed me, end of story, so fuck off!*" She screams again, turning to end this silent exchange.

"*I'm not your...*" The veil closes once more as she slams the door. I kick the chair I had my feet propped on, frustration and rage flood my system. I will make her listen; she will never be free of me.

Coming Soon.

Made in the USA
Middletown, DE
01 March 2024